Secrets
IN THE
Snow

KIRI PATTERSON

To my beautiful babies,
Ellie, Ethan, Garen, and Benson.
I hope you will always have the courage to be true to you. The world needs your uniqueness and beauty. I am beyond excited to see what each of you achieves in life. Thanks for letting me be a part of your story.
Mommy loves you, just how you are, with all that I am.

To Teachers:
Your influence for good and kindness changes our world for generations. Thanks to all those who helped shape me and my children for the better.

---

* For content warnings see my website www.kiripatterson.com/contentwarnings

Chapter One

FAITH

I straightened the papers on the short table, built for my adorable second graders' height. Coach Peters — Hillsdale's most eligible bachelor and one of my second-grade student's father, would be in my classroom any minute and I was going to barf.

I wiped my hands off on my pencil skirt as my eyes flicked to the door.

Adults are terrifying. Parent teacher conferences stressed me out for days, but meeting with parents outside those guidelines... nightmare inducing.

And if that wasn't enough to fray the nerves, I was hardcore crushing on Danny's dad, who was Henry Cavill yummy with a happy-go-lucky Ted Lasso type attitude.

The man hardly noticed me, let alone talked to me. The few times he did, my mouth went dry, and I lost all coherent thought. Last month he wished me a happy birthday weekend at parent pickup (yes, I was wearing the standard elementary birthday crown), I said, "You too..." and no, we do not share a birthday.

I glanced up at the analog clock above the whiteboard. He was ten minutes late, and I didn't know whether to be annoyed or grateful.

I stood and paced back and forth, trying to expel the antsy energy. I flexed my fingers and counted to three as I inhaled and exhaled. A panic attack right now would be beyond embarrassing, which meant my body was happily prepping for one.

I will not puke. I will not puke.

I looked over to Danny's desk and pictured his bright blue eyes and stoic expression.

I knew what it was like to not quite fit in, and to struggle in certain social situations. I rolled the fidget ring on my right ring finger. The birthday present from Marissa, my close friend, was trying its best to ground me and not let me spiral.

Doing this right before Thanksgiving break was maybe a bad choice; but the bonus was I wouldn't see anyone for at least a week once I was done. I was exhausted and ready for it. Baking and bubble baths were high on my wish list.

I checked the clock. Fifteen minutes late. The high school Gymnasium was a few minutes walk away. The entire K-12 school campus wasn't more than a five to ten-minute walk.

I'd never lived anywhere that was small enough to have K-12 all together. The school campus was a hodge podge assortment of new add-ons, portables, and buildings that dated back to the early 1900s. It felt a bit like walking through time as you went from one end of the campus to the other.

My classroom was in the oldest section. But the heat worked, and the large windows let in plenty of sunshine, so I didn't mind.

Do I wait longer? My stomach flipped at the thought of rescheduling this meeting again. Despite knowing it was coming for weeks, I still wasn't sure how to broach the subject.

'Excuse me, but I'm pretty sure your child is neurodivergent.' Was hardly a pleasant conversation starter, more like straight into confrontation land.

My favorite.

My hands shook, and I flexed my fingers again.

Almost twenty minutes late. I rubbed my eyes. I would give him till thirty, and then I was bailing. A bubble bath, and panic attacks for that matter, could only be put off for so long.

There was a loud knock on the door, the kind that announced a jovial presence, dun duh duh dun dun... DUN DUN.

Mr. Peters came bursting in, wearing an enormous grin. He weaved around thankful leaves that hung from the ceiling.

"Sorry I'm late, Ms. Lyons."

I flinched. How many times did I need to ask everyone in this town not to call me by my new last name. The parent - teacher conference we had was months ago, but still.

He shook off his coach jacket with Hillsdale's colors of maroon and gold, showing a fitted dark T-shirt and large forearms underneath.

I reminded my brain to make sure I didn't drool and I tried to focus.

"It's the first week of basketball practice, we ran longer than expected, and then Mom was late grabbing Danny from my office." He shrugged and chuckled. Waves of a carefree attitude rolled off his massive shoulders. "Anyway, I rushed over from the high school gym as fast as I could."

He paused, waiting for a response.

I shook my head, hoping to restart my thoughts. I held out my hand. "Please call me Faith, Mr. Peters." His hand dwarfed mine in a handshake.

"Call me Adam." He smirked. "Or I answer to Coach if you prefer. Mr. Peters feels so stuffy." He scrunched his nose.

I took a silent breath and held it. Okay, no time like the present. But where to start?

"Thanks for coming, Adam." I gestured over to the two foot table that held the papers I had put together for the meeting. I walked over and sat, rolling my fidget ring one last time. I watched as he stalked towards the table, looked at the child size chairs, and pulled out the tiny chair and sat gingerly on the edge, his knees bent up almost to his chest.

I had an adult size chair on the other side of the table, but he must not have seen it, and I wasn't sure if I should point that out now.

Besides, he seemed less scary, scrunched like this, and honestly downright adorable.

"So what's up?" Adam smiled in my direction, and I wondered if that smile would stay in place when I brought up testing and support for Danny.

I bit my bottom lip and slid the folder towards him.

Breathe in for three, hold, then out.

"I called this meeting because I am worried about Danny."

His head reared back. "What do you mean?" His eyes no longer held amusement. He grabbed the folder and began flipping through it, looking at the half done assignments.

"For one, he is exhausted, and often falls asleep in class or is completely zoned out."

Adam flinched. "That's probably on me." He scratched the back of his neck with his right arm, and I was proud of my restraint for not staring at his bicep. "The neighbor's fence broke, and his cows got out, and then we had a few late basketball practices this week." He shrugged. "If I go, he comes with me. There's not much I can do about that."

I could feel the energy shift in the room, the little sting of confrontation poking at my skin.

"I am a single dad. What do you expect?" He folded his arms across his chest; his biceps pushed forward with the effort. "Look, I'm sure you mean well, but I get enough advice on how to raise Danny from everyone else in this town." He raised his left eyebrow.

This was not going well. "As his teacher, I thought I might provide a different insight to Danny, that's all." I held my hands up between us.

Adam sighed. "I will try to get him to sleep earlier this week. Maybe he can go to my mom's more." He looked down at the stack of papers of unfinished homework assignments. "Are we done?"

I cleared my throat. "I'm afraid not." I tried to fill my tight lungs with a deep breath. "I have some other things I was hoping to discuss."

He side-eyed me and leaned back into the chair, causing it to nearly snap before he surged forward. "Is Danny misbehaving in class?" His eyes held worry, but his body was rigid.

"No, it's not that. It's..." Maybe I should have practiced this conversation with someone, this was hardly a wing-it situation.

I clasped my hands in my lap so I would stop fidgeting. Might as well get it out there as fast as I can. "I have noticed some signs that make me wonder if Danny is perhaps neurodivergent and would benefit from testing and further assistance. I am not qualified to diagnose, but—"

"Neuro what?" He tilted his jaw towards me. It seemed like he was still trying to process everything I had said.

I tried to swallow. "Neurodivergent. It just means their brains work a little differently from others..."

"Are you saying he is stupid?" His voice and eyebrows sank lower.

"NO!" I leaned back, and waved my hands in front of me. "I would never!"

"So, what is he doing that's wrong then?" He gestured with his hand over the folder. "So he missed a few assignments... big deal. That is as much on me as on him."

The cheery, carefree side of Adam was nowhere in sight, replaced by his angry papa bear side. This was definitely a side I'd never seen from him.

I cleared my throat trying to loosen the tight muscles. "Again, not wrong." I hated that anytime someone was different, we labeled it as wrong. "I'm simply stating his brain *may* function and perceive things differently than some of his peers."

"Why?" he growled. His brown eyes pierced mine and left no room for hiding.

I blew out a tight breath and dropped eye contact. Maybe I should have left things alone. But I hated to think some child out there might feel misunderstood.

"Why," Coach Peters repeated, his lips in a scowl.

I steeled my shoulders; this was for Danny. I could puke later. "He never makes eye contact, has problems if the schedule has an unexpected change, certain noises seem to bother him, he has a hard time understanding others' emotions and regulating his own—"

Adam tossed the papers back onto the table. "He's seven, lay off. He will figure it out." He pushed himself and the chair away from the table and stood.

I was trying to help Danny, and Adam wasn't listening to me at all. Why do parents always assume different is bad? Moments from my childhood flashed in my memory. It didn't have to be like this.

My palms pressed down on the table and I stood. "It's not something for him to figure out; it's more for us than for him." I didn't need Adam looking down on me. I eyed the chair behind me suspiciously.

What were the chances of standing on it in my heels without either looking ridiculous or falling off?

Not great. I focused back on Adam.

"Right. So what..." Adam's eyebrow raised. "You want to test him. Give him a label?" He scowled. "You're not from here, but I know this town. They would make him carry that his whole life." He grabbed his jacket off the ground and slammed it over his shoulder; it must have fallen when he stood up. "He isn't stupid, and he doesn't need a label."

I placed my hands on my hips, feeling my blood heat. "Again, I never said stupid. I said different."

"Danny's fine how he is." Adam shoved the small chair back under the table hard.

So hard, it bounced off the table and fell to the floor. The movement caused a box of crayons to fall, and a few scattered pieces rolled off the table and onto the brown stained carpet.

This conversation reminded me of my mother and her need for perfection and for me to fit a certain mold that I desperately tried to, but I never could.

I stared at the pieces of crayons, shattered and broken. This conversation could not have gone worse. I took a deep breath and held it, I smelled something citrusy coming from Adam's direction.

Why was I getting so worked up about this?

Was this because of Danny, or my past?

My thoughts kept flicking to my past and my mother, and I knew too much of my own scars had resurfaced during the exchange.

The thought cooled my anger, and I rubbed my forehead.

"This isn't about a label." My voice was soft, broken like the crayons. "This is about trying to understand Danny, so that you as the parent, and me as his teacher, can have the tools to help him, now and in the future."

I gestured towards the toppled chair. If my second graders had to pick up their messes, surely that applied to adults as well.

His icy expression melted as he bent down and righted the chair and scooped up the crayons into the bin. Seeing Adam scoop up the crayons, my awareness and anxiety rushed back into me.

My reaction, plus my nerves, were over the top.

Adam stood, shoulders hunched in. "I shouldn't have acted like that. I've had—"

Tears pricked at the corners of my eyes. It was obvious my body was done masking the panic. It had too many big emotions and was collapsing. This conversation wasn't going anywhere, and I needed to leave. Now. I shook my head. "The choice lies with the parents if they want to pursue that or not." I tried to breathe with my belly. "Let me know if you would like to discuss my concerns about Danny at a different time, but I think we both need some time and space." I pointed my hand toward the door, praying he didn't notice how much it shook.

His gaze took in my shaking hand, and his eyebrow raised.

I was not so lucky.

I clasped my hand into a fist.

He nodded. "I'd better go get Danny." Adam went towards the door, but glanced once more in my direction before he left. He looked ashamed of his outburst, but I was even more so.

I was seconds away from crying.

Well, that went absolutely terrible.

Of course, Danny was fine. Danny was wonderful; I just wanted... Well, never mind what I wanted. Parents got to choose and shape their kids' lives, and that was how it should be. I wished sometimes they were less rigid about how that plan needed to look.

I walked to my desk, shook out my hands, and sank into my chair. I might need to work through some worksheets when I got home. I hadn't been to therapy in over two years, but I still used the cognitive behavior therapy worksheets from it when needed.

I breathed in for four, held for four, and then slowly released. Energy coursed through me. Maybe I would feel better with movement. I walked the length of my little classroom.

I straightened my shoulders and exhaled. I would have to see Adam after Thanksgiving break at parent pick up, but that was a future me problem.

What would I even say to him next?

Sorry, I accidentally brought all my childhood drama into our conversation about your son. Sorry, I didn't help you pick up the crayons. Sorry, I didn't listen to your apology and treated you like a child...

So many options to choose from.

He would probably ask for Danny to be moved to the other second grade class. I rubbed my forehead and the oncoming headache. I hoped he wouldn't do that. I loved Danny and honestly felt like we were finally making progress on some of his transition struggles.

My phone vibrated on the table. It was an unknown number.

Weird.

"Hello?"

"Astrid?" the voice sounded sad.

My breath caught in my throat. It couldn't be. "Mom?"

"Astrid Luxe, you have some major explaining to do!"

The sadness was gone, replaced by her familiar frustration.

Speaking of disappointed parents who still tried desperately to shape their kids' lives... How did she even get my number?

Chapter Two

ADAM

As I flew down the road just outside the edge of town headed for home, I honked a hello at Frank on his green John Deere tractor. He smiled and tipped his cowboy hat back at me. It seemed he was still on cloud nine after winning the pumpkin contest last weekend—first prize for biggest squash, eight hundred pounds.

I drove past the Anderson and Bailey fields with brown dusty dirt, now that they had dried and stored their hay. I normally hated being away from Danny, but this time I was grateful for the twenty minutes to collect my emotions.

Neurodivergent...What did that even mean?

Failed parent? Too much time on electronics?

Was I inattentive? Was it because of the divorce?

Even if he was different, how would giving him a label for the whole town to focus on help him?

He needed more time from me, more support. I was sure any shortcomings were due to me and my parenting, not from him.

I rubbed my forehead. I felt like I was drowning.

Drowning in debt, failures, and expectations.

I slowed my speed and turned onto the gravel road.

I'd always prided myself on being able to keep calm and collected in charged conversations, but apparently that didn't apply when it was about Danny. I couldn't believe I had knocked down the chair and crayons. My outburst and behavior were nothing short of embarrassing...but I was impressed that Ms. Faith didn't back down, even with our size differences.

Even if my opinion hadn't changed.

I pulled my old diesel truck into Mom's dirt driveway and shifted into park. I needed to cool it. Danny felt others' emotions strongly and would pick up on mine in an instant. That wasn't fair to him. I wondered if there was time for a run to burn off the frustration real quick.

I leaned my head back, resting it against the multicolored striped fabric of the bench seat, and pulled out my phone. It was covered in cracks and dents, just like my truck, but it still worked fine. No need to throw something out just because it ain't pretty, regardless of how my ex felt.

I texted Mom.

Adam: Can I go for a twenty-minute run? Had a long day.

I knew I would pay for it with inquiring questions and motherly smothering, but I would pay for it later, and *later* was the key.

Mom: Yep. I am making pancakes. Danny liked them last time. =)

Adam: Here's hoping he hasn't changed his mind. Thanks, Mom.

Danny might have in fact changed his mind. He would love one thing and eat it over and over and, without warning, he'd decide he would never eat it again. That Mom struggled in the cooking department didn't help, and I wasn't much better.

I grabbed my running shoes from the duffel bag I always kept nearby in case I needed to burn off some negative energy. I tightened the double knot on my laces. I put my earbuds in and selected my rock playlist.

The current plan: push my body until I can no longer think of all my failures.

I ran past cattle pastures and hayfields, letting the loud beat of the music soothe my soul. The air was crisp and cold as it filled my lungs. I could do this run with my eyes closed. This was the same run I'd done in high school.

The only difference was that back then I would run to meet my now ex-wife Cassie and make out with her near her barn. We were young and stupid, that we married right after graduation proved it. I dodged the pothole in the dirt road.

I passed the Parks' mailbox built out of horseshoes welded together at the end of their lane. I waved at Brad as he rode by on his horse. Must be bringing the cows in from pasture.

The life Cassie posted and bragged about now couldn't look more different from mine.

I pushed harder and faster. Trying to outrun the failures, guilt, and pain that clung on to me as Metallica's "Enter Sandman" blasted into my ears.

Not choosing me was one thing, but not wanting Danny would never make sense.

Danny. My reason for living and the brightest and best part of my life.

The run had worked its magic because I no longer felt anger and frustration. I wanted to be with Danny. I turned around and rushed back to Mom's.

I gasped for air, trying to steady my breath, as I walked up to the old ranch house with white paint peeling and makeshift particle board steps. I knocked as I stepped inside.

"Hey, Mom, it's me." It had been just the two of us for a while. Dad died of a heart attack when I was in middle school.

She glanced up from the faded blue plush couch, but her smile didn't reach her watery eyes.

"You okay?" I crossed the worn brownish-orange shaggy carpet toward Danny at the kitchen table.

"Yep, I'm good." She gave a small nod.

Hm. "You ready, Champ?" He nodded but said nothing, nor would he look at me or his grandma.

Something happened, but I wouldn't push the issue today. Danny needed to get home, and I would be back in the morning anyway. We could chat then.

"Okay, I'll be back at ten to winterize the sprinklers. Snow can't be far off." I had to scrape the frost off my windows every day this week.

She shrugged. "Hard to tell with Idaho, But Frank's knees were acting up and he swears snow's coming this weekend."

I smiled. "I know better than to bet against Frank's knees." I grabbed Danny's errant sock. The man was correct more often than the weather man.

"Let's bring out the Christmas decorations from the shed tomorrow too." That would cheer her up; she loved Christmas decorations, and I would get to finish early. Between frozen fingers and slick shingles, early meant less likely to fall.

It would take the whole day. First blowing out all her sprinkler lines and then loading up her house with big, gaudy plastic reindeer, Santa, elves, and tinsel. Her favorite was the plastic yard nativity. Even though a light had shorted out and melted part of baby Jesus's face years ago, it still went up every year. She insisted Jesus wouldn't care about looks anyway.

I gave Mom a hug. "Cya in the morning." She felt smaller against my chest than she used to. Had she been helping with Danny too much?

I grabbed Danny's backpack off the floor where he had left it, and helped him into his neon orange sweater. He had been wearing it every day. I tried to wash it last week, and Danny insisted he wouldn't go to school without it. After a heated conversation where neither of us budged, I finally asked why. He didn't think his friends could find him without it.

I bought an extra one that day. I had better look for a neon winter coat. I held the truck door open and Danny climbed onto the bench.

I drove the truck six miles up the dirt road. Danny had taken to wearing his hair longer. I'd tried to cut it for the last month, but every time I tried, he said he liked how fuzzy it felt and he didn't like the sound of the buzzers. I rumpled his blond hair with my hand and smiled. This kid was my entire world.

I loved my coaching job, and doing the PE classes with the kids. I loved my son. I loved my life, and I loved Hillsdale, even if it could be a bit much for some. It was my home, and they were proud of their own.

Danny started humming a Christmas song. Was he struggling in school? Why hadn't he told me? I should probably look through the piles of papers he brings home instead of throwing them out. "Hey, Champ, how was your day?"

"Good." Danny looked out the window at the neighbors' grazing horses as we passed. He yawned. It wasn't great to have him come to morning practices. But I couldn't leave him. Maybe Mom would come over, but she was doing so much as it was.

"Hey, Danny?" He continued to stare out the window.

"Danny." I prompted again.

Nothing. I reached over and tapped him on the shoulder, and he looked at me as if he was hearing me for the first time. "Did you eat at Gran's?" When that boy went to another place, he was gone.

He shrugged. "Kinda. She made pancakes. I didn't like them though. They were burnt."

I winced. Danny's blunt honesty could hurt Mom's feelings sometimes. That must have been why she was upset.

"Danny." He was looking out the window at the passing fields. "Look at me, please." He quickly made eye contact, then looked away. "No, Danny, I need you to look at me, so I know you're listening."

His bright blue eyes met mine.

"Danny, did you hurt Gran's feelings again?"

He sighed. "I don't know. I just said they were black." His brow furrowed. "And that she should use less butter if she wanted to lose weight."

Great. I would need to call Mom tonight. I was so tired, tired to a level that my bones and soul felt a constant ache. I rubbed my stubbled chin.

"Danny, that is hurtful," I whispered. He was listening. There was no need to raise my voice. Another area where my ex and I differed.

His eyes shot to mine and then away. "Why? I just told the truth. She was talking about how her pants were tight and she wanted to lose weight. I remembered a YouTube video about fats in the body."

I had to explain these things more and more, but it didn't seem to stick. I recalled what his teacher had said about eye contact and not making social connections with the other kids. I dropped it for now. I leaned back in my seat. "I love you, bud."

"Hmm." His attention went back out the window.

"Can I ask you a question?" I asked.

His golden hair bobbed yes, but he didn't look my way.

"When I ask you to look at my eyes when I am talking, so I know you are listening, how does that make you feel?"

Danny shook his head. "I hate it. It makes me nervous, and my hands get wet. I don't know what to do with them. Why do they think I can't hear them if I am not looking at them? The different aids and specials teachers say it over and over. Look me in the eye, Danny. Eye contact, Danny. Danny, listen with your eyes, Danny." His forehead creased. "That's not even possible. Right?"

I leaned back. That was the most he had said about anything in a while. *Okay. Don't make him look me in the eye. Got it.*

Chalk that up to another parenting fail.

I reached over and rubbed his shoulder. "Sorry, Champ. Daddy's still trying to figure parenting out. I'll stop asking you to look at my eyes, okay?"

He shrugged. "It's not so bad with you. I don't like when the lady at lunch does it. She won't let me leave the line until I look her in the eyes and say thank you."

It sounded like a reasonable request to say thank you. But since Danny was talking, I didn't want to interrupt him.

"I didn't want to do it. And she couldn't make me." He glanced my way and then back to the field. "So I decided to skip lunch, but then Ms. Faith found out. She talked with the lunch lady about how it made me uncomfortable and how we could come up with different 'strategies.'" He made air quotes with his hands. "She likes that word." Danny's brow furrowed. "Now when I give the lunch lady a thumbs-up, she knows it means I'm saying thank you." Danny kicked his feet swinging from the bench. "Ms. Faith went with me to get my lunch a few times, and now it's okay again." He looked out the window again.

My pride crumpled. Ms. Faith. It sounded like I needed to apologize for more than my childish behavior. I didn't know he wasn't eating lunch because he was uncomfortable. I also didn't know why he couldn't just say thank you.

"Do you like Ms. Faith?" I flexed my fingers around the steering wheel.

"Yes. We are doing a business fair where we can win a real prize. I want to get first place."

I nodded. I thought about our discussion earlier that day.

Discussion was a bit of a stretch. I shut her down and didn't listen to her reasoning at all.

I tapped my fingers against the steering wheel. Danny had been through so much. He didn't need more difficulties in his life, including some label.

"When we get home, we can throw the ball around?" I asked Danny.

"No, thanks."

He never wanted to throw the ball, but sports was the only way I knew how to play. Before long it would be too cold to do much of anything outside. Danny asked to build LEGO sets once, and I tried, but I always seemed to do it wrong.

There was a list of rules somewhere, but I wasn't privy to it.

"Is there something you want to do together?"

We pulled up to our simple ranch-style home with broken shutters and a crumbling shed in the back.

"Nope, I'm good."

"Are you hungry?" I asked.

"Yep, I already told you Grandma burnt the pancakes."

I nodded as I turned off the truck. Danny opened the door and hopped out, rushing to the front door. I shut the door of the old truck and fumbled through my set of keys as I listened to the constant sound of the neighbors free-ranging chickens.

Inside, Danny took off his shoes and his shirt and went and grabbed his favorite blanket and wrapped up like a little burrito. This wasn't the life Cassie wanted, but it was a beautiful life, and it was mine.

Chapter Three

FAITH

I hadn't heard my mother's disappointed voice since I left home just over three years ago.

The panic increased a hundredfold. This very well might send me spiraling right back into my therapist's care.

"Mom?" I whispered. "Are you okay?"

A part of me was excited to hear her voice, and I allowed that part of me to hope that she might say she loved me or even missed me. My heart betrayed me as it picked up speed, with hope.

"Don't call me that!" came the quipped reply.

My eyes widened and I inhaled a sharp breath. I'd know that anger anywhere, but I refused to call her Meredith. She would do anything to maintain the persona that she was in her early thirties.

Surgeries, Botox, crazy fad diets, and mostly not acknowledging her aging offspring.

"Is everything okay? You sounded sad."

"Of course I'm not sad. Don't be ridiculous." The rough edge of her voice left me raw.

"How did you get my number?"

"Honestly, Astrid, stop being so simple minded." Her annoyance grew louder through the line. "I am tired of waiting for you to end this tantrum."

I chewed on my bottom lip, unsure what to say.

"Time to come home. I refuse to make any more excuses for your absence at the Christmas Eve Gala. You know Jane Knolt's told everyone at her New Year's party that her daughter, Mandy, had joined the family business." She scoffed.

I wondered how often Mom wished she had Mandy as a daughter instead of me. Mandy seemed to love the "esteemed" life.

"She announced it to everyone! I know she did it to embarrass me. You're making us a joke—the LUXE line a joke. It's time to grow up."

I had grown up. The problem was I grew into someone she didn't want.

My heart dropped. She didn't miss me, all she wanted was for me to come back, work for the company, and control who I was.

I kept my breathing slow and deep and waited for my hands to stop shaking. In therapy, I'd learned about setting boundaries. It was such a simple word to say, but so much harder to do.

I took a shuddering breath and tried to hold back my emotions. She wouldn't take my emotional outburst as anything but weakness, anyway.

"Please don't call me again." The words felt sharp on my tongue, even at a whisper.

I hung up the phone and refused to acknowledge the pain falling from my eyes.

I flicked my fingertips across my cheeks to banish the tears and glanced around my classroom sanctuary. The thankful turkeys hung all over the walls.

Turkeys colored by little fingers and smiling faces. They were all so different. Different colors, different placements of feathers, feet, eyes, and beaks. Two were turned into unicorns, and another looked like it was an explosion of feathers and feet. I chuckled. I was not sure where Mason had gotten the extra feet from. But each child handed their turkey to me with such pride and happiness in their eyes.

Each one different, each one wonderful, and each one accepted.

Hillsdale was my life now; this was where I wanted to be.

I looked at Danny's desk, and my heart shrank from the feeling that I might have failed him. But at least I had tried.

Why did parents feel their worth was on the line every time a child was different than they expected? I admit I could do without my own differences—I spun my ring—but Danny was different in a beautiful and subtle way.

My head was ringing and I wished I could undo the last hour of my life.

My phone rang again with the same unknown number. I sent it to voicemail and then saved the number as Mom. It hurt, but it was better than the alternative.

I stood and walked around my little second-grade sanctuary, pushed in orange plastic chairs, and put away pencil boxes. It was healing to my soul, like I was putting the pieces of myself back together. Lydia must have gotten new scented markers because her desk was now sporting some bubble gum–scented hearts, Mason left his plastic dinosaurs out, and Caleb was still wiping boogers on the desk. Gross.

I grabbed the disinfectant and wiped down the tables. Technically, the janitor, Jim, would be by later, but there was no need to add to what was already a tough job.

I turned off the lights and went down the hall toward the exit, giving courtesy nods and smiles to people as I passed.

A week of bubble baths, cozy pjs, and *The British Baking Show* was calling my name. Rose, my roommate and one of my best friends, was going to Haven Falls for the weekend, and I was glad she didn't pressure me into coming this time. I had already gone to her birthday celebration with her family and the one we had a few weeks ago at Scott and Marissa's Bed & Breakfast, so she decided my presence at three birthday celebrations wasn't necessary.

She loved dance clubs, loud music, shopping, and I was more of a comfy couch, baking, and romance novel girl. We were so different, but somehow it still worked. Now, I was extra glad that I hadn't gone this weekend. I really needed to spend some time processing and decompressing.

I opened the door of my dependable Corolla and sat as my phone vibrated with an incoming text from an unknown number.

[Unknown Number]: Astrid Luxe, stop being so selfish and come home! You're making us look like a joke.

So, she had multiple unknown numbers at her disposal.

If home was where the heart is, then I guess I had no home. Just cold, perfectly decorated walls, fake friends that only liked you when you were popular, and a mother's failed expectations.

Right after I graduated high school, I took my credits and used my large "allowance" to cover the fast track online college classes. I also paid a college student and my new friend from COMM 101, Sarah to teach me how to drive. She was studying to be a therapist, and I appreciated all the free mental health tips I could get.

Mom was never too worried about how I spent my money as long as I did as I was told. I still had two years left of my degree when I found the rural school program where you can finish your degree as you teach. It was in a small town in the middle of nowhere, and it was perfect.

I got the job and left New York for Hillsdale, Idaho. I changed my name and my number and never looked back. I wanted somewhere no one knew about Luxe fashion. I wanted to start over, to find myself.

I pulled out of the school parking lot, avoiding the largest potholes and mud puddles. The good thing about the upcoming freezing weather was maybe the ice would take care of the mud that was being tracked into the classroom.

When I changed my name to Faith, I hoped it would help me

gain the ability to create a life I was proud of. The last name Lyons I completely regretted. Not only because it sounds like lying, which was what I had been doing to everyone I'd met in Hillsdale, but also because I chose it thinking it would help me be brave. But I wasn't. I was still me: anxious, embarrassed, and a bona fide crowd hater.

I stopped at the one stoplight in town, watching as Randy wrapped the streetlight with red and silver tinsel, prepping for the upcoming Christmas decorations. He was using a weird spinning gadget. I couldn't tell if it was helpful or making things more difficult.

My phone vibrated again, so I set it to silent.

I knew this was not the end of the conversation; it would now never end. The thought made me tired.

Growing up, my mother's constant negativity at my attempts drained my soul, and I wasn't excited to restart the exchange.

The sensible thing would be to change my number again, but she would just find it again. Money has always had its perks.

And I was hoping she had grown to accept me and my choices. That maybe she wanted to get to know each other as adults. I shook my head. Stupid.

I was born to continue the Luxe fashion empire. My parents had gotten it from an investor and had built it into the icon it was today. Dad was quiet to my mother's demands. She had my life all mapped out: I would be LUXE Brand Ambassador, or as she called it *the face of the business.* Which is why if my face was ever seen, there were strict expectations for it.

The light turned green and I continued down main street, passing Letty's cat strolling down the road. I made a mental note to text her when I got home in case she was out searching for her again.

At home in NY, I always had to be *on,* you never knew when people would be watching, and they were always watching. I shivered remembering the paranoia. I did interviews, needed to be seen at galas, and was always on parade.

My perfect life, fit into her perfect gilded frame.

The only problem in her equation was me.

I drove past the Bed & Breakfast and a group of boys shooting basketball in hats and mittens. I could see their breath in little clouds in the air. It was really cooling down.

I hated the spotlight. I hated being in the papers and all the fake connections and very real money flaunting. I puked before most social gatherings and panicked in crowds. The more I tried to be who she wanted, the more I struggled.

"Anxiety is normal. Take a pill and push through."

"You don't have a stomach ache, you are just dramatic."

"Everyone wants to be you, can't you see that? Stop embarrassing me."

So I tried harder to be the popular debutante. The one who thrived in attention and loved crowds. I hated the person I became during my senior year, even if my mother had never been prouder of me.

I was popular, but I was mean. Like in those stereotypical high school movies with the popular mean girls, the ones you hate, and you love when they get their eventual comeuppance. Let's just say I didn't resonate with the hero of those movies; I was the villain.

I still hated watching any movies about high school.

I hid my anxiety and sadness behind a mask of bravado and bite. My therapist told me to forgive myself and move on. But some things I'm not sure should be forgiven, because then they might be forgotten. Words have consequences, and I used mine to hurt, and I would never go back to being that girl.

I turned down Park Street, and my little duplex came into view. There were only six, so I was lucky to find something to rent at all. It was the smallest thing I had ever lived in, and I loved it more than anything. It was mine.

Well, mine and Rose's and the person who actually owned it, but you know, basically mine.

I would try to be worthy of this new life I was creating. I would try to set healthy boundaries and create the life I wanted.

Mom didn't care about me. Mom didn't know me, nor did she want to. She wanted a puppet, an empty vessel to shape, mold, and control.

I would need to spend my time and energy on things in my control, on my life in Hillsdale.

I walked into my apartment and turned on the lights as I went. The pressures and expectations of the world easing away.

My house smelled of vanilla and was blissfully quiet. I took off my blue high heel shoes and put them with my collection of heels. One good thing about being raised the way I was, I basically learned to walk wearing heels. Most teachers refuse to wear heels, but I loved how they made my legs look and helped me reach things on shelves.

I went to the bathtub and started the hot water. Hopefully, a bubble bath would help release the tight muscles in my neck and shoulders.

If not, I could try a new recipe as a distraction. I had wanted to try macarons for a while. It looked extremely complicated, which would be perfect.

I sank down into the bubbles and hoped the soap would wash away all thoughts of my past, my mother, and Adam.

Chapter Four

ADAM

I was always late. I growled as I threw my truck into park. Granted, the snow-slush mix everywhere didn't help. I expected my players to be respectful and on time, even on an early Monday morning practice right after Thanksgiving break.

And yet, here I was, late.

I was doing my best.

My best to build a team and teach these boys to believe in themselves. On top of that, play the right players and avoid angry parents and town gossip. Throw in the mix be a single dad and hopefully not ruin Danny's life.

I pulled Danny past the signs for the upcoming high school dance and into the gym. He refused to get dressed this morning. Kept pulling off and throwing his shirt. He wanted the one with no tags, but it was dirty. I even tried ripping off the other shirt's tag, but he still refused. I finally found another shirt with no tags, and then he made a huge ordeal about his socks.

The boys lined up on the black out-of-bounds line and were running ladders. The team captain, Jacob, had taken control of the group.

They were good kids.

Danny followed me, rubbing his eyes, and walked over to the bleachers, four rows up and into the middle, his designated spot he always chose. He yawned and turned on his tablet.

I felt guilty everywhere I looked.

Guilty I had let the boys down by being late, and guilty that I hadn't let Danny sleep in longer. These early morning practices were going to kill me. I made sure Danny had what he needed, changed my shoes, and rushed onto the court.

"Sorry I'm late, guys. I know it's not respecting your time." I looked at Jacob. "How about we have a shoot off to see how many pushups I have to do after practice?"

He chuckled. "You're on." It was important to me that they saw I didn't ask them for something that I wasn't willing to do.

The team rallied around me. Jacob said they were done with warm-ups. We spent the rest of the forty minutes working on plays, running drills, and ended with a free-throw competition that had me doing thirty-five pushups. I ran laps at the end with the team until my lungs and legs burned.

"All right, boys, circle up." I motioned my finger like a lasso in the air. The team tightened around me. "Remember, we have a game tomorrow. Keep those grades up and get a good night's sleep. Treat yourself to a carb-friendly dinner tonight." The boys nodded.

I looked at Jacob. "Captain, count us off."

Jacob smiled and put his hand in the middle, the team followed his lead. "Okay, Eagles on three. One, two, three, Eagles!"

The boys headed to the bleachers to grab water bottles or off to the locker room and the showers. We had about thirty minutes until school started.

I leaned against the wall, catching my breath, and stretching out my calves. There was something about the high energy and competitive nature that made time fly.

I was exhausted, but in a good way. Not from life or things I couldn't control. But from pushing my body to its limit and having it answer.

Jacob took the stairs two at a time up to Danny. He gave him a high five and said something. Danny nodded but didn't meet his eyes. I remembered what he said about it making him uncomfortable. Was it okay that he didn't look them in the eye when they talked to him? Would the boys care?

Ethan was by Danny too. He was a freshman on JV, but we often practiced at the same time. He liked to help Danny with the water bottles at Varsity games when JV wasn't playing. I'd been impressed with his work ethic and his kindness to Danny.

I made my way toward the bleachers.

Two teenage girls opened the double doors facing the outside. They were giggling as one pushed the other farther into the gym.

"Can I help you, ladies?" I asked as the girls turned bright red. Jenny, the cheer captain and Jacob's girlfriend, stepped forward.

"Umm...yeah." She cleared her throat and pulled her blond ponytail over her shoulder. "If you are done with practice, I was wondering if Jacob was here."

She held a poster board with candy bars at her side. Looks like someone was getting asked to the dance.

"Jacob," I called toward the bleachers, "someone's here to see you." I nodded at the double doors. "Danny, let's go to my office until I need to take you to class, bud." I looked at Ethan. "Nice hustle today, Ethan."

Ethan gave me a small smile. "Thanks."

Danny stood and walked toward me, eyes glued to the tablet.

"Whoa!" Jacob grabbed his shoulders before he tripped down the stairs. "Better keep your eyes on the prize. Which, in this case, is not falling down the stairs." He grinned, and Danny peeked at him as Jacob jogged around the corner to the girls.

"Jenny!" He pulled her in for a hug, lifted her in the air, and her face lit up with joy.

Watching Jacob with his girlfriend was hitting a little too close to home. High school sports star and his head cheerleader girl-friend. I could see my younger self and Cassie in them, like looking into a mirror of the past. I hoped Jacob knew who he was and what he wanted in life. I was so confused at that age. So many people asking about what you wanted "to be," scholarship offers for basketball at different schools, and the entire world felt like it was staring and demanding answers.

Danny clipped his ankle on the last step of the bleachers and almost fell. I caught him and grabbed his tablet. "How about I hold on to this until we are sitting?"

I didn't regret all of my decisions though. I'd do it all again to have Danny. We walked out of the gym, through the hall, and toward my office. Through one last double doors, I rounded the corner and saw Brandy, the cheerleaders' coach, waiting in front of my door.

Crap.

The doors closed behind me, along with my escape. She'd asked me several times to help with the different fundraisers throughout the year. I might have hinted I could help with the next one, hoping she would forget. I turned on instinct, hoping she wouldn't recognize me...

"Coach Peters," she called in a singsong voice. "You are a hard man to track down. It's no wonder no one has caught you yet." She smirked, proud she had trapped me.

"Sorry, Brandy, but—" I turned back around to face her.

"It's not happening." She placed her hands on her hips. "This fundraiser is for the entire sports program, not just the cheerlead-ers. You really need to help. Since you won't sell tickets or partici-pate in the PTO bake sale or anything else I've suggested, I signed you up to chaperone the upcoming dance."

What?

No.

My hands were sweating. "Come on, the dance? There has to be another option. What am I going to do at the dance?"

Danny started rocking and bumping his shoulder into me over and over while clearing his throat.

Brandy eyed him curiously. "You literally just stand there." She waved her hand. "It's easy! Keep people from getting too rowdy. Should be right up your alley; most of the mischief makers in this school are on your team, and they'll be on their best behavior if you're there."

I glared. They weren't troublemakers. Granted, the one who stole Ms. Bates's gnomes, and the group that threw rotten pumpkins at cars are still running extra laps, but they were good kids.

Danny kept up with his fidgeting, and I handed him his tablet. "Fine. I'll chaperone the dance."

"I'm so glad! Thanks." She spun on her high heels. "Oh, you need to bring a date."

"Whoa! Wait, no way." I held my hands up between us.

She turned back around. "Yes way, or else the other mom chaperones will spend the night trying to dance with you and not actually do their jobs." She rolled her eyes.

"Not interested." I folded my arms.

"I don't care." She grinned. "I'm sure your *friend* Jessica could come." She turned and left.

Jessica *was* just a friend, regardless of what everyone in this town assumed. She had wanted to be more than that when I first came back to Hillsdale, but I wasn't ready for a relationship then, not that I am now.

I don't know if I could ever trust anyone like that again. For relationships to work, you have to be vulnerable and open. You have to believe the other person cares about your happiness.

I learned the hard way that that isn't always the case. Sometimes people just want to manipulate and control.

People will change. They hide parts of themselves until it's too late. After I married Cassie, everything changed. I could no longer make her happy. I had tried for ten years to be who she wanted. Giving every piece of who I was into hoping she would accept me and be happy. I went to the college she chose and studied the degree she thought would get us the most money.

Money that she spent before I could earn. The credit card debt clung to me every step I took, even now.

Danny shrugged as he headed toward my office. He reached under the couch and grabbed a blanket, took off his shoes, and wrapped the blanket around himself.

I did a lot of things wrong with the divorce three years ago.

Like assuming all the debt and giving her all my assets just to stop the fighting, but in the end I was the winner.

I still couldn't believe Cassie didn't fight for Danny, and based on every lawyer I talked to, she couldn't change her mind now since she signed away her rights.

Danny clicked on one of his games, the sound bouncing around the small office.

"Turn your volume down, please."

I repeated myself three times before he heard me and turned down the sound.

I shook my head. Seriously...a date?

What was I supposed to do with that?

If I asked Jessica, she might think it meant more than it does. That I'm ready to date, and namely that I wanted to date her. I pinched the bridge of my nose.

But if I went to the dance alone, I'd spend the whole time making excuses and dodging handsy women.

I had Danny and the team, plus taking care of my place and Mom's. My life was full and busy. I didn't need or want any drama with a woman. At least the dance wasn't until January. I would worry about it later.

I signed on to my desktop and went into my email. I scrolled and noticed one from Ms. Faith about upcoming school events and her asking for volunteers, and was reminded I still needed to apologize to Danny's teacher.

Chapter Five

FAITH

It was Monday morning, and my students were currently hyped up on too much sugar and not enough sleep. I was excited about being back in routine, but not for all the emotions.

The Thanksgiving break had raced by, peppered with a few passive aggressive voicemails from Mom.

I had four failed macarons attempts where I couldn't get the foot part right, and I made it to the library and checked out a bunch of Christmas romance novels.

"Ms. Faith," Lucy shrieked. Her green doe eyes were wide, her tiny lips quivered. "Danny said chicken nuggets are made from baby chickens!"

Oh boy, not sure I was awake enough for this. I needed caffeine and quick.

My mental state wasn't much better than my students'. I really shouldn't have stayed up so late, even if the enemies just became lovers in my novel.

Today, I think my current reading addiction and I were enemies.

I stood up from my chair, promising my head I'd find caffeine before lunch, and made my way over to table three.

"What did you think chicken nuggets were?" Danny's eyebrows scrunched down as he stared at the table. "It says chicken in the name."

"Danny, let's stay on topic for now. You should practice your spelling words, please." I pointed to the nearly blank paper in front of him.

"I hate spelling," he grumbled. "I'm trash at it." He gripped his pencil so hard his knuckles turned white.

I leaned down beside him. "I know spelling is difficult for you, but we still need to practice." I shrugged. "Everyone has things that are difficult for them, even if you can't see it. That's just how the world works." I patted him on his back as he refocused on his paper.

I went over to Lucy. She had big alligator tears in her eyes. "Are you doing okay, Lucy?" I squatted down at eye level with her.

"Is it true about baby chickens?" She whimpered.

I exhaled slowly as I thought of how to handle the situation. "I haven't seen chicken nuggets being made, but yes, they are made of chicken, though not the babies."

She blinked rapidly, and I could tell her little mind was imagining horrors. This was not going well. "There are laws in place to help the chickens live healthy and happy. If you have any more questions about it, maybe ask your parents tonight, okay?"

Lucy wiped at her watery eyes with the back of her hand. She had such a sweet soul. "I ate chickens," she whispered in pain.

Danny fidgeted in his chair as his eyes shot between Lucy, me, and then the table. "Danny, would you like to say something to Lucy?"

Danny shook his head.

I squeezed Lucy's shoulder. I needed to focus her attention elsewhere. "Your letters are looking great! I like how your capital G goes all the way from the ceiling to the floor."

Lucy smiled.

"And I love your pink glittery pencil."

Lucy then launched into a story about how she got it at a birthday party. Once she was refocused on spelling, I made my way to Danny. "I can tell you are working hard, thank you."

He huffed and whispered, "Was that one of the things that wasn't nice to say? My dad tries to remind me, but I can't remember them all." His eyes shifted, focusing anywhere but on me and Lucy.

My heart melted even more for this child. "You're all right. Let's just focus on schoolwork, okay?"

The last thing I needed to be thinking about was his father. I replayed the exchange until it was burned into my brain. I could see places where I could have explained things differently and cringed at the fact that I had let my past influence the conversation.

When I saw him today, I honestly did not know what I would do. Try to hide, obviously, but if not that, then what?

Pretend it didn't happen?

Maybe I could go home sick?

I sighed. I was being ridiculous. I was a teacher, and he was a parent. I would simply apologize. And then panic about it later.

I walked over to table five and reminded Sophie that the paper was for writing on and not eating.

"All right, class, we have five more minutes to finish your spelling paper and then you have specials. It's music today!" Of her twenty-four students, some were excited; others were not. The new music teacher seemed sweet, although eccentric in her tinsel sweaters and huge dangly earrings. "I think you are preparing for the Christmas Music program."

The class turned in their papers, and I walked them down to the music room. I had a few minutes and needed to check emails and catch up on the group text with Rose and Marissa.

Last text I read, Scott, Marissa's husband, had eaten one of Marissa's favorite cookies, and then left the box on the table, where their dog London ate the last one.

Marissa was not happy. The newlyweds were a perfect match. Even if Marissa was missing cookies, soon she would text Scott's praises.

Emails first. I steered my pink heels to my desk.

The business day planning meeting was tomorrow, and I still needed parent volunteers. I sent three emails and still hadn't seen any offers.

If I didn't get some help, there was no way the student business day would work out. After all, the business plans of second graders could be tricky. Sam was planning on building a rocket, and Lucy wanted to start a unicorn research team.

I opened my email and scanned through it.

There was one from Adam Peters, subject: Volunteer and apology.

My cursor froze over the message in my inbox. I clicked open.

Ms. Faith,

I need to apologize for my behavior at our last meeting. I was tired and caught off guard on a long day, but that is no excuse.

I noticed you asked for parent volunteers several times for the business fair at the end of January, and I figured the best way to apologize and to spend time with Danny would be to help. He has been talking about this business day nonstop, and for Danny, that's saying something.

Thanks again, and I'll be at the meeting tomorrow night.

Adam

Wait.

What?

Adam was volunteering?

Oh no! This wasn't a good idea.

There was no way I could work that closely with Adam. It would require spending a lot of time together and constant communication. The saliva grew thick in my mouth as I tried to swallow.

I could barely even speak to the man without getting tongue

tied—unless I was scolding him, apparently. Not only that, but wherever Adam went, enormous groups of people immediately seemed to gravitate. That was the opposite of what I wanted.

I rolled my anxiety ring and pursed my lips.

I had no other volunteers, and I really couldn't do this by myself. I bit my bottom lip and went back to my inbox. Maybe I missed an email from another parent volunteer?

I scrolled through twice.

Nothing.

I picked up my phone and texted Rose and Marissa. My besties always came through in a crisis.

Faith:So, remember that meeting I had with a parent before the break?

I had told them about the meeting with Adam but had left out names. I never wanted to start a rumor about anyone. I learned back in New York how hurtful words and gossip could be, and I wanted to err on the side of caution now.

Rose: You mean the one you let past-mama-drama enter the convo and had you baking all Thanksgiving break? (eye-roll emoji)

Marissa: I still can't believe you wouldn't tell us who it was with.

Rose: Right? And I don't buy the excuse that you were worried I might retaliate.

I smiled. I loved our Three Musketeers trio. The Rose threat wasn't far off either. I took the blame, but Rose was still ready to go fight my battles. That she owned the only salon for thirty miles meant she could start a rumor fire quickly and do some serious damage. She wouldn't without my permission, but still.

I felt like names were necessary now for them to understand the situation.

Faith: Yep...well... It was Coach Peters, and he also just volunteered to help the class for the business fair...to apologize and spend time with Danny.

Rose: Hunky Peters!!! Girl, you are going to get one-on-one time with him! (flame emoji) Lucky! He'd better be nice though.

Marissa: At least you finally got a volunteer? I'm so sorry about the anxiety spike over Thanksgiving. No fun! We should do a girls' night.

Marissa had always been a bit more level headed than Rose, not that that was saying much.

Rose: A hot, muscly volunteer. He could just pick you up if you need to hang signs above 5 ft.

Faith: Ha ha...

She wasn't wrong. At barely taller than five feet—without heels—I always had a step stool handy.

Marissa: Want to come over for ice cream so we can discuss the plan of attack? I will grab Ben & Jerry's.

The B&B Marissa was running with her hubby Scott had become a great place when we needed to meet up and didn't want the audience and eavesdroppers that came with eating out in this small town.

Faith: Cherry Chocolate, please

Rose: Cookie Dough

Marissa: Got it! See you ladies tonight. 6?

Faith: 6

Rose: 6

Could I spend all this volunteering time with Adam?

I decided for now I would not answer the email; I needed time and space to see it better.

I PULLED UP AT THE MULTIPURPOSE B & B, WHICH served as a community center and events center as well as law office, and shut the door on my car. Looks like they finished painting it over Thanksgiving. I know they were rushing to finish before the hard freeze. The B&B was a Victorian-style house that held charm and history. It had dark purple shutters and a freshwood railing around the porch. They had been working hard to get it fixed up, but because of the historical funding and guidelines, they had run into a few logistical bumps.

I was in my usual after-school attire, leggings and a loose sweater. I love my pencil skirts and heels, but there was something amazing about taking off the professional layer and being all about comfort. My mother would be horrified that I was in public like this.

The sign at the door said DOORBELL BROKEN YELL DING DONG. They had fixed the doorbell, but Marissa would never take down the sign; she laughed every time she saw it.

I knocked softly.

"Come in!" Marissa hollered from somewhere inside.

I opened the old wooden door and was met by London, their golden retriever. She wagged her tail in excitement as I rubbed behind her ears. "Hey girl!"

She eagerly licked my extended hand, hoping for a secret treat.

I squatted down as I reached for the treat in my pocket. Her brown eyes shone as her tail picked up speed. I held out the little cookie bone. "Here you go." I was never allowed pets growing up, and I couldn't wait until I had my own place. I would have to be careful, or I would eagerly take in every animal I saw.

London took the cookie and rushed into the kitchen.

I walked through the foyer into a small kitchen with mismatched cupboards and faded yellow wallpaper. Marissa was in her usual 80's band T-shirt and jeans; her jean jacket was hanging on the hook behind her. It was threadbare and sported a few patches now. Her cellphone was pressed against her ear and a planner was in her hand.

Scott really had changed her. Maybe changed was the wrong word.

He made her feel safe and able to explore who she was. She used to run from anything that resembled planning, and now look at her.

I walked to the freezer and grabbed the three little cartons of ice cream.

Marissa nodded and took down a few notes. "Yes, that weekend is available for both a wedding ceremony and reception."

I set down the ice cream and grabbed spoons.

"Yep, I put you on the calendar. Thanks so much for thinking of us."

London came back over to me and barked.

"Shhh, London." I had brought only one treat, and she was obviously ready for another.

"All right. Yep. We will be in touch." Marissa hung up and smiled at me. "That's going to be our third wedding next year."

"That's great!"

She sighed and plopped down in the chair next to me as I passed her the Chunky Monkey ice cream.

Rose threw open the door. "Don't start without me!"

Rose's heeled boots clicked against the aged wooden floors as she made her way to the kitchen. London greeted her with kisses and a wagging tail. Rose hated animals, and I think London could sense it and was determined to change her mind. She raised up and put her paws on her black shirt.

"London! Down," Marissa called.

London dropped to the ground but licked Rose's hand on the way.

"Ugh! Sick!" She wiped her hands off on her pants. "Go away, London." She threw her hands out. London doubled her loving efforts, jumping up on Rose again.

Marissa stood and grabbed London's purple collar and took her over to the kennel.

"Where is Scott?" I opened my ice cream. He usually wasn't far from wherever Marissa was.

"He's in Clifton, helping his parents with some stuff with their house. He will be back tonight though."

Rose brushed any stray hairs that might have landed on her black pants, washed her hands, and then sat at the table.

"Okay." Marissa smiled. "Let's unpack this Coach Peters situation."

"It's Adam, apparently." I put my head in my hands.

"Ohhhh!" Both girls squealed in unison, then we all giggled.

I dug my spoon into the soft texture and took a bite. The cold sugar coated my tongue and worries. The best things in life are usually packed with sugar. My five-foot-nothing frame had some things not going for it, but a fast metabolism was a point in my favor.

My phone rang, and I silenced it without looking. It was probably spam. I didn't allow myself to wonder if it was Mom. I had broken down and answered an unknown number over Thanksgiving break only to hear about my car warranty that didn't exist.

Rose raised an eyebrow and nodded. "Okay, which first, mommy issues or hot daddy issues?"

I rolled my eyes. The girls knew I had a complicated relationship with my parents, namely my mother, and that she was beyond disappointed when I became a teacher and left the life that was set up for me.

I told Rose that Mom had gotten my number recently and I was trying to ignore her. I still listened to her passive aggressive voicemails, even though I should have deleted them.

I shouldn't keep my past from Rose and Marissa, but my past was complicated, and honestly, I wanted to start over, without carrying it around with me.

"There is not enough ice cream in this town to talk about mommy issues. Let's stick to Adam." I took another bite.

"So why does he want to volunteer?" Rose took a large bite. "Does he feel bad or something?" The frigid ice cream made her mouth pronounce the words as if she had a cold.

"He says Danny loves the fair and wants to be involved in

something he enjoys, and yes, he apologized for how he acted in the meeting, even though I'm as much to blame."

"Awww...I love that." Marissa said.

"I bet he is a great kisser, and he could definitely lift you off your feet with those biceps." Rose wiggled her eyebrows.

The image instantly played in my mind, and I enjoyed the daydream more than I should have. "Rose! Not helping. And not interested." My cheeks heated. Okay, maybe some interested.

Rose pointed her spoon at me. "Umm, girl, everyone with a pulse is interested."

"I'm not." Marissa fluttered her fingers in the air, showing off her wedding ring.

"Is Scott already forgiven for the cookies then?" I asked, with a raised brow.

She was so happy she practically glowed. It was inspiring the way she adored her husband, and he obviously returned the sentiment. I wondered if my parents had ever been that way. It seemed more like they sprouted from an ancient business transaction rather than anything resembling affection. They often slept in different rooms and barely seemed to acknowledge each other's existence.

"Well, he bought them, and I ate four of the six, so..." She shrugged.

I chuckled. "Fair."

"But, back to Adam." Marissa raised her eyebrows.

I set down my spoon inside the lid. "Admittedly, he is gorgeous. But he also seems very extroverted." I shuddered. "Besides, everyone has said he isn't interested in dating." I shrugged. "Not that I have thought about dating him or anything." My cheeks heated.

"Riiight." Rose quirked an eyebrow.

Marissa lifted her spoon in the air. "People saying they aren't dating isn't always the barrier you think it would be." She gestured around the room, grinned, and scooped another bite.

"Facts." Rose pointed her long acrylic nails at Marissa.

I shook my head. "True, but Scott didn't stand a chance of not dating you. This is me we're talking about."

Marissa rolled her eyes. "Whatever, Faith, you're too hard on yourself. You're gorgeous and kind, and anyone would be lucky to date you."

I was short, which in the fashion world was basically a sin, plus I hadn't always been kind, so there was at least a piece of me that was ugly and mean.

"I think Jessica has already called dibs on dating him anyway." I looked up at the ceiling. "The way she is always talking about him, it's obvious she is crazy about him."

"You can't call dibs on a person. They get to make their own choices." Rose gave me a flat look.

"None of this matters anyway. He isn't asking to date me, just to volunteer." I held my hands up.

"We'll see." Rose gave a wicked grin.

Marissa shrugged. "Regardless, you will do anything for those kids, and like it or not, you need help, and Adam has offered."

"True." I scooped another bite, holding it in my mouth as it melted.

"Looks like you're stuck." Rose raised her eyebrows.

I leaned back and blew out a small breath.

We all knew I would put myself through a lot for my students' happiness. Including accepting help from the hot and outgoing Adam Peters.

"So, maybe the question is how do I get over my crippling anxiety about it? I can barely form sentences around him, and I still need to apologize." I would need to learn how to hold a conversation with him, and fast.

"Oh, I know!!" Rose clapped her hands. "Don't they say that to get over your nerves you picture the other person in their underwear?" Rose bit her bottom lip and wiggled her eyebrows.

Heat rushed to my face, and I put my head on the table before Rose could comment on my blush.

"Oh, my gosh! ROSE, not helping!" I groaned.

Chapter Six

ADAM

I walked into the elementary library for the business fair meeting. I was a few minutes late, which I hated, but it couldn't be helped at this point. Danny's teacher was brief in her reply but said she would be happy for my help. I hoped this meeting was short. I still needed to grab a few things from my office, and I promised Danny we could get pie from Merritt's tonight.

Among the staff sitting at the round wooden table was Jessica, rolling her pencil back and forth along the scuffed surface. The minute our eyes locked, she lit up and smiled. "Adam!" She motioned eagerly to the seat beside her.

I'd tried to talk myself into dating Jessica once, just to appease Mom. But every time I tried to get myself to feel "more" for her, I couldn't. She was solidly placed in the friend zone. That didn't surprise me; the thought of dating anyone made my skin itch.

I walked toward the empty chair. My eyes flicked to Ms. Lyons —I shook my head, I mean Ms. Faith. Where Jessica was demanding attention in bright neon colors and dark makeup, Ms. Faith was the opposite, avoiding eye contact and attempting to dissolve into the background. Maybe that was why Ms. Faith stood out to me. She wasn't yelling for my attention.

She was beautiful with her petite frame, hair pulled back into a messy bun, blue eyes, and quiet vibe. I knew better though. I'd seen the fire in her gaze when we were discussing Danny. She could hold her own when necessary.

I glanced in her direction, and she gave a barely perceptible nod back, but then avoided eye contact. It was obvious she was happy to avoid me. I chuckled.

"What's funny?" Jessica asked.

"Hm?" I refocused on Jessica. "Oh, it's nothing."

Jessica's forehead creased, then she cleared her throat and pivoted to face me.

"Sorry, practice ran late." I announced to the room.

"Oh, that's fine. The sports program does so much for this school." Jessica reached out and laid her hand on top of mine. "Do you guys think you will make it to the state basketball championship again this year?"

Wide eyes around the table went to Jessica's hand over mine. I gently pulled my hand out from under hers. "Hope so, and hope to actually win this year too."

"No one blames you. It was so close last year, even going into overtime." Jessica leaned back, looking a little hurt that I'd pulled my hand away.

I didn't want to hurt her feelings. Maybe I'd grown too lax in allowing physical interactions between us. Not much beyond hugs and arm brushes, but I also didn't want to make a big deal about things either.

"Oh, plenty of people blame me." I had many emails that proved so. Sam, the man who ran the only bakery in town, had cornered me the following weekend and let me know I could no longer buy his maple bars if I didn't win next time. I never was sure if he was joking or not.

"As I was saying..." Helen Sparks, one of the fourth-grade

teachers, cleared her throat. She was a no-nonsense spinster sort and had scared me to death when she was my fourth-grade teacher. I could still feel her eyes boring into my soul as she gave me papers covered in red that said DO OVER. Her last name of Sparks I always thought was fitting. She seemed moments away from combusting.

Maybe that's when I would officially be a grown up, when I looked at Ms. Sparks and did not feel fear.

"There will be one more mandatory group meeting where we go over the finalizing details, but you will mainly work with your assigned teacher, and often."

I glanced at Ms. Faith, and her cheeks turned bright red as she stared at the table. How would it be, working with Danny's teacher? We hadn't parted on good terms, but I knew Danny liked her, and although Danny was blunt for some people, he was an excellent judge of character.

Ms. Sparks scowled then turned her piercing eyes on Ms. Faith. "Ms. Lyons, have you been able to get your two assigned volunteers?"

"It's Faith, and not yet. I have sent out emails, but—"

"No excuses." Ms. Faith shrank in on herself, and I tried to shoot her a commiserating smile. She didn't see it.

Why didn't she mention I was a volunteer?

"Adam, why are you here? This is an elementary fundraiser, are you a volunteer?" Ms. Sparks turned on me.

Jessica's hand shot into the air. "He can help me!" She bounced in her chair.

I panicked and looked at Ms. Faith.

"Adam has offered to help with my class since his son is a student of mine." Her eyes flicked to me.

I nodded, grateful that she had spared me an awkward situation. A small smile formed on her lips before she focused down on her papers again. When she blushed, I could see her freckles better.

Ms. Sparks sighed. "Very well."

Jessica looked between Ms. Faith and me, her eyebrows drawing together.

"But, Adam." Ms. Sparks pushed her glasses up her pointy nose. "I know life has been hard with Cassie and whatnot, so don't tell Faith that you can do something if you can't." She raised her eyebrows.

I leaned back, still shocked that everyone in town felt they knew all the pieces of my failed marriage and that they didn't hesitate to comment on it. I wanted to tell her to butt out, and that I was an adult. Instead, all I managed was a nod and a "Yes, Ma'am."

"I'm right here..." Ms. Faith muttered as she gestured with upturned hands. I pursed my lips against the naughty smile I didn't want Ms. Sparks seeing form on my face.

"All right, teachers, I suggest you use the rest of the hour to set up schedules with your volunteers and organize. At next month's meeting I would like a list of the class's chosen business topics and any materials you require." She waved in dismissal.

Principal Dotty rushed in, flustered and with flushed cheeks. "I'm so sorry, my timer was set, but it didn't go off. What did I miss?" The new principal missed most things. Her wide eyes took in the room, and her head lowered.

Ms. Sparks, Dotty's aunt, rolled her eyes and power-walked toward her. "Dotty, you missed everything." She growled.

Everyone stood and wandered around the round tables. We had seen this family situation play out before. I nodded at Jessica, stood, and walked over to Ms. Faith. Standing over her made her shoulders shrink more, but I couldn't do anything about my size. "All right, where to?"

"Um." It came out barely above a whisper. "We can go to my classroom?" She gestured about my height. "But I think we learned you won't fit at the tables." She grinned at her joke and looked around the room. "Maybe we just find a table in the corner?"

I was glad to see she wasn't afraid to tease me. I needed to apologize, and all apologies are better with food. I snapped my fingers. "I know, let's go get pie. I need to apologize for our last meeting."

Her left eyebrow raised. "You already did in your email. Also, I wasn't exactly the picture of controlling one's emotions. I'm still so embarrassed." Her cheeks turned pink, and I couldn't stop my answering smile.

"Yes, well, I wanted to apologize in person, and all apologies are more sincere with sugar. Let's go grab a slice at Merritt's. You can bring the planner"—I gestured to the stack of papers in front of her—"and I can get out of this building."

She shrugged. "No arguments here."

We stood. "Perfect. Want to meet me at Merritt's or ride together?"

Her eyes widened. "Um, I can drive." We walked toward the exit.

"Adam...where are you going?" Ms. Sparks called out.

I felt like I'd been caught passing notes in her class, and my spine went rigid. I cleared my throat.

"We are still planning, don't worry." Ms. Faith chimed in and speed-walked to the door.

I held the door open for Ms. Faith, she rushed by me with her arms loaded with papers. Jessica caught my eye and her gaze narrowed at Ms. Faith's back. I gave her a small smile and closed the door behind us.

Ms. Faith took a slow, deep breath. "Thanks." She sighed. "She makes it hard for me to breathe."

"She terrifies me too. All right, Danny is waiting for me in my office. I'll go grab him and meet you at Merritt's."

Ms. Faith's eyes brightened. "Oh yes, please bring Danny. He's so excited and will love planning with us." She shrugged. "Plus, then it won't look like a date."

I stopped walking, and Ms. Faith bumped into me with the sudden change of pace. Ms. Faith didn't think I meant it as a date, right? My gaze flicked to hers.

Her face flushed with embarrassment, and she fidgeted with her ring on her right hand. "I know it's not a date, but this town has a lot of opinions and well... Ugh, never mind." Her head dropped as she closed her eyes.

I raised my right shoulder. "I really don't care what others think." I added in a flat tone. I lived too long trying to be who someone else wanted.

Well, honestly, that wasn't completely true. I had found I was starting to worry a little about Jessica, but it was less about me caring about people's opinions and more I didn't want her to trust the gossip and think we were more than friends. She was nice to talk to sometimes, and she was a good listening ear when I first came back and needed to work through some things about my ex.

"Must be nice." Ms. Faith grumbled and rolled her eyes. She sighed. "All I do is worry about others' opinions." She chewed on her bottom lip. "I'm going to turn off the lights and grab a few things from my room. I'll meet you at Merritt's." She called over her shoulder, rushing away from me, avoiding eye contact and avoiding me.

I chuckled and tilted my head to the side. I had a feeling I wouldn't mind spending time with Ms. Faith. I enjoyed watching her switch from shy to bold and then right back.

Chapter Seven

FAITH

Ugh, why had I made that date comment? I knew it wasn't a date, and I was sure Adam would never consider dating me. So why make it even more awkward?

I rubbed my forehead with my hand. I knew rumors could be vicious and do way more damage than the truth.

Besides, he was a parent of one of my students, which has to be inappropriate. I turned off the lights and did a final walk through my classroom.

I could do this. I steeled my shoulders and spun my ring.

Adam had me at pie, though I would do a lot for sugar. Plus, Danny would be a wonderful buffer, since Adam intimidated me. Nothing about the man was quiet. From his presence in a room to his commanding voice.

I went to my car and drove down Main Street to Merritt's. I pulled into a parking spot and tapped my fingers on the steering wheel to the Christmas music on the radio.

I loved Merritt's, but I usually came with Marissa and Rose. They knew my quirks and didn't care if I sometimes got nervous. I took a deep breath and reminded myself that the next best thing to being brave was pretending to be so.

I looked around the parking lot but didn't spot Adam's truck. I would look weirder just sitting in my car though, so I decided to wait inside.

I avoided the mud and ice patches and pulled open the front door. My stupid hands sweat, and my stomach tightened. I glanced around the dining room. There were a few groups of people, but most of the tables were open. One held a group of teenage boys, all laughing and hitting each other.

"Hey Faith, are Marissa and Rose coming?" Jesse greeted me with a smile.

"Um, no." I shrugged. "Just me, and one of my students."

Jesse raised her eyebrows. "Okaayy?"

I raised my hands between us. Oh, my gosh! That sounded wrong. "I mean, I'm meeting a student and their parent." That didn't sound right either, I closed my eyes. "Not because they are in trouble or anything."

Jesse tilted her head.

I took a slow breath to stop the rambling. "We're meeting about a school project." I exhaled.

Jesse nodded and pointed toward the tables. "Pick any table you like."

I turned to scan the dining room, and my shoulders dropped. There were about twenty empty tables. I chewed my lip and looked around the room.

Do I pick one by the front window? Or maybe closest to the door? My eyes flicked over the room, looking for some proof of where I should sit.

What if it isn't where Adam and Danny wanted to sit, or randomly too close to someone else?

Why didn't Jesse just tell me which one?

The teenagers chuckled, and a salt packet flew in my direction.

I took a fortifying breath, and I went in and sat at the closet table in a booth, plopping onto the bench to put me facing the door.

I sighed and rubbed my forehead. Why was I like this? Why couldn't I walk into a room of people and be rational? First I stumble over my words and then panic about a table.

It's just a table. It doesn't matter.

I flexed my fingers, relaxing the tension that had built in my knuckles as I spun my ring.

The door opened, and Adam and Danny walked in. Danny saw me, waved, and skipped in my direction. Adam leaned over and grabbed Danny's shoulder to talk with him. I didn't want to intrude, so I studied the grain of the table.

"Hi, Ms. Faith." Danny plopped into the booth across from me. Danny saw my spinning ring, and his eyebrows pulled down. It was obvious he was picking up on my nervous energy, so I pulled my hand under the table.

Adam's phone against his ear, his eyes met mine, and he pointed to the phone and raised his right shoulder. I smiled and nodded.

"Dad said I get to have pie, and I love pie." Danny was still looking at where my hands had been.

"Me too. Do you have a favorite type?"

"I like the red ones. I like that your ring spins. Can I see it?"

I pulled my hand up from under the table to show him my ring and the inner circle that spun. He reached over and rolled it back and forth.

"That's cool."

"Thanks, I sometimes get nervous, and when I spin it, it reminds me to take slower breaths."

"And it has pandas. I like pandas." I sensed no judgment or shame. This was why kids were the best. They accept and love so easily. Danny looked up at his dad and scooted farther into the booth as Adam put his phone into his front jeans pocket.

Adam slid in next to Danny. "Sorry about that, I had a parent who wanted to talk about a new play they made." He rolled his eyes. "All right, what does everyone want? Ms. Faith, you too."

"Oh, I can get my own." I raised my hands between us.

"Nope." Adam shook his head. "This is apology pie. I have to buy it."

Danny glanced up at his dad, his eyes curious. "Did you say something not nice?"

My breath caught in my throat. He openly suggested a flaw in public. My mother would have berated me for hours for a stunt like that. Adam faced Danny, and I reminded myself to breathe.

"Yep. Remember, Daddy is trying his best, but he makes mistakes too."

Danny nodded, his blond hair jumping with the movement.

"Well, Daddy accidentally wasn't very nice to Ms. Faith."

Danny scowled. "Why? I like her."

I released a breath I didn't know I was holding, and my heart soared at his comment. I wanted to hug Danny, although he didn't particularly like hugs.

"I know you do, Danny. I'm sorry I hurt your friend's feelings. I did something not nice, and I'm trying to show your friend that I'm sorry that I hurt her feelings. Does that make sense?"

Danny tipped his chin to the side, thinking about it. "Yep. And you are getting one for me too, right?"

He chuckled and ruffled Danny's hair. "Yes, I am."

Danny grinned, appeased that he also got to get pie.

Watching him interact with Danny, something inside of me melted. He wasn't like my parents. Adam might not want to pursue testing, but he loved Danny, and he wanted what was best for him. He wasn't concerned about how it made him look.

Danny looked at me. "Dad said we get to help with the fundraiser!"

"I know." I clapped my hands in front of me. "Are you excited?"

"Yep!"

Adam looked chagrined. "Is that okay? I should have asked.

It's just that Danny is so excited about this project. And I can't stand to be away from him more than I have to..."

I shrugged. "I was supposed to come up with two volunteers. Looks like I found both of them."

Danny fist-pumped. "Yes!"

I sighed. "I should let you know, Danny, that I also wasn't very nice. I got frustrated and forgot to breathe through the zones." I twisted my fingers and refused to look at Adam, although I felt his gaze on me. "I kinda yelled at your dad. I know your dad is also your friend, so I'm sorry."

Danny looked back and forth between the two of us, his eyebrows pulled down, thinking through the situation.

My eyes flicked up to Adam's. They were kind and patient as he gave me a small smile.

Jesse came over with a notepad. "Heard you guys are getting pie."

Danny sat up straight. "I want a red one. And my dad is buying Ms. Faith's because he was accidentally not nice." Danny scrunched his nose. "I'm accidentally not nice sometimes too."

Adam reached over and gave Danny a side hug. "You're great, Champ."

Jesse chuckled. "Trust me. Most people are not nice from time to time." She winked. "Okay, one red... Would you want straw-berry rhubarb or cherry?"

"He likes the rhubarb one with whipped cream, please." Adam added.

"I will take apple, please," I said to Jesse.

"Make that two for the apple," Adam nodded.

Jesse grinned. "Sounds great! I will have those right out." She turned and headed toward the kitchen.

I watched Danny and Adam interact, and their relationship was so different from what I'd first assumed.

If I ever had a family, this was what I wanted it to look like. I wanted to embrace and love my children and their differences. I wanted them to feel safe to be who they were.

And if I married, I wanted to marry someone like Adam. Someone who didn't stand in the shadows on the sidelines, but who was right in the middle of it all, actively loving them as well.

I cleared my throat and shook my head to clear the sudden onset of emotion. Okay, it was time to rein in this Norman Rockwell painting. I reminded myself and my ovaries that Danny was my student and I shouldn't be thinking about my future family and him and Adam in the same thought.

Boundaries, woman!

I grabbed a notebook from my purse. "All right, so, about the fundraiser." I opened the notebook and laid it on the table. "Okay, my class has twenty-two students, and I was hoping some of them might work in teams. My biggest concern was the business ideas and getting them to agree on something that actually feels manageable."

"What business were you wanting?" Adam asked Danny.

Danny shrugged. "I thought maybe I could just ask for money."

Adam shook his head and grinned. "I don't think it works like that."

Jesse came and set down the pie plates.

"OHHHH, Coach Peters got a date!!!" The teens in the booth ahead of us started laughing and making kissing noises. My breath caught.

Would this cause problems for Adam? Would it cause problems for me?

Danny's eyebrows pinched down. "Date? What's a date?"

I could tell he was feeling concerned. I forced a shaky smile. "No, Danny, it's not a date." I smiled at him, trying to give him comfort I didn't feel.

"But they said..."

I shrugged, pretending I didn't care. "People say things all the time that aren't true." I leaned in and whispered. "They probably don't know we are working on a project."

Danny nodded, but glanced over at the teens, his eyes held concern.

"Excuse me." Adam stood from the bench and stalked across the linoleum floor. The teenagers went silent.

I chewed my lip, unsure how to react to the upcoming confrontation.

"Hey boys, what is rule number one?" Adam tipped his head to the side.

They must be on his team.

"Respect others and yourself," the boy with the blond curly hair mumbled and avoided Adam's gaze.

"Right. So what do you think about how you're acting?" Adam's voice wasn't loud, but it was firm.

"Sorry, Coach," the boy mumbled.

"We were just joking," added the one in glasses and an over-sized hoodie.

"Yeah, we didn't mean anything by it," added the third in the group, as he raised his palms.

Adam rested his hands on his hips. "Right, but words can hurt."

I thought back to high school. It had been so easy to say I was joking, that the pain I caused was meant in good fun. My shoulders drooped. I wished I could go back and erase the person I was.

"The words you use show more about you than the recipient," Adam continued. "And to me it shows you boys need more direction. After practice, you will stay and run laps until I decide otherwise." Adam's voice left no room for argument.

"Yes, Coach," they replied in unison.

Maybe I should run laps too. Would it earn me the right to move on from my past? I spun my ring.

Adam leaned toward them. "I will run them with you. If you can beat me, I will cut down the time."

They grinned and nodded. "Deal."

He had reprimanded and then diffused the tension. That was amazing.

"All right, see you boys at practice."

They nodded. He walked over and sat down as though nothing had happened. "Now. About that school project," Adam said.

Right, school project.

BACK AT MY DUPLEX, I WEIGHED AND MEASURED THE flour for a new gingerbread recipe.

I'd come a long way since I first moved in. Poor Rose got stuck with me, dying our sheets pink and burning ramen noodles. She'd just mutter under her breath something in Spanish and teach me what to do. Between her and the internet, I figured out most things, and if not well, at least functionally.

Now baking had become therapeutic for me.

I poured the flour into my pink KitchenAid mixer. Then, I scrolled through the recipe I'd found earlier that day. My emotions felt as if they had been through a mixer and turned to jelly.

"Oh no! You are baking again!" Rose came in from the front door and plopped down her haircutting bag on the floor and walked over to the bar stools and sat. "Wanna talk about it?"

"Can't a girl just bake for fun?" I shrugged.

Rose raised an eyebrow. "Yes, they can. You, however, never take on a new recipe without cause. The cause being a reason to distract you from your thoughts. And at this rate, I am going to be back at my middle school weight if we don't work through some of these things. Your baking is too good to pass up," she swiveled on her stool. "Is it Mom or school?"

I should tell Rose about my background. I know I should. But there was some safety in no one knowing. Plus, I knew she struggled with bullies in middle school.

"How is your mom doing?" I asked, deflecting the question and putting the carton of eggs back in the fridge.

She raised a manicured brow. "Spastic and hanging by a thread," she smirked. "So, nothing new, but nice try."

"Fair." I smirked. This time my emotions weren't about Mom, at least not directly. It was more about Adam and Danny and how being with them together made me wonder if I could have a future family and what it could look like.

Rose reached down and unzipped her right boot and then her left.

"I had a meeting with the coach about the fundraiser," I said. "He and Danny are both going to help. We actually went and got pie at Merritt's together."

Rose grinned a knowing smile. "Oh, I know."

My mouth dropped open, and I blinked rapidly. "What?"

She shrugged. "I cut Ashley's hair today." She rested her elbows on the counter.

That was all the explanation needed. Ashley was the town gossip. If she knew or assumed something, soon everyone else would too.

"Do I even want to know what she said?" I braced myself for the worst potential outcome.

"She asked me if you were dating the coach, and that Jessica would not be happy, since she has been trying to date him for two years." Rose checked her nails.

I raised my palms. "We're just working on a project." I rubbed my forehead. How many people would she tell that I was trying to date Adam? Would it make it awkward between us? "You corrected her, right?"

Rose smirked.

"Rose?" I covered my face with my palm.

She sighed. "Yes. I told her you had a school project you were working on. But she also warned me that if Adam is ready to date, you wouldn't be the only one in line."

I rolled my eyes. "True, she and everyone else would be. I have no delusions there." Well, nothing I would be mentioning. Especially not that I compared him to someone I might want to marry someday.

"Admit it, that man is fine." Rose took out one of her gold hoop earrings and placed it on the countertop before starting on the other earring.

"Of course he is." I blushed, thinking about how he handled being patient with Danny. "You know, he seems like a great dad too."

Rose scoffed. "What would that have been like?"

"Right?" I raised a shoulder. We didn't talk about daddy issues often, but I knew hers was angry, and she knew mine was basically absent.

Rose smirked. "Well, you already love his boy. You spend enough time with Adam and you're a goner."

"He would have to want to actually date, and then want to date me." I forced a soft laugh.

Rose rolled her eyes. "Oh please. No one actually means that, it's just an easy excuse until they find someone they want to date.

I shook my head no. "Nope. It would never work, he is too intimidating." I shuddered. "He stops and talks to everyone."

Rose chuckled. "Maybe some eye candy is worth being social for?" She raised her left shoulder.

"Nothing is worth being *that* social for." I turned and grabbed the sugar out of the cupboard.

Rose wiggled her eyebrows. "Maybe…"

"Stop!" I tried to force my smile away.

She grabbed her earrings. "In the meantime, you better learn to cut your recipes down to quarter batches or start giving them to Adam."

Maybe I should bake him something as a thank you for helping me out? I immediately started feeling antsy and tight in my chest.

Or maybe I would just eat it all.

"If you fatten him up, maybe some other men in this town would stand a chance at getting a date." She stood and grabbed her boots. "I'm going to go shower," she called over her shoulder. "I have another date with Blake."

I stared after her. "Wait, the guy from Haven Falls?" I left the sugar on the counter and rushed after her. "That makes three dates!"

Rose smirked. "Well, tonight we are going bowling, and I don't plan on losing, so we will see how things go after that."

Chapter Eight

FAITH

I stapled the last reindeer with the red cotton ball nose in the hallway near our classroom door. It was a Friday, and my headache had been growing for hours, but the kids would love coming in Monday morning and seeing their artwork.

I went back into my room and grabbed the stack of homemade snowflakes attached to a string from my desk.

I didn't want to go through the trouble of finding a ladder, and I took my step stool home last week and forgot to bring it back. I grabbed my chair and pushed it near the wall. High heels on a chair would be asking for an accident. I removed my shoes and stepped onto the chair.

The best part of being in the old part of the building was the ceilings were lower. With the strings in my lips, dangling snowflakes swung back and forth as I reached with the stapler posed above my head. I stretched up on my tiptoes. I could almost reach the ceiling. I pressed up on my tiptoes harder. There! The door flew open with enough force that it crashed into the wall. I sucked the string farther into my mouth as I nearly fell off the chair.

Danny rushed into the room with tears streaming down his face.

I hopped down and rushed over to Danny, snowflakes left on the ground around me. I reached him and placed a hand on his back.

"Danny? What's wrong?" I leaned down.

"My dad wasn't at parent pickup, and I couldn't find him in his office or the gym." He rocked back on his heels and tried to hold back his gasps. "I think he forgot me." With that confession, a fresh wave of tears was released.

"Hey, it's okay." I rubbed his back gently. "I'm sure your dad is here somewhere." I grabbed a tissue from my desk and handed it to him. "Maybe we could find him together?"

"No, he isn't here. He left me." Danny's shoulders drooped.

"Oh Danny, your dad would never forget you. He may lose track of time, but he will never forget you."

Danny's breath calmed. His eyes took in the classroom and snowflakes littered on the floor. "What are you doing?"

"I'm putting up some Christmas decorations."

He wiped his tears with the back of his arm. "Can I help?"

It might be good to keep his mind busy, but I'm sure Adam was looking for him somewhere. "How about we look for your dad first, then we will decide?"

Danny didn't meet my eyes, but nodded.

I turned around. "One second." I slipped my shoes back on.

"I hate to wear shoes too." Danny pointed at my feet.

I smiled back. "All right, let's check the front office first, then maybe we can check his gym office?"

"I already checked it." Danny shook his head.

"I'm sure you did. Maybe someone in the office knows new information now."

Danny shrugged but started toward the hallway.

"Sorry you can't find your dad. I'm sure that feels scary." I quickened my steps to keep up with his fast pace.

"I used to have a mom, but now I don't." Danny stared at the floor but maintained his speed. "Grandma said it was because she left and didn't come back." His eyes shot to me before they darted away. "Do you think Dad will leave me too?"

My heart instantly broke, and I stutter stepped. I reached for Danny's hand, pulling him to a stop. I kneeled down so I was eye level, and I squeezed his hand in mine. "No, Danny, I don't think your dad will leave. Your dad loves you very much."

He stared at the brown woven carpet. "But moms are supposed to love their kids too, right?"

I walked right into that one. I grasped at what to say. I didn't know the details of his parents' relationship, other than the gossip around town. Which was basically that she left them both for a more prestigious career.

"Yes." I thought of my mother, I had almost called her last night. I hit dial and then hung up. She wouldn't want to get to know me, she would just want to change me. I pursed my lips. "Some people aren't very good at loving. Maybe they just don't know how to." My forehead creased. "I have watched your dad though. He knows how to love." I pictured Adam as he held Danny and his eyes when he looked at his son.

Danny looked back at me with his eyebrow raised.

I squeezed his hand again, stood, and nodded toward the office. "Let's see what we can learn."

I walked into the foyer, which was scattered with a few chairs and a long desk. Margo sat behind the desk. She glanced up and smiled. "Hey, Faith."

"Hey, Margo."

Her eyes went to Danny at my side. "Oh no, did a parent forget to pick up again?" She tilted her head. "Wait, you're Coach's kid, right?"

I placed my hand on Danny's back. "Yep, looks like maybe there was some confusion over pickup?"

"Hmm..." She sat back in the swivel chair and clicked her

keyboard. "Let me check." She focused on the screen. "I'm not seeing anything... Oh wait, yep." She looked back at me. "Looks like we relayed a message to the coach from his mom that she was having some car problems a few hours ago." She shrugged. "My guess is they got delayed. I'll call him. Do you want to wait here?" Margo looked down at Danny.

He stiffened and took a small step closer to me.

"That's okay. Danny was going to help with a few things in my room, the door will be open. When his dad gets here, will you send him there?"

"Yep." Margo nodded. "Sure thing. I'll call right now." She picked up the phone and started dialing.

"Thank you." I said and headed toward my classroom.

"Are you hungry?" I asked Danny. "I have some gingerbread cookies I made that I need someone to try."

Danny scrunched his nose. "Why do you want people to try them? Are they in a competition or something?" Danny's shoulders had softened now that he knew his dad was coming. I was hoping the cookies would help him relax even more.

"Nope, I simply haven't made them before, so I was trying something new."

Danny shrugged. "Sure."

Back in the classroom, I went to my desk and grabbed the Tupperware with cookies. I was going to drop them off in the teachers' lounge since Rose refused to eat any, but then I got nervous.

Would people think it was weird that I was randomly bringing cookies?

What if they liked them and thought I was searching for compliments?

What if they didn't?

So the cookies stayed at my desk.

I opened it up and handed it to Danny. "Have as many as you like."

He picked up a cookie and took a bite, and his eyes lit up in surprise. "These are good." He reached in and grabbed two more. "My grandma tries to make cookies," he mumbled between bites, "but I think she tries to sneak veggies in them, 'cause they taste weird, and she burns them." He scrunched up his nose. "My dad will sometimes buy cookies though."

I nodded. "Well, I am glad you like them. I love to make cookies, but I have no one to eat them." I sighed.

His forehead crinkled in thought. "Well, my dad and I always eat the cookies he buys." He shrugs. "We could eat them."

I chuckled. This adorable boy's logic was sound.

"All right, you finish those cookies there so you don't get crumbs everywhere. I'm going to keep working on the room. Once you are done, you can help."

He quickly shoved the remaining two cookies into his mouth. "I'm ready. What can I do?" Crumbs fell to the floor as he tried to keep the cookies inside his mouth.

I looked around to see what Danny could help with safely. "How about you hold the strand of snowflakes and I can staple them up high?"

He stood tall. "I'm tall for a second grader."

"True." I slipped my shoes off. "I'm short for a grown up, so that might come in handy."

He followed me over to my chair. "It's probably because my dad is tall so it's in my garnetics."

I smiled at his pronunciation of genetics. He used the most adult words sometimes. "I'm sure you're right." I steadied myself as I stood on the seat of the chair. "Okay, will you hand me a snowflake?"

"This one?" He grabbed a snowflake off the ground.

"Yep."

We worked like this for a bit. Me reaching to my tallest and stapling and then moving my chair, and Danny holding the snowflakes as high as his arms could stretch. He hummed "Frosty the Snowman."

"Do you like Christmas music?" I asked as I stapled another snowflake.

"Yep." Danny bobbed his head to his song.

"Me too."

"We're going to get a Christmas tree tomorrow."

I stretched and stapled another snowflake. "Fun, like at the Merc?" The mercantile store was an eclectic mix of hardware, farm tools, seasonal decorations, alcohol, groceries, and, at times, questionable bulk sales. I'm still questioning last year's bulk onion sale. What would someone do with forty pounds of onions?

Growing up, Christmas trees showed up at my house, huge, fake, and pre-decorated. The Merc had real trees for sale this year, and I wanted to get one.

Last year, Rose and I borrowed one of her family's old fake trees for fun, and it was my favorite part of Christmas. Decorating the tree and putting on the lights was my favorite part. It felt like magic.

"Nope." Danny picked up another snowflake as I moved the chair. "Dad takes the truck to the mountains, and we cut it down, plus we get one for grandma."

"Huh?" I had never thought of getting a Christmas tree that way, but I immediately wanted to try. "That sounds awesome! Where do you go?"

"I dunno, a mountain." He shrugged and handed me another snowflake.

I chuckled. "Fair."

A thumping sound came from down the hall, and a six-plus-foot man sprinted into my classroom, eyes searching desperately until they landed on Danny. I saw his shoulders crumple as Adam rushed over and pulled Danny into a big hug, anxiety and worry rolling off of him.

"Oh, Champ, I'm so sorry I was late." He leaned back and

searched Danny from head to toe. "Grandma's car fell apart, and then as I was fixing it I ripped my pants, then on my way here I hit a patch of ice and skidded straight into the snowbank." He sighed and his shoulders dropped. "Then I had to wait for Randy to come help pull me out, and he was insistent on trying this new gadget he made, and it took longer." He pulled Danny into his chest for another hug.

"It's okay." Danny shrugged.

Adam knelt on the ground and looked at Danny's face. "I know it makes you nervous when I'm late, and I told you I would be early, and I wasn't here. I am so sorry."

My heart melted as they hugged, Danny's smile growing by the second. I bet Adam's hugs would make anyone feel safe, not that I wanted him to hug me, it's just his muscular arms would feel amazing. I shook my head and reminded myself I was staring, and I forced my gaze elsewhere.

Danny gasped. "Wait, is the truck broken? Can we still go get a Christmas tree?"

"The truck's fine. I just got stuck." Adam ruffled Danny's hair.

"Phewf," Danny added. "Ms. Faith said you wouldn't leave me here, and she gave me cookies. You should try one, they are way better than Grandma's."

Adam chuckled, and his eyes met mine. They held such gratitude. "Thank you."

"Of course." I looked away from his intense gaze. "It wasn't a big deal. I needed to stay late anyway."

Adam looked at Danny. "It was a very big deal." It came out so soft I could barely hear the words.

Danny left his arms, rushed over to the Tupperware, and grabbed the cookies for his dad, who had sat on the floor, the exhaustion evident in his features. Danny grabbed a cookie and handed it to his dad and Danny sat right next to him on the ground and grabbed another cookie for himself. Adam gave Danny a soft smile. "I had better ask Ms. Faith first, Champ."

The boys peered at me with their kind eyes, and my heart swelled. "Please." I nodded toward the cookie.

Adam stood and walked toward me. My hands shook so I clasped them together.

"I am so, so, so sorry about Danny not knowing where to go. But it means everything to me you were here for him and helped him feel safe. I owe you big time." Adam closed the distance between us. The air around me heated.

Danny grinned widely. "Nice. What does she get?"

"I guess that is up to her." Adam shrugged and raised his eyebrows as he looked at me.

My mouth went dry, and I couldn't swallow. I couldn't ask for a hug. That would be weird. Right?

"Um," I looked at the cookies. "I could really use some taste testers for my baking. I love to bake when I am stressed...like a lot, and my roommate is refusing to try my recipes anymore." I sighed, hoping to convey the confidence I didn't feel.

Adam raised an eyebrow and I watched him in what seemed like slow motion as he raised the cookie to his mouth. My heartbeat raced like a herd of second graders released for first recess.

I cleared my throat.

Maybe it was just anxiety?

Adam slowly chewed, not breaking eye contact. My throat went dry, and I reminded myself to breathe. His eyebrows raised as he went in for another bite and finished the cookie.

"Ms. Faith, that was amazing!" He held his hand in front of his mouth as he smiled. "I might be saying that because of a steady cookie diet of Chips Ahoy and my mother's attempts..." He shrugged. "So maybe I am not the best judge, but I will happily eat anything you bake."

My cheeks flushed and I spun my ring.

Danny stood up and grabbed Adam's hand. "We can be your cookie testers!"

Adam quirked an eyebrow. "That just sounds like I owe you for two things now, Danny and cookies."

"Nope, I'm good." I put my hands up. "Honestly, I was happy to help."

Danny clapped. "I know!" He grabbed his dad's arm. "Ms. Faith has never picked out a mountain Christmas tree. She should come with us tomorrow."

Oh boy, this was not what I envisioned. Yes, I wanted to try the tradition, but going with Adam and Danny would be a terrible idea. My heart and ovaries might never recover from seeing this sweet family in all the holiday magic.

"That's so sweet, Danny. Thank you for thinking of me." I placed my hand on my chest. "I really am good though."

Adam tipped his head to the side. "Are you getting a Christmas tree?"

I pursed my lips together. "I was planning on getting one from the Merc once I convinced my roommate Rose."

Adam's nose scrunched. "Those pre-cut trees die so fast, and don't smell near as good."

"Well, they smell better than the fake one I used last year." I raised my right shoulder.

"A fake tree...that is blasphemy." Adam stepped away from me. "It's settled. You need to come get a tree the real way with us." Adam smelled like citrus and warm spices, and he was still too close to me.

"Oh, uh, I dunno."

Danny grinned. "It's a lot of fun, and Daddy lets me use the saw."

Adam flinched. "With lots of supervision," he added, looking at me.

I chuckled. This might be a once in a lifetime opportunity. It sounded so magical, and I admit the idea of spending some time with Adam and Danny sounded good too. I sighed and decided to be brave. I realized I wasn't nervous to spend time with Adam because he was intimidating, I was starting to feel nervous for an entirely different reason.

"Sure, why not?" The words were out of my mouth before I second-guessed everything, and I held my tongue.

"Can I still help Ms. Faith decorate? She needed me to hand her things when she was standing on the chairs." I watched as his blue eyes searched for his dad's confirmation.

"Seems like it's the least we can do." Adam looked back at me. "Put us to work, Ms. Faith."

"And can we listen to Frosty the Snowman on your phone?"

At this, Adam grimaced but agreed. I moved my chair and stepped back onto it.

"Here, let me." Adam held out his hand to help me down.

I stared at his extended hand. "Um, are you sure?"

He rolled his eyes. "Ms. Faith, whatever you are doing, I've got to be able to reach it easier."

I shrugged. "I guess if you put it that way." I moved strands of hair behind my ear.

He raised his eyebrows and gestured to his hand.

I set mine softly in his, and tingles danced up my arm. His eyes locked with mine as I stepped down. I was so close to his chest, I almost brushed against him. I blushed and took a few steps back.

Adam nodded toward the chair. "Right." He cleared his throat. "Tell me what to do."

Before long, I knew why Adam wasn't excited about Frosty. Danny didn't want to listen to a bunch of Christmas songs, he wanted to listen to Frosty the Snowman and only Frosty the Snowman, over and over and over.

Adam didn't show any signs of annoyance after the initial one, although I'm guessing he had listened to the song for far longer than twenty minutes. As he stapled the last snowflake, we gathered up the supplies, put the chairs away, and headed for the door.

Danny led the way, skipping down the hall, and Adam fell into step with me. "Sorry about that," he said softly. "Frosty is the current song of choice, and I didn't think of a way I could warn you without potentially hurting Danny's feelings." The smell of citrus and spice surrounded me.

My heart warmed. What would it have been like if my parents had supported and shielded me the way Adam did for Danny? Instead of worrying more about their own image or that of their colleagues.

I smirked. "Well, I think it was worth it to watch Danny's drum solo on the desk every time the chorus came on."

Adam chuckled. "And, again, I'm so sorry about being late today."

"Honestly, I didn't mind it." I looked toward Danny. "Danny calms me somehow."

Adam tipped his head toward me, his eyebrows lowered.

I clasped my hands behind me. I said too much. What was he supposed to think about that? "And he is a great helper." I thought to earlier when he decided he would rather spread paper confetti everywhere than pick up his paper scraps. "Well, when he wants to be." I smiled.

Adam put his hands in his pockets. His coach jacket sleeves pulled against his arms. "I was wondering if it might be easier if we exchanged numbers. Between the fundraiser and our role as permanent cookie testers and what not?" Adam shrugged but didn't meet my eyes. "It might be an easier way to communicate."

Aah!! Was he asking for my number as a friendly gesture? A teacher-parent kind of I need your number? Or could it be that he actually wanted *my* number? I spun my ring as my gaze flicked to his. I took a fortifying breath and told myself to chill out.

"Sure." I grabbed my phone from my little shoulder bag, unlocked it, opened a new message, and then held it out to him. "Just put your number in here and I will text you." My fingers brushed against his palm and I walked faster.

That sounded normal, right? Did I sound too excited? Or did I maybe sound like I wasn't excited at all?

Chapter Nine

ADAM

I walked out of the school toward my truck, exhausted from the surge of adrenaline seeping out of my muscles after I'd realized I was going to be late to pick up Danny. Ever since Danny's mom left, he hasn't done well when he thinks he's been forgotten—understandably so.

Danny's backpack slipped on my shoulder as I helped him navigate around the icy patch on the sidewalk.

The relief I felt when Margo told me he was waiting with Ms. Faith was almost palpable. Maybe that wasn't fair, but I knew Danny didn't handle unexpected changes well, and I could tell he felt safe when he was with his teacher.

As we crossed the parking lot, Danny reached up and took my hand. I stiffened at the unexpected physical touch and tried not to react. He rarely sought any physical contact, and that he did now made me want to scoop him up in my arms. I squeezed his hand gently as I helped him into the truck.

I thought about Danny and his problems with eye contact and being overwhelmed. I probably should look up the neurodivergent thing, but I wasn't sure I was ready to admit that something might be different with him. Then I would be faced with the questions of why or what it meant.

I closed down that thought process and focused on buckling Danny.

"I'm glad Ms. Faith makes better cookies than Grandma." He smiled, showing his gapped tooth grin. He'd lost another tooth last weekend.

"Let's keep that info just between us." I winked.

Danny got a serious look on his face as his eyebrows scrunched together. "Like a secret mission?"

"Sure, bud." I shut the door and started walking around the truck.

I'm not sure that asking for Faith's...I mean Ms. Faith's number was a good idea. I kept replaying the feeling of her hand in mine as she stepped down off the chair. She smelled sweet, like flowers or something, and was close enough to me that I could feel her breath on my skin. I shook off the thought. Maybe I was just craving physical attention?

I opened the door and climbed into the truck. I thought back to Jessica's hand on mine. The feeling I got was definitely different.

What was I expecting out of this? Surely not dating Danny's teacher. I started the truck.

Then what? I continued to search my mind for a reasonable excuse to rationalize my behavior and feelings.

A friend?

A friend to Danny or to me?

I put the truck in reverse and backed out of the parking lot. I shook off all thoughts about Ms. Faith and focused on the little boy beside me.

"Are you excited for tomorrow?" Danny didn't get excited about a lot of things, but picking out a Christmas tree was one of them.

"Yep!" His little legs swung off the bench. "Do you think Ms. Faith knows to dress warm?"

"I'm sure she does, Champ."

"I think she will like getting trees."

So much for keeping my thoughts away from Faith. My thoughts swirled like the snow flurries drifting across the windshield. I came up with a bunch of reasons it was a bad idea to spend time with her based on how I was drawn to her, but I couldn't deny I was still excited about tomorrow.

THE MORNING AIR WAS SHARP IN MY CHEST AS I LOADED the four wheeler in the back of the truck and strapped it down. I loaded the ramp for later. There was a skiff of fresh snow, which meant we probably had a good foot or so of new snow in the hills.

I walked inside through the tight hallways that brushed the side of my jacket as I made my way to Danny's bedroom. He was still on his tablet and hadn't touched his clothes, let alone his breakfast I set at the table. I sighed.

"Hey, bud, let's focus up, okay." I paused his tablet. I pointed to the layers of pants, socks, and a sweater on his space-themed bed. "I need you to change into these and eat. I'm going to go grab the winter gear."

Danny's bright blue eyes met mine. "Did it snow?"

He had been so bummed when the current snow froze over and couldn't be used for snowmen.

"Yeah, just a little, but there will be more where we're headed."

Danny fist pumped. "I love snow!" He reached for his tablet.

"Not right now. We're getting trees, remember." I grabbed the tablet to take with me and remove the temptation.

"Oh yeah!" He nodded and reached for a sock and pulled it onto his foot.

I was grateful I had Faith's number now; we were going to be later than I planned. I opened my phone and clicked on contacts. I scrolled down to Faith. I pursed my lips. Should I change it to Ms. Faith instead?

I tipped my head in thought. I mean, she calls me Adam, so Faith is fine.

Right?

Adam: Hey Ms. Faith, looks like we might run a little late. It's going to be pretty cold, so bring layers.

I checked that Danny had grabbed his pants and was getting dressed before I walked toward the hall closet. My phone dinged, and I grabbed it out of my pocket.

Faith: That's okay, no rush. Just let me know when you're heading my way.

The difference between Faith and Cassie was far reaching, it seemed. I texted mom.

Adam: Hey Mom, just a reminder-I'm getting trees and will be outside cell range today. I should be back by nightfall.

Mom: Sounds good. Be safe. And don't forget to grab a tree for me too. And HAVE FUN!

Subtle mom, really subtle. I stuffed the snow clothes and extra gloves in a duffel bag to take to the truck. Mom usually came with us to get trees, but when I told her our plans to bring Danny's teacher, she decided she might be coming down with a cold and shouldn't risk coming along.

I went out to the truck and placed the duffel bag behind the seat and checked that we had everything we needed. Hand saw, work gloves, tarps, extra gas, and rope. Once satisfied, I went to check on Danny.

He was playing with his matchbox cars, one sock on, and no sweater.

Seriously. I sighed.

"All right, Champ, let's focus up." I clapped, and Danny looked up at me, startled, like this was the first time I asked him.

I rubbed a hand down my face and went and sat on the floor beside him. I put on his other sock.

He moved his foot away from me. "No, not like that." He reached down and spent several exhausting seconds readjusting the line in his sock so it hit the spot he wanted.

I knew better than to rush him. I learned early that it only stressed him out and made him slower. After the sock was in the perfect place, we added the sweater and boots, and I grabbed his breakfast to take with us and some extra goldfish and granola bars.

Loaded in the truck, I texted Faith we were on the way.

Fifteen minutes later, we pulled up to Faith's little duplex. I shifted the truck into park. How was I already exhausted and it wasn't even eleven in the morning?

Danny threw open the door and jumped out of the truck, rushing toward the doorbell.

I hopped out to follow. "Danny, only once!" I hollered as his little finger pumped the doorbell button. *Great.*

The door opened, and Rose Torres grinned up at me.

"Good morning." She raised an eyebrow.

"Hey, sorry, Danny gets excited to ring doorbells." I shrugged.

"Oh sure, Danny's the only one excited about today." She smirked.

What did she mean by that? I didn't take the bait, but I took a subtle sniff of my cologne. Had I put on too much? I remembered Rose a little; her older brother Lucas was in my graduating class, and I think she was in elementary school then.

I flinched. I hated when I got those unexpected reminders of my age. I was only thirty-three, but somehow it felt drastically older than Faith when I thought about high school. I think there was about eight years between us.

Is that okay? Or is this creepy? Not that I was doing anything or expecting anything. I shook my head.

"Faith, your Christmas date is here," Rose called into the house.

"We are actually not a date." Danny stated with no pretentiousness, just facts.

"He's right," Faith hollered back from inside the house. She appeared in the hallway behind Rose, her cheeks flushed bright pink. Her blond hair was pulled up in a pony tail and the blue of her sweater matched her eyes and fitted her small frame. She grabbed her jacket. "We're not on a date." She glared at Rose as she passed her, grabbing her hat and gloves.

"Sure you aren't." She dragged out the first word and then winked at me.

I gestured to the truck. "Do you want to come?" I asked Rose, showing her this wasn't an exclusive event. Part of me really hoped she said yes; it would keep things from getting too "family-ish," but if she did, it would be a tight fit on the four wheeler.

Rose took a step back. "Go freeze and walk around in the snow for hours to find a tree infested with bugs? No thanks."

Wow, tell me how you really feel.

I chuckled. "Fair enough." I turned and headed toward the truck, Danny and Faith already ahead of me. I'm not sure when it happened, but she was no longer Ms. Faith, Danny's teacher in my thoughts at all. Instead, she was just Faith, our friend.

"Be careful." This time her voice didn't hold sass but worry.

I turned back to her. "We'll have your roommate back in no time."

She closed the door. I rushed to hold the door open for Faith and Danny. "Are you sure that coat is warm enough?" I nodded to her coat.

She shrugged. "I'm sure it will be fine. Thanks for checking."

Doubtful, but I had a few extra down feather coats in the back if needed. We turned out onto the main road and headed out of town and toward the mountains. As we drove, I was relieved when I lost cell service and could no longer play Frosty the Snowman on repeat from YouTube.

Danny was on the bench seat between Faith and me. He was unusually talkative. Telling Faith about the new game he downloaded and the different levels he'd beaten. She asked questions and encouraged the conversation.

The road turned rough with potholes and high snowbanks on either side, pushing the rare traffic and slush all to the middle of the road. We drove through several cattle guards, past some broken wire fences, and to a wide turnaround where we would leave the truck behind.

I stepped out of the truck, and the heaviness of silence, pine trees, and snow-covered mountains pressed in on me. I loved being in the mountains and away from everything. It was peaceful. It was just you and nature. We used to fish and camp a few miles up the road when I was a kid. I went with Grandpa John and Dad sometimes, although Dad wasn't much of a fisherman.

Maybe Danny would like to go this summer? Not sure he would like the idea of potentially hurting the fish though.

I unloaded the four wheeler and secured the saw to the front along with the tarps and rope. Faith stared up at the mountains and trees. "This is beautiful," she whispered, and her breath billowed around her as it rose. "I've never seen anything like it." I watched her spin, trying to see everything at once. Her lips parted as she smiled. "Wow." It was obvious she enjoyed the view. I shook my head when I realized I was doing the same, only I wasn't focused on the mountain. I cleared my throat and went back to the truck to grab an extra coat. Faith's cheeks were already turning pink, as well as the tip of her nose. It was obviously colder outside than what my body was feeling.

I walked back toward her and held out the coat. "Would you like to borrow one of my coats?"

She stopped looking at the mountains and focused on me. I resisted the urge to stand taller.

Her brow furrowed.

"This coat is down feather, and is pretty warm; it can get pretty cold out here, especially with the wind as we ride." I was stumbling over my words. I set the coat on the four wheeler. "It's there if you want it, up to you."

"Thanks." Faith slid out of her jacket. I pried my eyes away from her. I never felt this pull to be near Jessica, to touch her flushed cheeks. I shook the thought away, but as I turned, Faith held the jacket up to her nose and smelled it.

I smiled and then cleared my throat. "All right, let's load up." I called over my shoulder to where Danny was studying some animal tracks he found in the snow. They were small, maybe a rabbit. I sat on the four wheeler and Danny hopped on behind me, his arms wrapped around me tight. Faith stood to the side unsure, the arms of my coat reaching well past her fingertips. She chewed her bottom lip.

"You okay?"

"Um, yeah?" She eyed the four wheeler apprehensively. "I've never been on a four wheeler. I thought there might be seat belts or something?"

"Weird." I couldn't imagine an existence where I'd never been on one. It was the main mode of transportation for kids outside of town. On the farms, changing pipes, feeding cows, or just driving into town. "Just hop on. You can squeeze behind Danny and hold on to my coat or the bars behind you."

She took a deep breath and exhaled. "Okay."

Danny slid closer to me.

I moved my foot out of the way as Faith climbed on. If she had never been on a four wheeler, it seemed only right I showed her what they could do. "Ready?"

"Umm, yes, I think?"

"Perfect."

I gunned it. Faith screamed and pulled hard on my jacket as I laughed into the cold, frozen air.

Chapter Ten

FAITH

I was going to kill Adam! He floored that machine as he whipped around corners and dodged fallen logs. After my initial scream caused him to cackle, I refused to make another sound and encourage him. Plus, Danny had flinched and didn't appreciate my volume. I would have said so many words if Danny wasn't there, and none of them would have been appropriate for him to repeat.

Adam pulled over and cut the engine. "This looks like a good place to start." He grinned, clearly pleased. "So, how was your first time on a four wheeler?"

Danny pushed against my arms that caged him between Adam and me. I forcefully pried my fingers off Adam's jacket, stood on shaking legs, and let Danny get off. My stomach was still doing loop de loops, and I clenched my fingers as I tried to bring the feeling back into my hands.

Danny exhaled loudly. "That was kinda scary and kinda fun." He stood to the side of the four wheeler and stared at the snow.

Adam turned to face Danny and closed his eyes. "Shoot, sorry." He squatted so he was eye level with him. "I didn't mean to scare you. I should have asked first."

He shrugged. "It's okay."

"I'll ask next time." Adam tilted his jaw toward Danny. "But if you ever want to tell me to slow down, just slap the back of my jacket."

Danny nodded. "It's okay. I think I liked it."

Adam stood and went to the front of the four wheeler. As he unstrapped the saw and tarps, his eyes searched mine and then his shoulders dropped. "You didn't like it either?" He sighed. "Sorry." He looked at his feet.

"It was just a lot really fast." I flexed my fingers and studied my footprints in the snow.

"Fair." He pursed his lips and looked down. "I should have asked first." He flinched and gave me a partial smile. "Sorry 'bout that."

I brushed my hair out of my face. "It's fine." I saw his sincerity in his expression. I couldn't believe how readily he apologized, even to me. My heart sped up and this time it wasn't because of the four wheeler.

He grabbed the saw in one hand and Danny's hand in the other. "All right, let's see what we can find." They started up the hill to the left, their feet crunching in the snow.

We were farther into the snowy peaks and they reached to the sky, like fingers of a hand reaching for the heavens. My family wasn't exactly outdoorsy. I had seen snow and mountains...but these mountains were huge, steep, and powerful.

The insignificance of my existence wrapped around me, and I reveled in it. I thought Hillsdale was quiet and in the middle of nowhere, but this was something different entirely. There was a heavy blanket of silence that enveloped my fears.

"Can we build a snowman?" Danny's voice drifted down toward me.

I smiled, the boy was obsessed with snowmen right now.

"Sorry, Champ. We are going to have a full day of it as is. Let's race to that log instead." Adam pointed up the hill.

"I get a head start." Danny started charging up the hill. "Count to fifty," he yelled over his shoulder.

"Fifty!" Adam laughed. "No way."

Adam started counting. I rushed to catch up.

FINDING THREE TREES WAS APPARENTLY NO EASY FEAT. The trees weren't planted in neat little rows. They were spread far and wide with varied shapes and heights.

With the first one I suggested, Adam told me it wouldn't fit in any of our houses.

"That tree has to be fifteen feet tall." He smirked.

It looked a little taller than me, but three times? "No way."

"Trust me, everything is much bigger than it seems on the hillside."

I glared toward the tree, still unconvinced.

Adam chuckled and nodded. "Go stand by it."

I trekked up the hill to stand next to it to prove him wrong.

He wasn't wrong.

This tree seemed small compared to most. The vastness of it all was overwhelming.

We strolled over hills and around large rocks. Every tree Danny or I thought would be good, Adam refused. Finding a tree that was straight and had branches all around it that met Adams standards was like Where's Waldo in the wild.

"This is it!" Adam circled a tree. It was full and round and was, in fact, quite perfect. It looked like it was from a tree farm with its straight spine and bushy branches. He smirked, proud his perfectionist efforts paid off. "Now, that's a Christmas tree." He gestured toward the tree.

I rolled my eyes. "All right, I will give it to you, the tree is pretty good."

"Good?" Adam scoffed. "It's perfect!"

Adam helped Danny start sawing the tree down, I walked around for another Adam-standards tree nearby.

I wasn't sure anymore existed.

"Hey Faith."

I heard Adam call out my name, the sound echoing easily down the hill. My breath caught. I'm pretty sure that was the first time he hadn't called me Ms. Faith, but just Faith. My heart picked up speed and I wanted to squeal.

"Faith."

Oh right, answer. I turned to the sound and saw Adam near the tree, holding up the hand saw.

"Do you want to try?" Adam's voice called in my direction.

I looked back to the tree and Danny was no longer sawing but making snow angels farther down the hill.

"What?" I tilted my head.

"Do you want to cut down the tree?"

Like use the saw? Yes? No? Kinda.

Adam must have sensed my indecision and chuckled. "Come here."

I trekked back toward him. I mean, what's the worst thing that could happen, right? He taught Danny how to use it safely.

Adam handed me the saw and pointed to the tree. "Have at it."

Wait, what? That's it. I held the saw away from me at an awkward angle.

"No instructions, just go for it?"

What if I saw it wrong? Would he laugh? Would I break the saw? Would I break the tree?

Adam rolled his eyes, "Seriously, Faith, relax." He grinned. "You can do this."

I bit my lip but his eyes and voice held kindness, not frustration or annoyance. The fact that this man, who used to terrify me, was now a source of peace and comfort wasn't lost on me. I gave a forceful exhale. "Okay. But can you at least tell me how?"

Adam gestured for me to come even closer. "All right, scaredy cat, come here." And butterflies erupted in my stomach as I obeyed.

Tree. Focus on the tree. You have a saw in your hand, woman!

Adam squatted down near the base of the tree. "You see how it has a triangle cut out of the back?"

I squatted next to him and saw a small wedge cut out of the tree trunk, showing the pale bark underneath. I nodded.

"Okay, so that's how you control which way the tree will fall." He shifted and pointed to a strip of pale scratches on the front. "This is where Danny was cutting. I'd use the main, deeper one right here." His arm reached forward, and he brushed his glove along the groove.

I leaned closer to see better. "Okay, yeah, I see it."

Adam was so close to me, I could smell his cologne, and it was mouthwatering. Stronger than the scent on his coat, it was citrusy like orange, maybe, and cloves or something. I couldn't quite figure out the spice. Adam turned his head and jumped a little at finding our faces so close together. He raised a brow and smiled.

He knows I was staring at him.

Oh my gosh, how embarrassing. I cleared my throat. My cheeks flushed, my eyes flew to the base of the tree, and I begged the heat in my cheeks to go away.

Adam leaned back and then pointed toward the base of the tree. "Have at it."

I rushed in toward the tree trunk. Needing to pull the focus from Adam and my embarrassing self.

"Whoa, careful there tiger, it's still a sharp blade." He chuckled, and his hand rested on my arm. I ignored him and his hand.

"Okay, so I just put it in the slot and then what?" New rule for the day: no more daydreaming about Adam.

"You're just going to pull back and forth."

I put the saw into the deepest slot and pulled, it hardly budged. I frowned. I adjusted my weight and pulled again. Nothing. Ugh! Seriously. Danny could do it! I should be able to. I adjusted my hands for a better grip. Then I yanked hard, feeling a pull in my shoulder muscles. The blade moved that time but got stuck again when I went to go back the other direction.

"Am I doing something wrong?" I asked over my shoulder.

"It gets kinda tighter as it gets toward the end." Adam shifted position and stood.

I guess he thought this might take a while. I tugged hard and eventually I felt the saw give, and then I was sawing. I went back and forth, and it was easy now. I didn't stop even though my arms burned; I might not get it started again. I was cutting a tree down in the forest like some freaking mountain man, well, woman. I could dance in excitement, but I was busy...cutting down a tree!

I glanced up at Adam and found him standing over me, pushing against the trunk of the tree. He winked at me.

Tingling ran up my spine and my cheeks heated.

Wait. Why was he pushing on the tree?

I frowned. "Aw, I thought it was easier because I was pulling harder, not because you were pushing on it." I pouted.

Adam smirked. "Maybe it was both."

I rolled my eyes but continued to saw, and the tree groaned in protest.

"Okay stop, did you hear that crack? It's basically there," Adam said.

I froze. "Do I keep going?"

I could see the war in his eyes as he pursed his lips. "Actually, maybe let me finish. I don't want you to get hurt when it falls."

I'm not sure if it was the saw in my hand, but I decided I needed to cut down this tree. "Can you tell me how to do it safely?"

"Okay...here." He held out his hand for me.

I reached up and put my hand in his.

"No, the saw." He smirked.

Oh my gosh! Ugh, of course he wanted the saw. My entire body heated with embarrassment.

I grabbed the saw and handed it to him without making eye contact.

"Here." I heard the smile in his voice, and his hand extended to me again.

Nope, not falling for that again. I looked around for anything else I could hand him.

I looked up at him and waited, unsure of what to do.

"It's for you this time." He chuckled.

My cheeks heated, but put my hand in his. He pulled me to my feet and right into his chest. I was so close to him my other hand rested on his stomach. I was at eye level with his throat, and his Adam's apple bobbed. The chorus of Frosty drifted over to me, clearing me from Adam's spell.

Shoot! Stupid daydream rule! I dropped my hand and stepped away.

"Okay," Adam cleared his throat. "So now, um, push against the trunk." He pointed partway up the trunk. "Right here, then step back."

"Can I help?" Danny sat up in the snow.

Adam gestured him closer. "Sure, just be careful."

Together with Danny, we pushed, and the tree cracked and fell into the snow.

"Yes! We did it!" I jumped up and down with Danny cheering. "I can't believe I used a saw and cut down a tree." I spun in a circle. My face burned, but I couldn't stop smiling. "I can't wait to tell Rose and Marissa."

Adam wrapped the tree in a tarp and tied a rope around it. He glanced up at me, his eyes bright and proud. Warmth spread through my chest.

The sun had moved a lot since we started and was now almost behind the mountain. I checked my watch. We had been looking for trees for almost three hours, and we had only one tree to show for it. We started down the hill to the four wheeler, Adam pulled the tarped tree, and Danny walked next to me. Danny reached over and grabbed my hand.

I tapped down my excitement that he initiated physical contact with me. I wanted to squeal and wrap this little guy up in a great big hug. I didn't because I knew it would make him uncomfortable. This day was so magical. I wanted to freeze time and live in this moment forever.

"Did you know that there might be a manhole cover in space?" Danny kicked at the snow, sending a spray of it into the air.

If it wasn't video games Danny was talking about, or snowmen, it was space. "I didn't."

"They were testing some weapon thingy underground, and the cover blew off so high they thought it went to space." He let go of my hand and jumped up on a fallen log and walked along it.

"Seriously?" I turned to Adam.

He shrugged. "It's a sound theory. It was during nuclear testing and was on a space video we saw before bed last week."

"Well, if I ever go to space, I hope it's not on a manhole cover," I teased.

Danny looked up at me, eyebrows pinched down in concern. "Ms. Faith, if you were on a manhole cover when you left the atmosphere, you would die."

I forgot, Danny didn't always understand joking. "True. Good thing I don't plan on going to space then."

Danny relaxed and nodded. "I might one day, but if it's too dangerous, I might be a cashier instead and get to use all the money."

I chuckled. "Both are great options."

This boy was going to break my heart when he moved on to third grade. Danny grabbed my hand again and pulled me forward as we continued down the hill. I glanced back at Adam. He had stopped walking and was watching Danny and me. He looked stunned but then refocused on pulling the tree.

We made it back to the four wheeler and Adam dropped the tree and then started up the hill to the right.

"Let's do this one." Danny pointed at a tree that was close to the four wheeler, even though I could see it was too tall.

We had only gotten one tree, and I felt like I had walked around Disney World twice and then some. I was glad at least Danny was tired too. My calves were on fire, and my arms burned. Adam, however, showed no signs of weakness.

"Danny, it's too tall and is missing all its branches on the left side at the bottom." Adam eyed the tree uncomfortably.

"Let's just cut the top part then." Danny plopped back in the snow.

"Are you sure you aren't just tired of walking?" Adam raised his brows.

"Dad, we have been walking my whole life." He laid back in the snow.

I chuckled. "Hear hear." I sat down next to Danny. "Not everyone works out ten hours a day, you know. Some of us mere mortals need rest."

Adam rolled his eyes. "You know I'm like twice your age, right?"

I scoffed. "Gross! No, you're not!"

His eyebrows raised. "How old do you think I am?"

I wasn't sure if it was his way of checking to see if I knew he was older than me. I searched Rose's brother's yearbooks after she let it slip that they were in the same class, so I had a pretty good guess.

I shrugged. "Early thirties?"

He tipped his jaw up and nodded. "Thirty-three."

"And how old do you think I am?" I challenged back.

He pinched his lips and squinted. "Early twenties?"

"Twenty-five." I shook my head. "'Twice your age.' Pish!" I rolled my eyes.

Adam chuckled but looked relaxed as he nodded.

Danny sat up in the snow. "I'm seven, but I turn eight after Christmas."

Adam and I made eye contact and we both bit back smiles.

"That's awesome, Danny," I added. He plopped back down in the snow.

"Okay. I think I might need to stop expecting so much perfection out of Mother Nature." Adam looked back to the tree Danny suggested. "Let's get it!"

Danny jumped up and ran to Adam's side so he could help with the saw. It was not a fast process, and the sun dipped behind the mountains, taking any lingering hints of warmth with it. My toes were numb, and I finally understood why Rudolph's nose was permanently red. Once Danny was tired of sawing, Adam offered the saw to me, and I took it. Who knew when I would get to do this again, so I ignored the burning in my arms and sawed down another tree. This was so awesome.

We wrapped it in the tarp and tied the rope around it.

"How about we find mine back by the truck? I think I saw some good ones right at the start." I pointed in Danny's direction.

He was lying in the snow pretending to sleep.

Adam looked chagrined. "Sorry, I sometimes get carried away." He made his way over to Danny. "All right, Champ, let's get back to the truck." He pulled him up onto his feet.

I thought I was cold before I got on the four wheeler; it didn't even compare. We started off slow, but Danny and I both decided we wanted to go fast. Him because he decided he liked it, me because I was cold and wanted to get back to a warm bath.

The wind whipped around us, and the snow hit my face like pins of ice. I was totally numb in my toes. Adam loaded the four wheeler and trees before we lost more light.

I pointed up the hill to the left. "How about that tree?" It was at the top of the little hill, it bent to the right and had more branches on the left side. Either my standards were far less than Adam's or the cold was speaking louder. "I think it looks perfect."

Adam didn't argue the tree's virtues or lack thereof. "You sure?" He grimaced.

"Yep." I smiled.

Adam nodded, and we started up the hill hopefully for the last time.

"Can I carry the saw?" Danny reached for the handle.

"Sure. Just keep the safety guard on."

We continued up the steep slope, and I slipped on a patch of ice and braced my hands in front of me to catch myself. I noticed Adam smiling in my direction. "What?" I stepped nearer to him, just for his warmth. I lied to myself.

He reached up and touched my hair. "Your hair is frozen straight out." He smirked.

I gasped, hurried a glove off, and felt my hair; it wasn't the sexy windblown look; it felt like a crazy cat lady, or electroshock therapy hair. "Yikes!" I squeaked. I'd lost my hair tie on the trail somewhere, so I tried to tame my hair back into my hood.

Adam chuckled. "I like it."

I rolled my eyes. "Well, it's entirely your fault. With your crazy driving, my hair didn't stand a chance."

Adam reached over and pulled my hand away from my hair. "You should leave it."

Adam stopped walking and looked down at my ungloved hand in his, but he didn't drop it. The air got caught in my lungs, and everything went quiet. I searched his brown eyes, and neither of us stepped away. The entire mountain seemed to hold its breath, waiting, wondering what was happening between us.

Suddenly the mountains were far less quiet. Something cracked, and a large rumbling crash filled the air. A large tree trunk segment tumbled down the hill toward us.

Danny held the saw as he walked along a log, right in the falling tree's path. He was completely oblivious of the danger.

Adam and I both started running.

"Danny!" we both hollered.

Danny stopped and turned toward us. Adam was faster and got to Danny to pull him into his chest as my momentum carried me into Adam and we made a Danny sandwich. The snow broke our fall, all of us on our side next to the log, and Adam's instinct brought him rolling on top of us both. He grimaced and braced as the trunk met the log Danny had been walking on moments before and rocked the earth around us. Adam cursed as a jutting branch scraped along his back before the trunk flew onward then slammed to a stop in a group of trees. Everything went quiet.

If I wasn't lying on the ground, I would have wondered if I imagined the whole thing.

Then I heard crying. Who was crying? I searched Adam's now wide eyes. If it wasn't him, that left...

"Danny, are you okay?"

Chapter Eleven

FAITH

The saw!

I looked around frantically and found it lying on the ground to the side, thank goodness. But then, why was Danny crying?

Adam pushed off of us and kneeled in the snow. He scooped Danny up off my stomach and into his arms, his eyes frantically searching all over to see what caused him pain. Danny was holding his wrist at a funny angle as tears streamed down his face.

"Danny, I'm so sorry! Are you okay?"

Danny didn't answer; he just cried.

"I'm an idiot. I should've been paying attention." Adam growled.

"Hey," I whispered, "you were paying attention. That's why Danny only has a hurt wrist." I nodded toward the tree and the branch that ripped part of Adam's coat, and wondered how he fared underneath. "Is your back okay? I think it's scra—"

"It's fine. I'm fine." He shook his head.

I don't think he would even know. If Danny was hurting, he was all that existed. He scooped up Danny and hurried back toward the truck.

I rushed forward, pulled open the truck door, and climbed into the middle. I took off Adam's borrowed coat, ignoring the cold, so I could use it to prop Danny's arm and wrist. "Here, lean him on me and I can try to keep his wrist stable."

Adam's shoulders dropped lower, then he gently transferred a whimpering Danny to me.

Adam ran around to his side, slid in beside me, and roared the truck to life. He shifted into drive and cranked up the heat. I was so glad that we had already loaded the four wheeler and trees.

Adam kept his focus on pot holes as we started back down the dirt road.

I looked at Danny's face streaked with tears, and my heart couldn't take it. "Frosty the snowman was a very happy soul..." I quietly sang his favorite song.

He eventually relaxed against my side and fell into a restless sleep as I rubbed his hair.

Once we had driven far enough to get cell service, my cell phone pinged with notifications, and I ignored them all. We were still an hour from the nearest hospital in Clifton. I glanced over at Adam. He was reaching for his phone that was in a cubby in the dash between us.

"Here." I picked up his phone and handed it to him. "Or I can text someone if you want?"

"That's probably best." He unlocked the phone and handed it back. It had a cracked screen with a picture of Danny's young face.

"If you click on messages, can you text my mom and let her know we are headed to Clifton to get Danny's wrist checked?"

I forced myself not to peek through his other texts. His mom's contact was pinned at the top. I clicked on it, and there had been several recent texts from her asking to let her know when he was safe. I started texting. "Headed to Clifton to get Danny's wrist checked..." I spoke as I wrote. "Anything else?"

"Yeah, for her not to freak out, and I'll call her when we get there." He sighed and ran a hand through his hair.

"Okay... Don't freak out. I will call as soon as I can." I looked up at him. "Want me to hit send?"

"Yes." He nodded.

I sent the message and set his phone back in the compartment.

"I can drop you off in Hillsdale, but I need to go to the Urgent Care." We left the dirt road and mountains behind.

I shook my head. "I'm in no hurry. I can come." I could tell Adam was overwhelmed, and having someone with him might help calm him and Danny. I opened my phone and texted Rose that I would be home later than planned.

Adam pulled out onto the paved road.

The town lights of Hillsdale twinkled up ahead, dusk fully faded. We passed the gas station, Merritt's, and the old law office building. It looked as if someone was renovating it. Last I heard, Harry still owned the building, but since his wife passed on, he spent most of his time with grandkids. Scott and Marissa bought out the law office business and moved it to the B&B.

We drove through the outskirts of Hillsdale on the other side. Houses started to get farther apart. There were snow-covered fields and the occasional farmhouse with Christmas lights.

I glanced over at Adam. His fist was clenched on his leg, and the muscles up his forearms were tight.

"This isn't your fault, you know," I whispered to him.

He harrumphed. "I should have been more careful."

"You were. That's how you got him out of the tree's path."

He shook his head. "I should have watched how we fell." He cursed and smacked the steering wheel.

I saw his anger for what it actually was, fear.

I reached over and touched his shoulder. "Careful, anxiety spirals won't solve anything. Trust me." I put my hand on top of his clenched fist. I felt Adam startle, but he didn't pull away. "I know a thing or two about anxiety spirals. And what Danny needs now is love. He will feel your frustration and might interpret you as being mad."

"I am mad." Adam looked over at Danny with his head resting against my lap. "I'm mad at myself."

We passed a semitruck carrying hay bales as we got closer to Clifton.

Listening to Adam berate himself was crazy. He was the most caring father I'd ever seen. Adam was nothing like my father.

He cared, and he was doing everything he could to protect Danny. I hated to see him being so hard on himself.

We sat in silence for quite a while.

"Adam."

He didn't look at me.

"Adam."

He glanced in my direction.

"This is not your fault. You cannot stop Danny from hurt and pain."

He groaned. "Then what good am I as a parent?" He pulled into the urgent care parking lot and parked near the door. He turned off the truck and leaned his head against the bench seat, closing his eyes.

I rubbed his arm, his blue long-sleeved shirt had the sleeves pushed up against his elbows. "You're there to pick him up when he falls and tell him everything will be okay."

Adam sighed then shifted to open his door. As he turned, I could see a small amount of dried blood on his back through the shirt.

He came around to Danny and scooped up the seven-year-old boy like he weighed nothing. Danny woke up with a start, which caused him to move his hand and start crying again.

"I got you, Champ." Adam hugged him close to his chest and pressed his jaw into Danny's hair as he walked toward the entrance. I closed the door of the truck and quickly followed.

Poor Danny. Poor Adam.

Once the nurse called Danny back, Adam and I both went.

The nurse asked questions and took Danny's vitals. The doctor came in and ordered an X-ray for Danny.

"Would you mind checking his back?" I pointed toward Adam.

Adam shook his head. "Honestly, it's fine. I'm just worried about Danny."

The doctor turned and faced Adam and asked what had happened.

Adam mentioned the tree branch but how his old Carhartt jacket got the worst of it.

"Well, let's have a look." he gestured for Adam to remove the shirt.

I blushed and looked at the floor as Adam pulled his shirt over his head.

I didn't even look at Adam's chest as the doctor felt around his back. Okay, fine, I peeked. I totally checked out his abs, and they were as chiseled as I imagined.

Adam grimaced, and my eyes shot to his as they closed.

"Yep. Looks like you're going to need a few stitches."

After a few hours, Adam was stitched and wrapped in gauze with ointment, and his shirt was back on, which for my focus was probably for the best. Danny had his X-ray and it looked like all he had was a nasty sprain. He got a brace and both boys got pain medicine.

As Danny's pain reduced, Adam relaxed.

Once back in the truck with Frosty playing on Adam's phone again, we headed back to Hillsdale.

"Wait! What about the tree?" Danny leaned forward. "We only got two." His eyes were wide with worry.

"Ah, crap, I forgot!" Adam grumbled.

"Oh, no. I'm good. I was going to buy one from the Merc, anyway." I patted Danny's unbraced left hand. He didn't need to be stressed about that right now.

His eyebrows creased. "We could go back and get another one?" He looked at Adam.

I smiled. "Oh, I think one tree excursion is enough per year. I promise I don't mind." I reached over and side-hugged Danny. "I loved being there for the experience. I'm happy with a tree from the Merc. Thanks for letting me come with you though."

He slowly nodded. "Okay."

I looked up, and Adam was staring at me. He had tired eyes and a soft smile. Adam reached up and ruffled Danny's hair. "Sorry again about your wrist, Champ."

Danny yawned. "It's okay."

I knew one thing that would cheer Danny up even more. "Oh no," I feigned sadness. "Danny, you won't be able to hold a pencil, which means you won't get to practice your spelling for a few weeks."

Danny's bright eyes shone, and he showed a gap-tooth grin. "Yes!"

We all laughed.

"Hey, Faith."

I looked at Adam, and his brown eyes searched mine. "Thanks for telling the doctor about my back." He shrugged. "I get a little focused on Danny, but it was nice to have someone watching out for me for once." The right side of his mouth pulled into a smile.

I shook my head and blushed. "Haven't you heard about the oxygen mask thing?"

Adam's forehead scrunched. "The what?"

I looked at him. "You know, like in planes?"

He shrugged his shoulders.

"You have to put on your own oxygen mask first, and then you can help others."

"Hm." He nodded.

We listened to Christmas music on the radio as Danny slept on my shoulder as we passed farms outside of Hillsdale. The same peace I had on the mountain surrounded me in the cab of this truck. It was radiating calm and contentment. I reached over and touched Danny's hair; it was soft in my fingers.

Wait. What was I doing? My hand froze.

As his teacher, this was totally inappropriate. All day was.

I closed my eyes. Stupid.

Would this hurt and confuse Danny at school? I forced my hands to my sides and refused to move them.

We pulled into my parking lot, and I slid out from under Danny, laying his head onto the seat. Trying to force more space between myself and this little family. "Thanks for letting me come get trees. It was amazing," I whispered to Adam as I reached for the handle.

Adam rolled his eyes. "Yeah, hardly the outing I expected."

I raised my right shoulder. "True, but I still loved being in the mountains, and I got to cut down a tree. So overall definitely a win for me." I smiled and opened the door. "Good night, Adam," I called over my shoulder then shut the door and rushed away before I got pulled further in.

A door shut behind me, and I turned to see Adam walking up to me.

My throat tightened, and my hands shook. What was he doing? I remembered I was still in his coach jacket. I'd put it on after the urgent care. "Oh, sorry! Your coat." I slid it off my shoulders and handed it out toward him, instantly missing its warmth and the smell the second it was gone.

He grabbed the coat and put it over his arm and gestured toward my door. "I forgot about the coat. Figured I would walk you to your door, the least I can do after today." He stuffed his hands in his pockets and shrugged.

We walked the rest of the way in silence. I grabbed my keys from my pocket and inserted the key into the lock, unlocking the door.

"Sorry about earlier. I kinda lose my cool when it comes to Danny." His voice was soft.

I glanced over at him. "You're fine, and you kept him safe." I turned the handle. It was two a.m., and I was exhausted.

"Wait." Adam reached out and touched my arm. "I just…"

I took a quick breath and turned to him, searching his warm brown eyes.

"I wanted to thank you."

"Thank me?" I tilted my head to the side. "I didn't do anything."

"You did more than you will ever know." His voice and his eyes were soft. "You kept me calm, and you helped Danny feel safe." Adam searched my face, and his hand moved up toward me.

But then he stopped, stepped back, and put it back at his side. "Thank you, Faith."

I wondered how it would feel to have him say my real name. Was Astrid even my real name anymore? Who was I?

"I'm gonna get you a tree." Adam nodded, bringing me back to the present.

"No, Adam, please don't." I rested my hand on his forearm. "Honestly. I'm not worried about it. I wanted the experience more than anything. Plus, I even cut two trees down!" I smiled at the memory. "Christmas looked a little different growing up, this was wonderful."

Adam leaned against the house. "Where did you grow up?"

Crap!

"Um, on the East Coast."

"And they don't have Christmas trees there?" His forehead creased.

"Not like here, I guess." I did not want to talk about my past. "It's late. And I'm sure you and Danny are exhausted." I turned to the door and twisted the handle.

"Good night, Faith," Adam whispered behind me.

"Night, Adam," I said over my shoulder. "And tell Danny thanks for taking me to get trees." I went inside and shut the door before I did something stupid like hug him or ask if I could see him again.

SUNDAY PASSED WITH PINE-SCENTED CANDLES AND sugar cookies. The icing designs required a lot of focus, but somehow, my mind wouldn't stop replaying Christmas tree scenes with Adam and Danny.

Rose had some family drama with her siblings and would be absent all day, which gave me space to bake and process. I thought about texting Adam several times to ask how Danny was doing, but I wasn't sure if that was appropriate.

Was it bad not to text?

Would he think I didn't care?

But if I did text, would he get the wrong idea?

Which was what? That I wanted to spend more time together... That wasn't wrong...but was also so wrong. After I finished the snowflake pattern, I gave in to the impulse.

Faith: Hey Adam, I was just wondering how Danny is doing today. How's your back?

I set my phone down and went to frost another cookie so I couldn't obsess over whether he texted back. After I had finished five, I allowed myself to check.

Adam: Hey Faith, Danny is hurting a little and his pain meds make him sleepy, but overall doing much better. He is bummed that his sling is limiting his drum solos to Frosty the Snowman though. I'm also grateful for the pain meds, now that the adrenaline has worn off. But I'm good.

I chuckled.

Adam: I was going to ask you. Danny wanted to start decorating the Christmas tree later tonight and thought since you helped get it, you might want to come decorate it. I told him I would ask. Zero Pressure though. I'm sure you have things to do.

I had things. Baking things, cleaning things, anything to keep my mind from thinking about how much I wanted to join them doing adorable family things.

Boundaries.

Faith: Tell Danny thanks for inviting me. I have a few things I need to do here. Plus, honestly, I think me being at your house, as Danny's teacher, might confuse him. But maybe don't tell him that part. I don't want to hurt his feelings.

Would Adam understand? I didn't want him to think I didn't want to hang out with them.

Adam: I understand.

Ugh! What did that even mean?

Was he mad?

Did he want me to come, or did just Danny? Texting has to be the worst form of communication.

Adam: I'm not sure Danny will feel up for school tomorrow.

Faith: That's fine, whatever he needs to feel comfortable.

I started another batch of cookies. At this point, I could feed a homeless shelter with all the extra cookies I have piled up. After baking, cleaning, and frosting, I read. Unfortunately, it was a Christmas romance, and the MC looked suspiciously like Adam in my head.

Monday morning, I rushed out my front door. My breath was a big puff of steam against the cold air as I walked toward my car. I noticed something different on my left. A real Christmas tree was leaning against the side of the house with a note. I froze.

Wait, what?

I stepped closer to the tree. It looked like... No. I studied the saw marks at the bottom.

I knew this tree because I helped cut it down. It was *thee* tree. The "perfect tree" Adam found. I stepped around the little pile of snow and found a note tied to the trunk with a string.

Faith,

Thanks again for helping me stay calm and Danny feel safe. I couldn't stand you never having a tree that you cut down. So, Danny and I decided we would go get one for Mom later. I also picked up a stand, not sure if you needed one. Tell Rose I checked it for spiders.

Merry Christmas

Adam

Then, scribbled at the bottom, Danny also signed his name. He must have used his left hand, because it was bad even for Danny.

I rubbed the note softly, and my eyes filled with tears. I tried to wave them away before they fell. They gave me their Christmas tree. I didn't know if anyone other than Rose and Marissa had ever done anything so thoughtful for me.

I had gotten expensive, gaudy gifts growing up, but it was never anything I actually wanted. It was more about Mom being able to tell people how generous their presents were.

And they gave me this tree... This was Adam's tree. The perfect one that he searched forever for.

A sob caught in my throat.

This tree was like a piece of Adam and Danny. It held memories and smiles on every pine-scented needle. I reached over and rubbed the branches softly. I wiped a tear off my cheek.

Next to the tree was a stand propped against the house. I untied the note and held it to my heart. I wanted to call Adam and thank him and Danny. I wanted to see Danny and check if he was okay. I wanted to sit next to Adam and watch Christmas movies.

This was so bad.

Why were they making it so difficult?

I needed to instill some boundaries, or I was going to break my heart and, worse, hurt Danny.

They gave me a frickin' Christmas tree. I squealed and stomped my feet. I wanted to hug the tree, but figured it would probably prefer I take it inside and give it water.

Chapter Twelve

ADAM

Faith was right to take a step back. I needed to take a step back too.

Between Christmas trees and inviting her over, she consumed my thoughts all weekend. I kept thinking of wanting to hold her hand, the way her freckles stood out when she blushed, and how she smelled like flowers. I didn't think about her mouth and how she bit her bottom lip when she tried not to watch me take my shirt off at the doctor's.

I hadn't felt that pull of wanting physical touch from a woman for a long time; it seemed to come back stronger than I remembered. I should've been grateful she declined Danny's offer to come to our house and decorate our tree. I wasn't, but I should've been.

The ref blew the whistle loudly, pulling my thoughts back into the game. Focus. Foul. Number 44.

Great, that's three for Connor. I hollered down the line for Jackson to sub in for him. I waved Connor off the court, over to me.

"I'm sorry, Coach, I thought my feet were planted." I handed him a water bottle and nodded.

I also thought he was too, but admittedly, I was a little

distracted. "That's okay. Take a second to rest. You'll go back in after the half."

"Come on!! What kinda call was that!? He was planted," Connor's dad Tony shouted from the stands. "BOOOO!!"

I faced the stands and saw a bag of popcorn flying toward the court. I was going to have to ask him to leave again. I turned my attention back to the game. We were behind 28 to 33, and it was two minutes until half. Connor shook his head. "Sorry, Coach, I can't control my dad, I—"

"You're right, your father's actions are not in your control." I patted him on the back. "Just focus on the game." Connor sat on the folded metal chair. I needed to take my own advice.

I thought through plays and what I knew of their team. Their boys were getting tired. They weren't used to the fast game we played and should take a hit in the second half. Part of winning this game seemed to be outrunning the other team.

The boys hated all the sprints we did, but I could tell it was paying off.

"Come on, Coach! Put forty-four back in!" Now Tony was yelling at me. I ignored him. There was no use in me embarrassing Connor for the behavior of others.

The Panthers scored again. Dang.

The halftime buzzer sounded, and the team stood from the bench and clumped together as they went toward the visitor locker room. We were down, but not by so much that morale was down.

"If you don't want to lose, you better put 44 back in," Tony hollered.

I turned and took the stairs two at a time up to Connor's dad, who was fifteen or so years older than me, had weasel-stringy hair, and smelled of alcohol. I towered over him.

"I appreciate your enthusiasm, Tony, but you will leave the second half if you can't be respectful."

He scoffed and shifted his gaze to the people around us

watching the exchange. I hated making a scene, but I wouldn't let him continue to be disrespectful.

"Yeah? Who's gonna make me?" He smirked.

"I don't think he needs any help," someone hollered nearby, but I kept my focus on Tony.

I used my six-foot-five stature to my advantage. "I'm the coach. I say who plays and when." I stepped closer, so he had to crane his neck to see my face. "If I can expect a team of teenagers to be respectful, I can certainly expect it from a grown man." I glared at him.

He scoffed and huffed, but he wouldn't bite now, not with so many witnesses to watch him lose.

"This is your last warning. One more negative comment about the refs, or throwing food, and you will be leaving." I crossed my arms over my chest, fully aware of how it pressed my biceps forward. "Understood?"

"Whatever." Tony stood up on wobbly legs. "It's not like I wanted to stay and watch you lose, anyway." He pointed at my chest, and I held my ground. "You are the worst coach we have had."

I shrugged but refused to move.

He stepped gingerly around me and muttered something about suing.

"Get in line."

He stumbled down the stairs toward the exit.

"You'd better not be driving home," I called after him. I only hoped he wouldn't take his anger out on someone other than me later, namely his son. Even though Connor was a good foot taller than him, I don't think that boy had a mean bone in his body.

I rushed to the locker room. "All right boys, this next half is ours." I rubbed my hands together and met their eyes. "You guys are doing great." I sat on the folding chair, completing the circle. "Now, what have you noticed about their players?" I enjoyed the boys' opinions, and when they took an interest, they would be more invested in the outcome.

Jackson spoke up. "They recognize the gold play. They have started preemptively going where the ball will be passed." He shrugged. "Maybe we can change the name for the next half."

My brow furrowed and looked up. "I don't want to confuse our own team in the process."

Jacob raised his hands. "Please, we can handle a name change."

I raised my right shoulder. "All right, what do you want to change it to?"

"Let's change it to 'Danny,'" Connor added.

The boys nodded collectively.

My chest warmed at the goodness of these kids. "Deal. What else?" I asked.

"They are getting tired. What if we full court press and see if we can keep the pressure on?" Jacob added.

I snapped my finger and pointed at Jacob. "My thoughts exactly."

LAST NIGHT'S GAME WAS IN A TOWN FORTY-FIVE minutes away, so between that and the icy roads, we didn't get back to the school until past midnight, so I crashed on Mom's couch. Danny needed his rest, so we decided he would come to home games. Today was his first day back at school since he sprained his wrist.

He didn't love staying with Mom, but I also didn't have a lot of options. Cassie's parents had moved out of Hillsdale a few years ago. They sent him cards on his birthdays but never really wanted much to do with the day-to-day. I wasn't sure they would even recognize him. It was Danny, Mom, and me against the world.

I showered and got ready for the day, letting Danny sleep a

little longer. Then, I grabbed some clean clothes for Danny from the suitcase and went to my old bedroom and knocked on the door.

"All right, Champ, it's time to get ready for school." I opened the door and stepped over to Danny. I rubbed his back over his Spiderman pj's. He turned over and pulled the blankets up over his head. "Danny, bud, it's time to get ready for school." At least there was no practice after school today.

Danny began snoring again. I patted his back. "Danny."

Nothing.

"Danny, you've gotta get up." I pulled the blankets from over his head.

Danny stretched and rubbed his eyes with his non injured hand and yawned. "Hey, Dad, did you guys win?"

I ruffled his hair. "We did. By almost ten points."

I helped him take off his shirt. "Nice! Can I come next time? I need to hand out the water bottles."

I loved when he came with me. "It was an away game, bud, and I didn't get home till really late, and Faith"—I flinched—"I mean Ms. Faith said you need your sleep." I put on his blue shirt, the one he liked with no tags. "Next home game, okay?" Ugh! This was feeling way too complicated. I didn't know how to think or talk about Faith.

He scrunched his eyebrows. "Dad, Grandma burnt the pizza, her milk tasted yucky, and her internet didn't work."

Ouch. It sounded like Mom had had a rough night.

I changed his pants and grabbed his pj's to wash at home. "Sorry, Champ. We have to make it work sometimes. She loves you and is trying her best."

He hopped out of bed. "I know! I could stay with Ms. Faith instead. I could help her make cookies." He smiled up at me, eyes full of excitement.

Oh boy, I had better handle this. It looked like, once again, Faith was right with Danny. "I'm glad you like your teacher, but it's probably best if we don't mix up home and school things too much." I bit the inside of my cheek.

I grabbed clean socks and slid them on his feet.

"What do you mean?"

How could I say this so he would understand? He pulled his sock off, and we had to try twice more to get it lined up right on his toes. I chewed on my cheek. "Ms. Faith is your school teacher. And that's the role she needs to stay in. You understand that, right?"

Danny pulled away, but I needed him to hear this.

"Danny, Ms. Faith is a great friend, but she isn't part of our family." I searched his eyes. "You know that, right?"

"Yeah." He leaned away. "I mean...maybe."

Dang. I wanted to be all Danny needed, but I couldn't fault him when even I felt something special with Faith. But I didn't know who Faith was, not really. I asked around, and no one knew who she was before she came here. I knew she was from back east, but that was about it.

How could I navigate this without hurting Danny?

When we finally got sock two lined up acceptably, I grabbed his shoes where Mom had left them by the bedroom wall.

The best thing for Danny would be to not disrupt his life for an unknown relationship.

To be rejected again would be like starting over mentally for us both. That was too much pressure. It wasn't worth it.

I tied his shoes in a double knot and grabbed his backpack.

"But we are still meeting with Ms. Faith for the business thing, right?" He grabbed his tablet and charger from the wall.

"Yeah. Let's get you some breakfast."

"I don't want Grandma's cereal. Her milk tastes funny."

"Okay, how about we go get Sam's maple bars and hot chocolate?"

That put an immediate skip in his step as he rushed out the door and down the hall. In the living room, the Christmas tree was full of lights and homemade ornaments. I told Mom I would go get her a tree, but she grabbed one from the Merc before I could, and I was okay with one less thing to do. It didn't smell as good as the tree we got, but it was pretty and had a much better shape.

Maybe I shouldn't have given the tree to Faith, but it seemed like the right thing to do. Besides, she helped cut it down; she earned it.

Danny reached for the front door handle. I stopped him and bundled him in his orange sweater, coat, gloves, and hat. It was tricky, but we left the braced arm against his chest.

I opened the front door, and the cold air immediately made our breath a cloud of smoke around us. "When do we meet with Ms. Faith together again then?"

"Not sure, Champ." I sighed and helped him up into the seat of the truck and I reminded myself that Faith was Danny's teacher and nothing more.

I needed to stop thinking about Faith's bright, kind eyes, her pink lips, and how I couldn't breathe when she placed her hand on mine. In fact, I needed to stop thinking about her altogether.

Danny constantly bringing her up wasn't helping.

Chapter Thirteen

FAITH

My second graders were dressed in Santa hats and flannel. The Christmas music program was starting in twenty minutes, and Danny was struggling.

"I forgot my Santa hat!" Danny wailed.

"Danny, that's fine. I brought extra in case anyone needed one." I grabbed one of my extras and set it on his desk.

"I don't want that one, I want mine!" Tears streamed down his face as he picked up the hat and chucked it across the room.

"Danny. We don't throw things in this classroom. That's enough." I took a deep breath.

He rushed under his desk and folded his arms, refusing to look at me or anyone else.

"Danny, everyone else is willing to compromise. Landon forgot his hat, and he is fine with using an extra."

He spun away from me. "I don't want Dad to be mad that I wasted his money."

My eyebrows creased. "Danny, I'm sure your dad doesn't care that you forgot your hat."

"Yes, he does. He will be mad."

If I hadn't interacted as much as I had with Adam, I would've been worried. "Danny, come on. Please, just wear the hat." I crouched down under the desk near him.

"It could have germs. Do you want me to get sick and die?" He turned his body away from me.

I rolled my eyes. "Danny, this hat is clean. I just bought it."

"How do you know? You can't see germs."

I exhaled slowly and rubbed my forehead. "Okay, how about you come without the hat then?"

"No, I'm not going without it. You can't make me." He shook his head.

Danny was such a sweet boy, but changing his mind once it was set was something I didn't have the patience or ability for right now. "I will not sit here and argue with you, Danny. We are going to go down to the lunchroom in ten minutes. I really hope you decide to come with us." I stood and walked toward my desk.

"Can't you text my dad and ask him to bring it?" Danny asked.

I looked over my shoulder at Danny. Proud, angry, defiant. What was really going on with him today? "Sure, I can text him, but there is no guarantee he will see it before the performance."

Danny nodded and turned away from me.

I sighed. "All right, class, you have ten minutes to finish your letter to Santa. Please make sure you use your best writing and draw a picture in the box above."

I picked up my phone and scrolled down to my messages with Adam. We had been texting a little, but it had been only a very friend-zone vibe since I had decided not to go over to decorate trees. Even though every part of me wanted to run into Adam's arms when I saw him, I was sure space was for the best.

Faith: Hey Adam, Danny forgot his Christmas hat today and is refusing to go to the music performance without it or use one of mine. He was curious if you had his hat? I inserted a fingers-crossed emoji and hit send.

Danny reached up and grabbed his paper off his desk and vigorously scribbled all over it until his pencil ripped through the page. He grabbed the paper and crumpled it into a ball. Was it because he was struggling with his letter to Santa with his brace? I tried to talk to him about it and offer help. He told me he didn't want my help.

My phone vibrated, and there was a text from Adam.

Adam: Getting someone to cover my PE class early. On my way.

My stiff shoulders relaxed. I wasn't sure what else to do. I messaged back a quick thank you and focused on the rest of the class.

"All right, everyone write your names on your papers and bring them up to the basket, please. It's almost time to line up."

The kids handed in their papers and then went back to their tables. I looked at Danny, who was still not making eye contact and was crumpling his paper tighter and tighter. It was almost time to go, but I wasn't sure what to do.

I checked my watch and spun my ring. "Everyone grab your Santa hats and line up, please."

Lydia stood and made the way to the front of the line. She was the line leader today and proudly stood at the front.

"Mason, your shoes are untied, and Caleb, hands to ourselves, please." I sighed.

The door opened, and I turned to see Adam filling the entire doorway. His eyes searched the room and landed on me, and I gestured toward Danny. When he noticed Danny sitting under his desk, there was immediate sadness and exhaustion in his gaze.

The kids in the line had started fighting over space. "Okay, class, I am going to put Rudolph on, and I want everyone to practice the lyrics one last time." I pushed play on the video on my phone. The music started, and I made my way toward Adam crouched near Danny.

Danny openly cried as Adam held him and rubbed his back. Adam sighed and shook his head. It was as if he held the entire world up on those big shoulders, and he was collapsing under the weight.

"Can I help with anything?" I squatted down near them. Danny pressed harder into Adam's chest.

I think I was causing Danny more stress. I handed Adam the extra hat. "Here's an extra hat that he is welcome to wear if he wants."

Adam nodded and took the hat. He looked down at Danny. "He thinks he has been bad and Santa won't bring him a present because I got frustrated with him this morning." Adam whispered as his strong shoulders dropped.

Parenting looked so difficult sometimes. I gave Adam a small smile. "Hang in there. You're doing better than you think." I patted Danny's shoulder and headed back to the line. I checked my watch again. We were out of time. I sighed. "All right, class, quiet coyotes." Several kids held up their hands and made the shape for the quiet coyote. "Danny, your dad has a hat for you. I need to take the class to the gym for the performance, but we don't sing first, and I would love it if you would join us once you feel comfortable."

Danny's head stayed pressed against Adam's chest.

"Okay, are we ready, class?" I checked my little line. "Mason." His brown eyes met mine, his hand up ready to tug Lydia's hair. "Hands to our sides, please." He slapped his hand back to his side and away from Lydia's pony tail.

"Teacher. I don't want to leave Danny." Lucy's big doe eyes looked up at me from the line. "He is sad."

Several others joined in.

"Yeah!"

"Me too."

I was so proud of my little class. "I appreciate your kindness, and Danny does too. We're going to give Danny a few minutes to regulate, but hopefully, he will join us soon." I opened the door and gave Adam a little wave, and led the way down the hallway.

I really hoped Danny felt better in time. He loved music, and they even added a bit of Frosty because he wouldn't stop begging the music teacher, Mrs. Jolly.

In the gym, my class sat on our section of the bleachers and waited as Jessica's second-grade and two first-grade classes filled the space. I'd tried to implement some collab stuff with Jessica the first two years, since we both teach second grade, but everything always felt awkward and forced. We also approached class management so differently, I eventually decided it was best to just do my own thing.

I checked my watch. It would all start in a few minutes. I glanced toward the hallway we had entered from.

Nothing.

I sat in the front row of folding chairs set up for the audience, with empty chairs on either side of me. The other teachers and parents filled the space. My class searched out their parents and waved, their red Santa hats flopping with the effort. Parents stepped into the aisles to take closer pictures.

Mrs. Jolly raised her hand and pointed at the students with the bells, and tinkling filled the room as the first-grade class started sing-screaming Jingle Bells. Jessica, the other second-grade teacher and Adam's I-don't-even-know-what, plopped down on my right and plugged her ears without being obvious. I gave her a small wave, but she didn't return the gesture. She raised her eyebrows and shifted away from me.

Ouch. Got it. Not feeling friendly. Maybe I should ask Adam about him and Jessica.

I checked over my shoulder for Danny and Adam.

Still nothing. I spun my ring. Come on, Danny, you've got this.

The next first-grade class stood and started their group of songs.

I turned to see Danny and Adam walking in from the hall. I could barely hold back my cheer of joy. Danny was wearing a Santa hat and skipping next to Adam; both of their gazes were on me.

I stood and met them partway. "Oh! Danny, I'm so happy you made it in time." I gave his shoulders a little squeeze. "Our class isn't complete without you."

Danny met my eyes. His bright eyes were red as he rubbed his nose on his sleeve. Eye contact was a win, and I would take it as such. "Here, let me walk up with you to our class when this class is done with this song." I nodded toward the stage.

After Santa Claus Is Coming to Town, I walked with Danny to the front and pointed to his spot next to Mason.

"Danny!" Several of his classmates cheered his arrival and made room for Danny to find his spot. I reminded them to be quiet. Danny sat in his spot, and I made my way back toward the audience. Adam was leaning against the wall, watching his son. I stood next to him.

"Thank you so much for your help with Danny today." I sighed. "I was so worried I was going to have to leave him in the classroom or force him to come screaming and crying."

Adam grunted. "Yeah, that sounds about right." His shoulders dropped and he ran a hand down his face. He had dark bags under his eyes. I wondered if he wasn't sleeping well.

The first grade finished their songs, and my second-grade class stood. I pointed at the two empty chairs in the front row.

"There's an extra seat by me if you want." I gestured.

"Sure. Thanks."

I made my way back to my chair, and Jessica noticed Adam behind me and patted the chair I had been sitting in previously.

I stopped walking.

What do I do now? I looked at Adam and the tight smile on his face.

He nodded us forward, so I sat, leaving room for him to sit between Jessica and me.

Awkward.

My darling class put on little red noses and sang Rudolph the Red-Nosed Reindeer. They did their hand actions perfectly, and I almost teared up. Then they started a song about snow and snowflakes.

Danny frequently looked in our direction, probably at Adam to make sure he was watching, and every time Danny waved, Adam waved right back. They finished with Frosty, including the clapping/stomping part that was Danny's favorite.

I loved being a teacher. It was seriously amazing.

My class sat, and my heart warmed in my chest as I stared at their cute faces. Jessica's class stood, and Adam leaned closer to me. I smelled citrus and spice and felt his warm breath on my neck.

"Thanks for getting me today, and sorry Danny was difficult."

I turned so I could look him in the eyes. His face was inches from mine. I tried to swallow. "Danny is okay. He just got overwhelmed when he didn't have his Santa hat and had a hard time shifting focus."

Adam rolled his eyes. "That kid is so stubborn." He ran a hand through his hair. "I don't know what I'm supposed to do."

Do I bring up testing again?

Will he get mad?

I sat in silence.

He tilted his head and looked at me. "You can say it. I'm a mess. I have no idea how to parent, and it's all my fault."

I leaned back in surprise. "Wow, that's a lot of loaded language. Adam, you're doing great. Trust me. You care way more than my parents ever did."

His eyes held questions I could tell he wanted to ask.

I didn't want to talk about myself, so I guess I'm going to bring up testing. "Do you remember the first meeting I set up?"

Adam raised his right eyebrow. "The one where you made me sit in that tiny chair and I threw a tantrum?"

I blushed. "To be fair, there was an adult chair too, I just got too nervous to say anything once you sat." I shrugged, I'd opened the conversation, and now I would not push it. Adam's eyes went wide and then he laughed.

"Shhh!" Jessica leaned forward and glared in our direction.

I flinched and mouthed sorry as I shifted back in my seat and returned my focus to the stage.

"Are you sure being neurodivergent doesn't just mean you had bad parents?" Adam continued.

Didn't he see Jessica's death glare, or did he not care?

I rolled my eyes. "It for sure doesn't mean that. It isn't something anyone did wrong. They aren't bad or wrong either." My brow furrowed as I tried to think of how to describe it. "It's maybe like basketball versus football. They are both sports, but different. One isn't better than the other, but they focus on and practice different things...but both are good?"

His eyebrows raised, and he smirked. "Did you just give me a sports analogy?"

I chuckled. "Well, I tried to anyway, with my very limited sports knowledge. Did it work?"

He folded his arms across his chest. "I think so," he whispered, and his arm brushed against mine, and I held my breath.

I nodded. "Let me know if there is anything I can do to help."

"Are we still meeting about the fundraiser today after school for thirty minutes?" Adam asked.

I gazed into his eyes. "If that works?" I whispered.

"Yeah." He stared at my lips.

Energy pulsed between us, and the connection from Christmas trees snapped back into focus, like it never left. I met his eyes as he stared into mine.

The moment stretched and pulled. The corner of his mouth raised up into a smile.

"You better be frickin' joking me." Jessica growled as she pushed Adam's shoulder. "Is this why you haven't been returning my calls?" She gestured to me.

The gym lights flipped on, and my body flinched at her anger.

Adam closed his eyes. "No, look, Jessica," he turned toward her. "I was trying to stock up Mom's firewood last time."

"Mmm Hmmm." She scowled.

"I promise." He shifted closer to her.

I stared at the ground, my hands feeling clammy on my lap. Then my class came off the bleachers. *Hallelujah, a distraction.* "I better go," I called over my shoulder as I rushed toward my class.

"Okay, kids, if you have parents here, you can go say hi. When the bell rings, we are going to meet by the exit sign." I pointed to the green sign above the door. Some started to run. "Wait, where are we meeting?" Several kids pointed up to the sign and repeated the instructions, half ran off. I shook my head and shrugged.

Danny came over to me. "I remembered the actions this time!" He fist-pumped and looked over my shoulder.

"You did great!" I put my hand up for a high-five. "I'm so glad you decided to come." I would have been heartbroken if we were singing and Danny was sitting in the classroom sad.

He nodded. "Me too. Where's my dad?"

So much for ignoring Adam and Jessica. I turned to point to where we were seated, but Adam was now a few feet behind me.

"Oh!" I placed a hand over my heart. "I guess he is right here." My eyebrows lowered, my stomach turning sour from the image of him leaning toward Jessica and talking to her.

No, I wouldn't let it.

Because you and Adam are just friends. He is a parent to one of your students, I reminded myself. Plus, I had no idea if there was something with Jessica. If so I would feel like a jerk. Also I would feel like Adam is a jerk. How dare he look at me like that if he is dating Jessica! *Don't be weird.* I took a deep breath. *It's not like you're dating or something.*

Ugh! I was getting a headache.

I closed my eyes.

Danny ran up and gave Adam a big hug. Adam's body stiffened in shock and then his face lit up as his eyes met mine.

"Nice job, Champ!" He ruffled his hair. "I'm so proud of you."

Adam leaned toward me and whispered, "So, is the neurodivergent one basketball or football?"

I raised my right shoulder. "I don't think it matters."

His eyebrows lowered in thought as he slowly nodded. "Could we talk more later?"

Did he mean he wanted to talk about Danny and neurodivergent things? I mean, that was probably totally what he meant. "Sure." He kept looking at me, and I wasn't sure what to do with my hands, so I reached over and rubbed Danny's back. "I'm so glad you came to the performance, Danny. Everyone was so happy to see you."

He showed his big gap-tooth grin as the bell rang. I sighed in relief, grateful for the reason to add distance between Adam and me.

"Ms. Faith's class," I called over the voices, "to the exit sign, please."

Danny grabbed Adam's hand in his. "Can you walk me back to class?"

"Sure, Champ."

Danny stepped up next to me and grabbed my hand with his free one. "Sorry I threw your hat, Ms. Faith."

I looked into his blue eyes. "Hey, it's okay, Danny." I raised my eyebrows. "It's not okay to throw," I said, "but it's okay to get overwhelmed." I squeezed his small hand in mine. "We'll just have to come up with some different—"

"I know, strategies." His brow furrowed.

I wanted to hug this little boy until he popped. "Yep. Strategies."

If I had known how much my own therapy lessons could help my future students, I would have tried to learn even more.

Someone loudly cleared their throat behind me. I turned to see Jessica glaring angry daggers into my soul. If looks could kill, I'm pretty sure I would need a sub tomorrow. She fumed with her arms folded over her chest as she looked at the three of us.

We continued to walk down the hall, and I leaned toward Adam and lowered my voice. "Hey, so, um, about you and Jessica?"

Adam closed his eyes. "I swear, we're just friends."

"Does she know that?" I looked over my shoulder, making sure no one was behind me as we made it to the classroom. "You go ahead, Danny, I will be right in."

He nodded and gave his dad another hug and left Adam and me in the hallway. I leaned against the doorway cubby leading to my room. "It's just that I'm pretty sure she is planning my funeral."

Adam sighed. "I mean, I told her I wasn't ready to date anyone, and that I wanted to be friends."

I pursed my lips together and released them with a pop. "I see..." I scrunched my nose. "That's not exactly the same thing. But I guess it's none of my business." I looked at the ground. "Because, I mean, it's not like we're dating... We are also just friends." I looked up into his brown eyes and they held me captive.

He shook his head slowly. "Right."

"Right..." I waited, unsure what to say, and the English language completely failed me between what was spoken and what was left unsaid. I quickly exhaled. "Mkay, well, I better go." I turned and rushed into my classroom.

Chapter Fourteen

ADAM

I set the snow shovel in Mom's garage along the wall with random tools and food storage and stomped the snow off my boots.

The last meeting with Faith about the fundraiser had been super awkward. She avoided being near me or even looking at me. My life was simpler before I started hanging out with Faith. Not happier, but definitely simpler. I pulled off my gloves and rubbed my forehead.

I walked up the steps into Mom's house then removed my boots.

Was it because she thought there was something going on with Jessica? I wasn't sure what to do there. Was it possible to be friends without hurting Jessica? It was obvious she still wanted to be more. At the music performance, twice she shifted closer, and put her hand in obvious hand-holding range.

Or was it because we needed to back off and just be friends because of the whole parent/ teacher thing? That was what Faith said last time she stepped back.

Whatever the reason was, my heart wasn't listening very well. I slid out of my winter coat and hung it up on the hooks near the back door. But if Faith's blush and eyes were to be believed, she wasn't listening to those reasons very well either. The draw I felt to be near her was magnetic, and it was obvious she felt it too.

"Mom, I finished the sidewalk, but it's still slick, so make sure you're careful." I'd noticed her sidewalk needed to be shoveled as I was dropping Danny off before the staff party. She'd slipped and fallen last winter, and her wrist still bothered her sometimes. I was worried she might get hurt and no one would be here to help.

"Don't forget, I am the one who taught you how to shovel." She placed her hands on her rounded hips and scolded me like I was back in junior high. "I hit a random patch of ice. Even sports stars like you can fall sometimes." Her lips pinched into a scowl.

I held my hands up in defeat. I wanted her to slow down and take it easy, but I also knew better than to tell her what to do. "Where's Danny?"

"He put on snow clothes and went to make another snowman." She gestured to the sliding glass door that led to the backyard.

I nodded. That had to be his sixth snowman this week.

"So, what's this about Danny's teacher?" Mom raised an eyebrow.

I stutter stepped. "What do you mean?"

She raised her brows. "Please. I'm your mother." She grinned. "I see all, remember? Just like those frogs that you thought you could keep under the bathroom sink."

I went into the kitchen, ignoring her piercing gaze and questions. I picked up a cookie from the counter and popped it into my mouth. The good thing about it being burnt and dry was it took longer to chew.

"Now, don't you avoid me." Mom followed me to the kitchen and loosened her apron strings from behind her.

I reached for a glass, filled it with water, and cleared my throat.

"It's nothing, Mom." I took a big drink. "I'm just helping in Danny's class for the business fundraiser."

"Oh, yeah...nothing." She crossed her arms and raised an eyebrow. "Getting Christmas trees, texting, and oh, I don't know... sitting together at the Christmas performance, staring at each other." She shrugged. "Doesn't sound like nothing."

What? "How did you..." My forehead creased, and I tried to remember the performance. I looked at the ceiling and sighed. I'd totally forgotten that Mom had agreed last minute to come. I was so wrapped up in trying to get Danny to even go.

"Mom, why didn't you come say hi if you were at the performance?" I scowled at her. Of course, Mom came to watch Danny sing, and then she slipped out unnoticed when she thought I might be having a romantic moment.

She waved me off. "Oh, you seemed a little distracted, and I didn't want to be a bother." She nodded over to the worn kitchen table, and I followed her and sat.

"You're not a bother." I shook my head. "But, don't make a mountain out of a molehill either."

"Oh, I'm not. I'm just stating what's plain as day. I saw how you looked at her, and you were smiling." Her shoulders softened. "I haven't seen you smile at a woman like that since you moved back."

I rested my head in my hands. "Don't meddle."

"I'm not. Just asking you how you feel about her."

I leaned back in my chair. "I don't know how I feel." I rubbed my hand down my face. "On one hand, I have enough drama without adding a woman into the mix. I don't want to confuse Danny or hurt him more." I looked out the window to see him rolling a ball around in the snow. "Plus, I'm not sure I could ever trust another woman with my heart or with Danny."

It was a hopeless cause.

"And if that wasn't enough, she is Danny's teacher. This town has enough gossip about my failed marriage. Can you imagine if I started dating his teacher?"

Did I want to be more than friends with Faith? Did she want

to be more than friends with me? Her words sometimes said no, but the chemistry between us said something different.

Mom waited patiently. "And..." She motioned for me to continue.

"And what?" I held out my hands and shook my head.

"Well, I'm assuming those are the cons, right? What are the pros?" Mom repeated the gesture.

I grabbed the salt shaker off the table. "Fine." I sighed in defeat. "Faith is kind, humble, and so patient with Danny...and with me. She has shown she is everything Cassie isn't." I raised my right shoulder. "And I can't stop thinking about her."

Mom reached across the table and put her hand on top of mine.

"Mom, it's nothing serious. Don't go planning things that won't happen."

Mom lifted her eyebrows. "Oh, I'm not. Relationships are tricky. Sprinkle in kids and work drama and it probably feels impossible."

I nodded but eyed her skeptically. There was no way she was leaving things like that.

"But..."

Yep, I knew it.

She shrugged. "Impossible happens far more often than the word suggests." She tapped the table. "If you actually try for it."

I rolled my eyes. I had better change the subject before Mom launched into either a Bible lesson or wedding plans. I tapped my head. "Have you ever heard the word neurodivergent?"

Mom tipped her chin to the side. "Neuro what?"

I looked to the ceiling trying to remember it all. "Faith was talking to me about it the other day regarding Danny."

Mom's lips pulled down in a frown. "What does that mean?"

I could see the fight enter her eyes. Like mother, like son, I guess.

"It's not bad. It's like football versus basketball."

Her eyebrows pinched. "What are you talking about?" I guess the description worked better when Faith said it.

I had spent the last several days googling everything I could find on the autism and ADHD spectrums. I could see resemblances to Danny, but some things felt far off. I set the salt shaker back in the middle of the table.

"I don't know." I wasn't ready for this conversation. I stood, causing the chair to scrape against the linoleum. "I'm going to go help Danny finish the snowman and then get dressed for the staff party." I pushed my chair in. "Thanks again for watching Danny tonight."

"Of course, I love his company." Danny and I were both lucky to have Mom. "Since it's Christmas break, let's plan on him spending the night. In case you end up with later plans than you think." She failed to hide her smile.

I grabbed my gloves and raised my eyebrows. "I appreciate the offer, but I will be back right after the party."

Mom shrugged. "Up to you, but no rush. I'm not going anywhere."

I STEPPED INTO THE TEACHERS' LOUNGE WITH MY "ugly" sweater and my package of Oreos. I had left the plate of burnt cookies from Mom in the car. I would need to dispose of the evidence later. My eyes searched the room for Faith.

Her blond hair was curled softly around her face. She had on a knee-length blue skirt, and a sweater covered in tinsel. She was beautiful, all of her.

Her blue eyes met mine. What would it be like to date Faith? To hold her in my arms or run my fingers through her hair. My stomach tightened.

I set the Oreos by a glass plate with gingerbread cookies and intricate snowflake patterns out of frosting. I bet I knew who made those.

Faith waited over on the right, standing off a bit by herself. I started her way when Jessica waved her hands, catching my attention, and began hustling over to me. I stopped mid-step, unsure what to do.

I really wanted to go over to Faith, but I also didn't want to make Jessica upset. And if I caused a scene, Faith wouldn't like the attention or confrontation. Every time a confrontation happened around her, she seemed to make herself smaller or she left. I noticed it with the school meeting and Ms. Sparks, I noticed it when I went too fast on the four wheeler, and with Jessica at the music program.

"Hey, Coach." A firm hand slapped my back, making the choice for me. "Heck of a game against the Panthers the other day." Craig, my old basketball coach and the current middle school science teacher, grinned. "I thought we had lost for sure, but that Jacob kid. He is something else, isn't he?"

I chuckled. "Yeah. He is a great kid. On and off the court."

"Reminds me of a high school basketball star I used to coach." He bumped my shoulder.

I laughed softly. "He's way better than I ever was."

"Oh, I don't know." Craig shook his head and looked up at the ceiling. "I remember you scoring so much in that championship game your senior year. It completely turned everything around, and your three-point shot." He made an OK sign with his hands. "If I remember right, you got another scholarship offer on that game alone."

I nodded. True, but it was a community college, and even at a full ride, Cassie helped me decide we could do better at a more expensive, prestigious college.

A throat cleared loudly near the door, and I turned to see Ms. Sparks demanding attention with her stern gaze. "Thanks everyone, for coming. I'm sure Dotty will be here any minute." Her forehead wrinkled and she checked her watch.

"I still don't know why Helen didn't just become the principal instead of her niece. She runs everything anyway," Craig whispered with a mischievous grin. "I told her when the position opened, she should take it. I think she refused on the principle that she doesn't want to be told what to do." He stared at Helen.

"Something you want to share with the class, Craig?" Helen called him out.

He winked. "No, Ma'am."

"That's what I thought." It looked like behind that stern mouth, she might hide a smile.

Huh. Craig and Helen Sparks. Weird.

Dotty came rushing up the stairs in a bright sweater covered in tinsel and flashing lights and with a cardboard box in her arms. We were about the same age, but she was much further in her career than I was, not that I wanted to do anything with administration.

Ms. Sparks sighed. "About time, Dotty."

Dotty turned as red as the tinsel wrapped around her shoulders. Ms. Sparks turned to command the crowd.

"Now let's start the cookie exchange and—"

"I, um, actually planned something different." Dotty avoided Ms. Sparks's eyes.

Ms. Sparks cleared throat. "You what?"

Dotty straightened her shoulders. "Okay, everyone, I took a mystery item from each teacher's room and attached a number."

Gasps scattered around the room.

Her eyes widened in shock. "Nothing bad, I promise. You'll see. Here." She nodded her head toward the table. "I'll put the items on the table. Everyone, take a paper and try to assign each numbered item to its owner." She rushed to the table and laid out the items and stood to the side. "Let's see how well everyone knows each other."

Everyone glanced at the table, but no one moved.

"We don't do games," Ms. Sparks whispered angrily toward Dotty.

It's true, we never had games in the past, and this group of people didn't take change easily.

Dotty tugged on her sweater.

I didn't want to play a stupid get-to-know-you game, but I couldn't let the woman just stand there. I nodded at Craig and turned to set down my cup. When I turned back around, Faith was already halfway across the room. All eyes followed her, and her cheeks flushed pink with the attention, but she held her head high. Looks like my charity wasn't fast enough to beat Faith's.

Faith grabbed Dotty's hand and gave it a squeeze.

"What a fun idea!" She reached over and picked up a paper and pencil. "I'm sure all of us know less about each other than we think."

I knew very little about Faith, and I was definitely ready to learn more.

Dotty put her hands up and clapped. "Oh, I forgot, the person who gets all the answers the fastest wins a prize."

That seemed to break the trance everyone was in, and the rest of the staff rushed to the table, grabbing papers and pencils. All except Ms. Sparks, who had her arms folded across her chest and her lips in a scowl.

Chapter Fifteen

FAITH

Bonus points, I didn't trip or vomit. I hated being the center of attention, but apparently I hated people being unkind more. I clutched my paper and pencil and pretended to stare at the different objects along the table. But, I was actually just calming my breath and stopping my hands from shaking. I rolled the ring on my finger.

I normally didn't like work parties. Everyone else knew one another all their lives, and they sat in their normal groups of four or five and gossiped. I never felt like I belonged anywhere. I loved Dotty's idea of shaking things up.

After a few minutes, I stepped away from the table that was now surrounded by people and made my way over to Dotty.

"This is a great idea."

She rubbed the back of her neck. "You think so?"

"Yes. I feel like an outsider since I didn't grow up here." I realized Dotty was in a similar situation. She knew these people better than I did, but she wasn't exactly a part of them either. "It shakes things up nicely."

Her bright eyes met mine. "Right! I thought this would help us form different connections."

I pointed over to where elementary and high school teachers were colliding and wandering around, no longer in clique groups. "It looks like it's working.

Dotty clapped her hands in front of her. "It is, isn't it?" She leaned close and whispered, "Aunt Helen told me no games. That everyone would hate it." She grimaced.

Jim was trying on a clown's nose, and the surrounding group laughed. "Well, looks like maybe she was wrong. I'm proud of you for going against her." I shuddered. Helen Sparks intimidated me, like a lot.

"Yeah." Her shoulders relaxed.

"Hey, do you want to go to Merritt's tomorrow?" I wondered why I hadn't hung out with Dotty before. "My roommate Rose and I are meeting there for brunch."

Her eyes lit up. "Yes!" Her cheeks flushed. "Um, I mean, if you're sure?"

I laughed. "Of course! You will love Rose, and Marissa might come too."

Dotty raised her hands in front of her. "Oh, I don't want to intrude. Sounds like you guys already have a group."

I reached over and grabbed Dotty's hand. "I promise I want you to come."

Dotty nodded, her cheeks rounded with her smile. "I would love that. I hang out with my aunt some, but she is a bit intense for me."

I whispered again. "And older."

"Don't tell her that. I used to think she was immortal. She has had the same angry scowl lines since I was five." Her aunt started coming our way.

I smiled and looked at the table. "Okay, I'm going to see if I can get any of these right. Wish me luck."

Her bright eyes met mine. "Good luck!"

"See you tomorrow. Merritt's, 10:30 a.m."

She reached over and grabbed my hand. "Thanks for the invite. You're so kind."

I internally flinched. How long did unkindness cling to a person? Was there a magical time frame where past mistakes were no longer a part of you?

I nodded. "K, tomorrow."

Back at the black folding table, the groups of teachers ebbed and flowed around the objects. I looked at each item and my peers milling about the room, wondering who each item could belong to, from the red clown nose to a knitted sweater fit for a small dog.

I hadn't gotten to know anyone here very well. That was partly on me for hiding from my past, partly on them with their cliques and groups, and my social anxiety seemed to cover the rest. I always worried I might annoy or inconvenience people when I inserted myself into a conversation. Or I would say something weird. So, I usually stayed thirty minutes and then I panicked and left.

It's a real mystery why I don't have more friends. I chuckled and shook my head.

I saw my item; it was a small red glass bottle of perfume. It was from the LUXE fall line four years ago. I got to work with designers on it and it was one of my few pleasant memories with the business. I shouldn't have had any reminders of my past at the school, but sometimes a girl's just lonely. It seemed inconspicuous enough. The LUXE brand written in gold didn't help.

I recognized an orange sweater. It was often draped over a Minecraft backpack in my schoolroom. I picked it up, looking for a number.

"That's cheating." Adam's voice was close to my ear.

I jumped and squeaked.

"You scared me." I turned to see Adam grinning. "How am I cheating?"

"I'm pretty sure you are the only one that will recognize that it belongs to Danny," Adam whispered in my ear, causing goosebumps to raise along my spine. This man was dangerous. Especially if we wanted to be only friends. I mean, technically I said it first, but he agreed.

"It's not cheating if I am using what I know," I challenged back and set down the sweater. I put Adam's name on number nine.

His smile grew as his eyebrows raised in challenge. "I found yours too."

"What?" My stomach tightened. How? I reached for his paper. "Let me see."

He held the paper out of my reach. "Are you trying to cheat by stealing my answers? I will tell Principal Dotty."

"Dotty would be on my side." She knew what it felt like to be new in a town full of lifelong acquaintances. I tried to pull his arms down from over his head.

Adam chuckled, but his arms didn't drop. "Nice try," he whispered near my ear, and my neck erupted in goosebumps. His arm muscles flexed under my hand.

Wait. What? I realized I was making a scene. I dropped my hands from his arm and stepped back.

Could he really have found out about my past? Would this be the moment that the other shoe finally dropped and everyone found out who I really was?

"What do you know?" I whispered as my shoulders sank, ready to admit my guilt.

He leaned away. "With a reaction like that, I'm thinking I should look for a murder weapon..." Adam's eyes flicked to the table.

By his reaction, I could tell he was teasing before, and I'd definitely made it weird. Adam studied the table, his forehead wrinkled in thought.

I wasn't ready to ruin everything. Not yet.

I stepped closer.

"Gotcha." I reached out and slapped his forearm, hopefully convincing him of my lie.

He didn't look convinced, but he looked less like running.

Time to change the subject. "I bet the red lipstick is actually the science teacher, Craig."

Adam relaxed slightly. "I'm not sure it's his color."

"True. It would wash out his complexion for sure." I nodded over at Craig, who was standing near Ms. Sparks and was obviously trying to make her laugh. "Hey, do you think—"

"I noticed the same thing earlier." Adam smirked. "Not who I would picture for the guy," he shrugged. "But no one knows what a person and relationship are truly like besides the people in it," he added softly.

Hm.

That was cryptic, he must be referring to his ex-wife. She must be bonkers to leave Adam and Danny.

"Is that one yours?" Adam was pointing at a little carton of energy drinks

"I thought you already knew which one was mine."

"I was hoping you would give it away." He glanced down the line. "I got it, the signed picture of the Muppets."

"No." I giggled, but then remembered it belonged to someone, so I quickly covered my mouth and I shoved Adam. "Stop!"

He smirked. "Stop what?"

"Making me laugh. Someone might think I'm making fun of them." I pinched my lips tight in false anger.

"I like your laugh, it's so happy." His tone was low and sent shivers down my spine.

I blew out my breath, trying to ease the tension in my chest. I wanted to reach for his arm again, to feel its warmth under my hand.

"Hm." Adam tapped a finger to his chin as he studied the objects. "How about that one?" His gorgeous lips pulled up into a devilish smile.

I couldn't look away from his smile.

"Um, what?" I looked to see what he was pointing at. It was a CD of someone, but based on his raised eyebrow and my flushed cheeks, he noticed I had been staring at his lips. He winked and I blushed.

I stared anywhere but at him. "I'm pretty sure we aren't supposed to say, right, Dotty?" I searched for her blond curls and bright tinsel sweater.

"Yep. You cannot confirm or deny if an object is yours until the end."

I nodded back at Adam. "Now who's cheating?" I tapped his massive chest with the back of my pencil.

The night continued with lots of laughter and people revealing their items and the stories attached to them. I learned more about the staff in one night than I had in the two and a half years I had been teaching here. When it was my turn, I simply stated the perfume was one of my favorite scents.

Adam never guessed my item right, but I loved watching him try. Maybe because it kept him closer, whispering in my ear. His warm breath gave me goosebumps every time. The night was ending, and it was now the small-talk portion, which was arguably the worst part. I needed structure so I knew what was expected. With Adam standing close to my side, I found I didn't mind it as much. He was like an anchor in a sea of chaos.

"All right, but I picked which cookies were yours right away. Do I get any points for that?" He leaned closer to me, so his arm brushed against mine.

My cheeks flushed. "Do I get points for guessing which cookies you brought?" I asked.

He chuckled. "I'm an open book. See the package of Oreos. That's mine. But if Mom asks, I brought peanut butter ones," Adam whispered behind his hand with a grin.

The evening was wrapping up, and everyone was gathering their things.

Someone grabbed my arm from behind. "Faith! Hey!" I turned around to see Jessica. She was all smiles but had fire in her eyes. My mouth went dry.

"Hey." I did my best not to look at the ground. I'd done nothing wrong.

"What are you doing later?" Jessica asked me, but stared up at Adam.

"Um, not sure." I shrugged. "Probably a Christmas movie or maybe reading?"

Jessica laughed high and nasally. "What are you, fifty?"

I studied my feet.

Rude.

Why does it matter what I was doing?

It wasn't like we had ever hung out before.

"Come with us." Jessica reached over and pulled me near her. I instantly missed the warmth of Adam near my side. "We are doing drinks and karaoke at the sports bar."

"Oh... Um..."

Karaoke. Yikes. As if everyone staring at you wasn't bad enough, let's add a microphone and singing into the mix. Kill me now.

Jessica looked over my shoulder to Adam. "You should both come." She grinned.

Ah, that was why she was inviting me. It wasn't about me at all; it was about Adam.

Jessica squeezed my hand in hers. "I won't take no for an answer." Her eyes held a firm challenge, and so did her grip.

I stepped back, yanking my hand from her grip.

"Um, maybe." I raised my right shoulder.

Maybe when hell freezes over.

She pivoted toward Adam, closing me out of the conversation. "What about you? Are you finally going to come hang out? The first round of drinks is on me?" She reached up and left her hand placed on his shoulder.

By the volume in her voice, I wondered if she'd already had her first round.

Adam held a tight smile in place. "Thanks, Jessica. But I'll probably head home and see Danny."

Jessica rolled her eyes. "Come on! Live a little." She smacked him on his massive chest and then left her hand there. "I'm sure your mom can watch him. You never hang out with me anymore." She stuck out her lips in a pout.

"I'm good. Thanks for the offer." Adam grabbed her hand, released it, and stepped back.

"You're no fun." Jessica scoffed and her eyes shot to me.

I took a sharp breath and stepped farther away. I felt the ice in her stare. Around the room, all eyes were on the group of us.

Nervous energy pulsed through my veins. I took a deep breath and held it as my eyes searched for the nearest exit.

Ugh, this was so awkward.

Do I go start a conversation with someone else?

That would be weird. Right?

Jessica leaned closer, her fingers trailing up to his biceps. "You should let yourself loosen up." Jessica's eyebrows raised suggestively. "You used to be a lot of fun in high school."

What did she mean by that? My eyes shot to Adam. He stood stoic with his arms crossed, no reaction.

Nope. Not my business. I took a step back.

Adam said they were friends, but we were also just friends. Did she feel about Adam how I felt about him? Did he smile at her the way he smiled at me when I wasn't around?

I felt like a floating third wheel. Not really connected to the conversation, but not sure if I should walk away. I spun my ring, and took a deep breath and held it. My nerves were fuzzy, and I wasn't sure what to do with my hands.

"Um, I think I'll go." I shrugged. Adams' eyes flicked between Jessica and me.

"Yeah, I'm going to call it a night too," Adam said.

I stepped toward the cookies, wanting to grab my plate and escape. Adam took a step after me when Jessica reached out and grabbed his hand.

"You seem to have suddenly changed your mind." Jessica glared at me and gestured in my direction. "Last I knew, you were too heartbroken to date."

Adam sighed. "Faith and I are just friends."

I felt that one like a punch in my stomach. The air suddenly left my lungs, and I couldn't move.

I was the same as Jessica.

Wishing and wanting more in a relationship that would go nowhere.

I sighed; this was a great reminder. I shook the fog loose and walked over and grabbed my cookie plate. Straightening my shoulders, I faced the many eyes that were pressing into my back. "Merry Christmas, I'll see you after the break." I put a tight smile in place and left the room.

"Faith, wait!" Adam called my name, but I kept walking. I needed space to reframe things in my mind. I'd been so stupid, I shook my head. I knew he didn't want to date. I knew I said I didn't want to date him, but yet, I wanted to be near him. To feel his warmth and watch his mouth curve into a grin. I kept finding ways to touch his arms tonight, and he always seemed to try to get closer to me.

If I wanted to be friends, why did that hurt so bad?

I held my breath for three and blew it out.

This would be better for everyone, better for Danny. Just friends was for the best. To my mind, it made perfect sense. But my stupid heart kept forgetting to listen.

Stepping through the doors, I was met with a sheet of freezing cold air. The air frosted my lungs, and I welcomed the ice on my skin. It would help me ground and reset and get out of my head. I took off my jacket and walked to my car.

I unlocked my door, sat blankly in my seat, and stared out my iced-over window.

This was good. I stared at the ceiling.

This was the check I needed. I took a tight breath and released it.

Chapter Sixteen

ADAM

Faith slowed a step when I asked her to stop, but she didn't turn around, and I wouldn't chase her.

I turned to see Jessica behind me, her shoulders now drooping and her arms across her stomach. Her bravado was gone.

This sucked.

"Oh sure, now I have your attention." Jessica shook her head.

"Let's go talk." I nodded over my shoulder. Looked like we needed to have the "I don't plan on dating you" conversation again? Faith was right though; I never specified that I wasn't interested in dating her.

Her lips pursed together. "Okay." Her voice was soft, like she was already broken.

I grabbed my jacket as Jessica went and grabbed her things. We stepped through the foyer and out the double doors.

It was too cold to stay outside for very long.

I looked down at Jessica. "Want to go for a drive or something?"

She nodded and crossed her arms over her chest. "Actually, is this like a 'hey it's been fun but I'm not interested' or like, 'we haven't hung out in a while and I missed you' type of drive?"

I rubbed my forehead. Jessica had been a good friend. She even watched Lord of the Rings with me last year when I didn't want to watch them by myself. I shrugged. "Maybe both?"

She studied her shoes. "Um, I think I'm going to go do karaoke instead."

I nodded. "I'm sorry, Jessica."

"Are you dating Faith?" she asked.

I stiffened my back. "No. We really are just friends."

She raised her brow. "Didn't look like it tonight. You followed her around like a lost puppy."

I flinched. I didn't love that description. What did that say about me?

"Do you plan on staying friends?" Jessica took a shaky breath, looking up at the sky.

I sighed. I had used that "not ready" line over and over since moving back, especially with Jessica. But now I wasn't sure. I was thinking more and more about wanting to spend time with Faith, but regardless, Jessica would not be who I talked to about my feelings on it.

I chose not to answer.

She took a step back and lowered her eyebrows. "Oh, so just not ready for dating when it's me, then?"

The hurt in her voice dug at me. But she deserved the truth. The problem was I wasn't sure what the truth was yet.

"I don't know when I will date, but regardless"—I hated being this blunt, and I really didn't want to hurt her, but I needed her to know—"Jessica, I really do like being your friend."

"But..." she whispered.

My shoulders dropped. "But I feel nothing but friendship toward you. So even if I were ready to date..." I pursed my lips together and shrugged. "I just don't feel that way about you."

She looked away.

The cold air froze around us, the silence becoming heavier with each passing moment.

"It's not like you ever really tried," she whispered, "not like with Faith." She held her head high and walked toward her car in the parking lot.

I mean, what was I supposed to say, that I had tried before Faith, and I still didn't feel that way?

I doubted that would make her feel any better.

So, I left things alone, walked with her to the parking lot, and she opened her car door, started her car, and drove away.

I felt like a jerk.

Jessica was hurting and feeling like I used her, and Faith felt upset when she left too.

I ran a hand down my face. I feel like I've been playing ping-pong all night, but I was the ball. I wasn't sure what I should do or where I should be facing.

I walked over to my truck and started it. It took a few tries to turn over in the cold.

I backed out of the parking lot. So I guess now...I just go home? I sighed. I wasn't ready. I still felt like I wanted to talk to Faith.

When Jessica asked Faith about her plans, she said she would be home watching Christmas movies and relaxing. I checked my phone. It was barely past eight.

Would it be weird to just show up though? I ran my hand through my hair.

Earlier when I complained about only getting one of Faith's cookies, she mentioned she had extra, and that I could bring some home for Danny too.

Does that count as Faith inviting me over?

I drove out of the parking lot and onto the main road.

If I went to her place under the pretense of wanting cookies, she might invite me to stay.

I pictured Faith curled up on the couch in my arms, watching a Christmas movie.

I wanted to go over to Faith's, and it had nothing to do with cookies or Danny.

I thought about Jessica's comment about me following Faith around like a puppy. Did she think I was annoying?

Stupid Christmas.

Stupid loneliness.

Stupid cold.

My truck slowed at the stoplight, and I noticed the pile of burnt cookies on the seat next to me. I picked one up and shoved it in my mouth, hoping it would settle the uneasiness in my stomach. It was both dry and gummy. I shivered as I choked it down.

The reasons I should keep heading straight out of town, and back to Mom's, played on repeat in my mind.

But when the light turned green, I made a U-turn and headed toward Faith's.

I pulled into the duplex and silenced my loud truck's engine. I scrolled through my text messages, just in case Mom texted. I checked the updated school basketball scores in the other 4A division schools.

I checked my email, which I never did.

I was stalling.

It was late. I ran a hand through my hair and laid my head back on the plaid bench seat.

Would she be happy to see me? Why did that matter so much to me?

She hadn't seemed happy when I said we were friends earlier, but what had she wanted me to say? Did she want to be more than friends?

I knew what I wanted. I wanted to touch her hair, to hold her hand. I wanted to kiss her lips.

I closed my eyes.

This was stupid. I should leave. The truck roared back to life, and I put it in reverse.

The door to the duplex opened, and Rose Torres stood in the

doorway with her arms across her chest. She hollered something I couldn't make out. I rolled down my window.

Well, I tried. It was manual, and when it was cold, it always got stuck halfway down. I sighed and stuck my head out the gap. "What?"

She rolled her eyes. "I said, are you coming in or not?"

Heat flamed my face. "Oh, umm, I just wanted to make sure Faith made it home."

Rose raised her eyebrow in challenge. "Okay, silly me. Here I was thinking you wanted to come in." She shrugged and started to close the door.

"No, wait." I held up my hands. I put the truck in park and decided the window could stay how it was as I opened the truck door and jogged partway to the glowing inside of Faith's home.

Rose smiled a devilish grin. "Yes?" she said, drawing it out long and sweet.

This woman would not make it easy for me.

"Umm...cookies?"

Her nostrils flared. "Cookies! Are you serious?" She went to slam the door when Faith's hand reached around the frame to hold it open. Geez. I stepped back. Rose was a feisty thing; her brother always seemed so chill.

"It's cold. Did you want to come in?" She was quieter than Rose in every way. She gave me a soft smile and nodded inside.

I didn't want to go home. I wanted to spend every minute I could tonight with Faith. I had this draw to be near her I couldn't seem to satisfy.

I walked toward the door, trying to keep my steps from betraying my eagerness, and keeping my hands firmly in my pockets. I was a grown man. I shouldn't be acting like a hormonal teenager.

I closed the distance between us, stepped into her entryway, and she closed the door.

"We should probably talk about Jessica." Faith's arms were crossed over her chest, and she studied her feet.

I closed my eyes and nodded. "Yeah, I'm so sorry about tonight."

Faith gave a little shrug. "I'm understanding more of where Jessica might be coming from, I think."

My eyebrows dropped. "What do you mean?"

She raised her shoulder, but still avoided my eyes. "Just that... I dunno."

I waited.

She exhaled forcefully. "Oh, just that, even if we are only friends...it would be easy to feel more than that, to want more than that...and get hurt." Her voice trailed off to a whisper.

I stepped closer, placing my hand on her shoulder. Her eyes went to my hand and then to my eyes.

"I probably didn't handle everything the right way with Jessica." I acknowledged. "But I talked to her again tonight."

Faith's eyebrows lowered as she searched my eyes.

"I told her I didn't know how I felt about dating."

Faith lowered her head and stepped out of my reach.

"But." I moved barely closer to her, but I wouldn't touch her unless she wanted me to. "That even if I was, I wasn't interested in her in that way. I feel nothing but friendship toward her."

Faith studied my eyes in the quiet. "Are you coming to tell me the same thing?" Her mouth formed a tiny pout.

My eyes widened, and I shook my head no. "No, not at all."

She tilted her chin up toward me. "Then why are you here?" Her brow furrowed.

"I want to spend time with you, and I want to get to know you better." I shrugged. I sounded so lame in my ears, but it was true. "I don't know more than that though?"

"What about not being ready to date? What about the whole parent-teacher thing? What about only being friends?" She took a slow breath.

I could feel her nervousness. I sighed. "I don't have the answers to everything." I shrugged. "But we could also just see what happens, take things slow?" I ran my hand down the length of her arms.

She nodded and raised a brow, a smile lit up her face. "Are you sure you don't just want my cookies?"

"I mean, the cookies really are great..." I leaned in closer, and raised an eyebrow.

She chuckled.

I cleared my throat and whispered into her ear. "But in all fairness, I think I should warn you." She shivered, her face inches from mine. "If you let me in, I'm wanting more than the word friend with you."

Her eyes shot up to mine, and she pushed hair behind her ear and blushed. "In that case, come on in." She turned, walking farther into the house.

It took all the restraint I possessed not to scoop her up in my arms and kiss her right there. What was this madness that consumed me?

Take it easy, I reminded my heart and mind.

"So help me, if you are only here for cookies and you hurt Faith, I will slash your tires. Mkay..." Rose's dark brown eyes and raised brows met mine from down the hall, and she left no room for argument.

"Rose..." Faith groaned and leaned away from me. "Stop. Please."

Rose stood her ground. It was clear she wouldn't be moving until I gave her an answer.

"Consider my tires warned." I nodded in agreement, and Rose lost her sharp edge as she turned and disappeared down the hall.

"But...I mean, have you tried her cookies?"

Rose whipped around and glared at me. I couldn't hold back my laugh.

She shook her head and turned back around. "Christmas movie is starting."

We followed Rose into the kitchen and living room, and a plate of gingerbread cookies was placed on the island counter. I looked at Faith with raised eyebrows and pointed to the plate. "Can I?"

She chuckled. "Oh, just grab some."

"Yes!" I fist-pumped and went to the plate. "Want me to grab some for you guys too?" I picked up three cookies.

"Oh, I'm good, thanks." Faith waved off the cookie. "And Rose has sworn she won't eat any more of my treats till after Christmas."

I stared at Rose in horror. "Why would you do that?"

She rolled her eyes. "Look, not all of us are built like Superman. If I ate all the cookies I wanted all the time, I would need life support getting off this couch."

I shrugged and kept all three cookies for myself. "More for me."

I was glad that Rose had taken the far side of the couch, leaving space for me to sit by Faith. I wasn't sure if Rose would make me pass some tribal friend tests first.

Faith sat in the middle of the couch. She held up the gray plush blanket and gestured for me to come sit beside her. I all but ran to her.

Chill out.

I forced my steps to seem normal.

I sat next to her, and I mean right next to her.

Dating as an adult in my thirties was not something I was exactly skilled at. Not that we were dating, per se...

But it was the first time I had wanted to spend time (almost) alone with a woman, and whenever I left her I wanted to see her more, wanted to know her more. I'd been on several dates since the divorce to appease Mom or someone else, but with all of them I couldn't wait until I could leave.

Maybe I had finally been single long enough to work through it, or maybe it was Faith.

Her blue eyes glanced up at me, with a soft smile. I put my arm along the top of the couch, and Faith leaned into my side, her head resting on my chest. I had to fight the urge to flex my chest muscles.

Faith looked up. "You have some crumbs." She brushed her finger along the bottom of my lip.

My stomach tightened, my pulse raced, and I lost all coherent thought. I tried to form words, but I couldn't make sense of anything. I replayed the feeling of her smooth finger tracing my lip over and over.

"Sorry, what?" I blinked rapidly.

"Nothing." Faith blushed and pressed her face into my chest.

The Christmas music started, and the title appeared, *Seeking for Sexy Santa*.

"Seriously?" I chuckled and raised my eyebrows.

I gazed down at Faith. She was bright pink as she pressed into my side. "It was Rose's turn to pick."

Rose shrugged. "If your masculinity feels threatened, you are free to take your cookies and go." She smirked, knowing I would stay on that couch, even if we were watching Frosty the Snowman, which I'd seen more than twenty times in the last few weeks.

I rolled my eyes. "I didn't know you were into fat old guys."

Rose smirked. "Oh, you just wait."

Chapter Seventeen

FAITH

The movie definitely wasn't about old men out of shape. It was men in bow ties, Santa hats, and six packs, flaunting and dancing in a competition.

Well, this is going to be embarrassing. I shut my eyes.

I was right though. Being in Adam's arms was like being held by a Norse god and a teddy bear at the same time. I leaned against his chest, feeling the soft fabric of his sweater under my fingertips, and smelling the citrus and spice. He shifted slightly, pulling me in even closer. My heart picked up speed. Adam gazed down at me, and I felt like I must be dreaming.

The movie was a tad bit ridiculous, but Adam was a good sport throughout it. Well, he was until a group of the men started doing a two-finger push-up competition.

"Oh, come on!" Adam scoffed. He must have finally had enough. "There's no way they are actually doing that." He flipped his left hand. "Look at the guy's biceps." He pointed at the screen. "They're not even straining. Please." He looked toward us. "You see this, right?"

I pinched my lips together to keep from laughing.

Rose smirked. "Just because you feel threatened doesn't mean you need to take it out on them." She gestured to the screen.

Adam pointed to the TV. "No, I mean, see, his triceps aren't even engaged. Look." He shifted to stand, and I leaned back on the couch, curious. He took off the sweater and revealed a tight black T-shirt underneath. He started giving us a lesson on muscle structure as he did push-ups in the light of the Christmas tree.

Merry Christmas to me.

After a few rounds of explaining the different muscles used in push-ups and why you could tell theirs were fake, he realized neither of us were listening, but just watching him instead. He rolled his eyes and came back to me on the couch.

He put his arm back up for me to slide under, and I happily obliged. After the movie, I walked Adam to the door. He set the plate of cookies on the entry table. He put his hands on my waist and pulled me closer. He held me as I wrapped my hands around his neck and pressed up against his chest. I stared at his mouth. My breath slowed, and I wondered if he was going to kiss me.

"Thanks for letting me come over for a surprise visit."

I smiled. "I'm not complaining."

He chuckled. "Thanks for the cookies too. Danny will love them."

Right. "About Danny..."

"I won't tell him anything about us," he whispered.

I nodded in relief. His head leaned closer, and I closed my eyes.

I hadn't been kissed in years, and my stomach fluttered.

Then Adam's lips pressed against my forehead. "Thanks again for tonight," he whispered, and then he grabbed the cookies and went out the door.

For the record, I was definitely not counting that as my first Adam kiss.

Not that I was complaining.

Okay, maybe just a little.

THE NEXT DAY, I OPENED THE SWINGING GLASS DOOR AT Merritt's, following Rose inside. I still felt halfway in the clouds.

Marissa waved her hand so we could find her, even though Merritt's was nearly empty.

Rose plopped onto the red bench next to Marissa. "Faith is officially almost a stepmom."

Marissa leaned back in surprise.

"Oh my gosh, Rose!" I glared at my friend. Sometimes the things that came flying out of that woman's mouth made me cringe. "First off, hi, Marissa, how is married life? Blissful and wonderful?" Then I glared at Rose. "And no, I am not almost anything to anyone, especially something as significant as a mother. I may have cuddled a bit with Adam last night, but that's it."

Rose looked at the ceiling. "Oh crap! Mar, sorry if I hurt your feelings. I didn't mean anything by the kid thing."

Marissa shrugged it off. She used to flinch anytime anyone mentioned anything to do with children, but she seemed to be stepping into her own space a bit more. I wondered what her and Scott's future would bring.

Would they adopt? Travel around the world like some exotic couple? Marissa shook her head. "I can see a lot has been going on, and we need to get together more often."

I don't think we had gotten together since the ordeal when Adam volunteered to help. "True."

Marissa grinned. "So...cuddle buddies, eh? What ever happened to him being out of your league and disgustingly extroverted?"

"Oh, those are still true." I scrunched my nose.

"So," Marissa leaned close, "how was it?" Her eyebrows raised at me.

"The cuddling?" I sighed as I melted onto the bench. "Divine." I giggled.

Rose rolled her eyes. "So how's Scott?"

Marissa pivoted to face her. "Oh, he's good, happily running spreadsheets as we speak. He has an idea about a community center venue or something. When I asked what he meant, he informed me he needed to work out the numbers before he was ready to talk about it." She smiled. "James is talking him through logistics and planning on being an investor, I think."

Thinking of James, I smiled. He was a groomsman with me at Marissa and Scott's wedding. He was sweet, a bit eccentric, but sweet.

Rose grimaced. "Not the twin?"

Marissa raised a brow. "Michael doesn't have the cash to be an investor. Although yes." She looked at Rose. "Michael might add sweat equity." She spun her cup. "Why...are you hoping to bump into him?" She raised her right eyebrow.

Rose snorted. "More like I wanted to know so I could avoid him."

Michael was the groomsman with Rose at the wedding, and I had been worried he might end up with slashed tires by the end.

"How're things with Blake?"

I wasn't really sure what Rose was looking for in a guy. She loved dating, but sometimes it seemed like she wanted to prove that a relationship with her could never last.

She scoffed. "I beat him in bowling. He couldn't take it. I get plenty of drama from my family, I don't need it from a guy."

I looked toward the front door as Dotty stepped into the room. "I have a confession to make." I raised my hand at her and waved her over. Rose and Marissa turned to see who I was looking at. "This is my friend from work, Dotty. I invited her to join us."

Dotty walked to the edge of the table. "I really hope I'm not imposing. I'm heading back to Haven Falls tomorrow, and my only other invitation until I left was with Helen Sparks."

Rose shuddered. "I wouldn't wish that on my worst enemy. That woman still frequents my nightmares."

I scooted farther down the bench, making room for Dotty, and patted the seat beside me.

"It's nice to meet you." Marissa smiled at her. "I'm Marissa. How did you end up in Hillsdale?"

Marissa used to hate everything about Hillsdale, but it sneakily grows on a person.

When I first came, I was like a fish out of water, but I love this little town. It would break my heart to leave it.

Dotty shrugged. "Oh, not much to tell. I started teaching early, got my masters, and applied for principal jobs. I didn't have much luck, probably partly due to my age, but then Aunt Helen let me know about a position here. The rest is history."

Rose grimaced. "Oh...she's your aunt? Um, sorry about what I said."

Dotty giggled. "Don't be. I have called her far worse. I'm still not convinced she isn't the immortal witch I called her when I was seven."

Rose laughed. "Oh, you're fun."

Dotty blushed. "Thanks again for letting me join. I have missed talking to women my age. I like this little town, but it can feel lonely."

Rose raised her eyebrow. "I have a purely hypothetical question." She paused, looking at me. "Is there a no dating a coworker slash the parent of a student policy at the school?"

I gasped. "Rose!"

She shrugged. "What, just curious. I said hypothetically."

"Hypothetically, there isn't a law against or anything." Dotty grinned and winked at me. "It can be complicated, so definitely a gray area, but legally it's fair game."

"The coach might finally end up being caught." Rose chuckled. "Oh, so many women are going to hate you."

My stomach dropped, and panic rose in my throat at the thought of any confrontation.

"I thought he liked you. The whole Christmas party, the man couldn't keep his eyes off you." She picked up the menu. "What's good here?"

Even though we'd come for brunch, Marissa jumped in with her favorite desserts, starting with hot cocoa with cinnamon.

Chapter Eighteen

FAITH

Christmas break was going fast and slow at the same time. I texted and called Adam some, but I knew his time would be spent with Danny.

I missed my students and the routine of it all, but there was something healing about the quiet peace winter can bring. The fresh falling snow, the soft glow of all the Christmas lights, the music, and not to mention my Christmas tree that was front and center in my living room and my mind. I stared at it and replay the day in the mountains far more than I would admit.

It was Christmas Eve, and Rose was staying the night with family. Marissa was hosting a dinner with the guests at the B&B. Both had invited me to join several times, but it didn't feel right. I didn't want to be an outsider anymore. I wanted to belong. That probably meant I needed to be honest and face my past instead of running to baking therapy.

Honest with myself and others.

Where would I even start?

My phone started ringing on the counter. I wiped the flour off my hands and went over to it. It was Adam.

I smiled and answered. "Hey."

There was no voice, just a loud beeping in the background. What was that? A smoke alarm, maybe.

"Is everything okay?" I turned off the Christmas music and heard a loud banging through the phone. "Adam?"

"You've ruined Santa's cookies! I'm going to be on the naughty list because of you," Danny yelled in the background.

Adam sighed. "Hey, Faith." The smoke alarm stopped beeping.

He sounded so tired. "Hey, Adam. How's it going?" I heard a door close.

"Oh, you know, just ruining Christmas." I could tell he was both joking and serious.

"Hey." I went to my room and lay back on my bed. "It can't be that bad."

He gave a self-deprecating laugh. "That's what I thought, but Danny assured me I am incorrect."

My heart broke a little for both of them. Adam was trying so hard, and it was obvious Danny was feeling lots of emotions.

"Did you know that if you use store-bought cookies for Santa, he won't leave your presents?" Adam asked.

I shook my head. "I don't think that's a rule."

"See, that's what I thought." He sighed. "But once again I was mistaken. The cookies must be homemade." He paused. "And he told me this on Christmas Eve, naturally. I'm really wishing now that we hadn't eaten all those gingerbread ones that I brought home a few days ago."

"It sounds like you at least tried. That's all you can do, right?" I asked.

"Clearly, you don't know my child. Burnt cookies are worse than store bought."

Poor Adam. I pursed my lips. Why was Adam calling me in this crisis? Was he hoping I would come over and help? My heart sped up at the thought.

I tried to be brave and put myself out there a bit. "If only you knew someone who loved to make cookies." I held my breath.

Adam chuckled. "About that, I was thinking how perfect it would be if maybe I had this wonderful friend that might take pity on me and Danny and save our Christmas Eve." I heard Adam sigh. "But I also realized it would be selfish of me to ask since she probably has plans or things she would rather do."

"Hm." I bit back a smile. "I'm pretty sure she would love to come over and help. After all, she's all alone. Maybe you would be doing her a favor." I knew it was true with every part of me. I really wanted to spend Christmas Eve with this beautiful family. Making cookies, watching movies, the whole thing.

I only hoped my heart remembered it wasn't a permanent part of that family.

He paused. "Are you sure you don't have plans?"

My heart fluttered at the thought of spending time with Adam. "Hm, I think my plans just got decided."

"Danny doesn't know, so you don't have to worry about that."

"Yeah, I'll come." I nodded even though he couldn't see it. "But only if you want me there too. I don't want to intrude at all."

"I want you to." His voice was low and soft.

My stomach did somersaults. "It's settled then. What's your address?"

Adam rattled off his address.

"I don't deserve you as a friend, Faith. I feel you are saving me over and over. It bothers me that I haven't returned the favor." He sounded so tired, like his world was crumbling around a pan of burnt cookies.

"Maybe you save me more than you think." It was true; he saved me from my loneliness. From my false beliefs about what parents are. "I'll head that way in a few minutes." I looked toward my kitchen. "Do you need me to bring anything?"

"Nope. Unless you have my pride somewhere, I seem to have misplaced it."

I chuckled. "Oh no!" I raised my eyebrows. "Wait, I thought you didn't like the word 'friends' between us."

"Oh, I want to be friends," I could hear the grin return to his voice. "Just not *only* friends."

I gave a breathy laugh. "Oh, okay, got it." I hadn't felt like this with anyone. I was excited and terrified, like I was flying but knew I might fall.

"Thanks, Faith." Adam's voice was soft, and I was excited to be with him.

"Cya soon."

"Bye."

I drove my car on the icy roads outside of Hillsdale. The road narrowed on the sides as the snow banks grew higher. I pulled into the driveway and noticed Adam's truck in front of a small blue ranch-style house, complete with what had to be ten snowmen lined up like little soldiers along the driveway. I grinned.

The front door flew open, and Danny rushed out. He was in pj's covered with flour, and his hair stuck up in all directions. I opened my door and was met with my second grader's arms wrapping around me.

"Thank you," he said.

I hugged him back, and a warm spot grew in my chest. "I can't let you have a Christmas emergency and not help."

Danny grabbed my hand and began tugging me toward the front door, which now had Adam standing at the threshold. He looked exhausted. He was covered in flour as he rubbed a hand down his face, shook his head, and one side of his mouth pulled up in a smile. "Hey, Faith."

I wanted to reach out to him, to hold him. "Merry Christmas Eve."

And Adam, by his eyes, he wanted to hug me too. But Danny didn't give us the option as he helped me toward the kitchen. I tried to look at the walls in the living room that held pictures and drawings, a pile of toys, and Frosty on the TV as I was pulled into the small galley kitchen.

Danny grabbed the recipe that was set on the counter and pressed it into my hand.

I chuckled. "Okay, we better get started. Let me wash my hands."

The three of us spent the next thirty minutes measuring, scooping, and adding extra chocolate chips for good measure. Adam could only pick out the eggshells. Danny thought he might have bad luck.

It was like a Christmas card. The three of us standing in the kitchen, Adam brushing against me and touching my waist every chance he could, and Danny with his rigid demands. This was what I wanted for Christmas. I wished to hold on to this memory forever, to paint it in my heart and in my mind, never letting it dull or change.

Danny was afraid the cookies might burn again, which led to the three of us leaning against the opposite cupboard, sitting on the floor, and watching them bake.

I should have kept my focus on the oven, but with both boys pressed in on either side, I couldn't. As I was enveloped in the smell of warm chocolate chip cookies, my mind envisioned a different life than how I was raised, a life I now wanted in my future. In a simple home, with homemade presents, watching cookies bake, and surrounded by people I love.

Christmas Eve growing up was Mom's annual dinner party. She always took it as a competition between that and the Knolts' New Year's Eve party. Both centerpieces started as small ice sculptures that somehow grew into ones the size of Christmas trees.

The year before I left, Mom boasted of crackers that cost three hundred dollars each and cheese that was seven hundred dollars a pound. And each guest got an exotic truffle chocolate box from Vosges and a gold champagne flute.

There were no cookies, no intimate dinner, no matching pj's.

There was nothing about family at all. The party went super late, and then my parents slept most of Christmas Day. I could open my presents by myself whenever I wanted.

Danny yawned and leaned into my side, and I was brought back to this real life fairytale. The one with chipped linoleum floors, burnt cookies in the trash, and Frosty the Snowman on repeat in the background. Adam shifted and his hand slid down my arm and clasped my hand in his. I leaned my head on his shoulder, and his lips pressed into my hair.

I sat as still as I could, afraid to wake up from this dream.

This life could never be real, never truly be mine, until I was honest with everyone around me. They all deserved the chance to choose the real me.

Chapter Nineteen

ADAM

The not-burnt cookies were set out for Santa, and Danny was finally staying in bed. I walked through the hallway toward the living room. The lights of the Christmas tree guiding my path.

Our tree of Christmas past with Cassie was white lights only and matching wrapping paper. Everything used to look picture perfect, but behind the scene, it all was sad and empty.

Our tree now was full of handmade ornaments, bubble lights, and whatever random thing Danny added. The recent idea was small balls of tinfoil for shine. It all looked so different from before, but this was the picture I wanted to have with me forever. It was real.

Faith yawned as I sat on the couch next to her, the Christmas lights adding a soft glow to her skin. I'd be lying if I said a part of me wasn't wondering if this woman would be a part of our Christmas picture in the future.

"Danny is so lucky to get to have Christmas with you." She nestled into my chest. It had been so long since I was in a state of constant physical affection. I didn't want to go back to being alone. I hadn't realized how much I missed being touched and held.

I chuckled. "What are you talking about? We literally had to call in reinforcements for the cookies." I rubbed her loose hair in my fingers.

She looked up at me. "I mean it! I wish my Christmases could have been like this."

The comment was a reminder that I hardly knew the woman pressed against my side. I could tell she wasn't very comfortable talking about her past, but I knew if we were going to make things work, we would need to learn to trust each other.

I smiled. "Tell me about your Christmases growing up."

Faith stiffened at my side.

There was a pause, and I let the heavy silence fill it. If she wasn't willing to share about herself, it would kill me, but I knew I would need to step back.

She raised a shoulder and looked around my little mismatched living room. "It was the opposite of this in every way." She shook her head.

My eyebrows scrunched down. "In what way?"

She spun the ring on her hand. I noticed her doing that when she was nervous.

There was something in her past she wasn't telling me.

"Oh, we had Christmas. It was big, gaudy, with no magic, and no connection." She paused. "Thanks again for my Christmas tree." Faith relaxed back into my chest, and I rubbed her shoulder. "I think it's probably the most thoughtful gift I have ever been given."

I didn't know what that feeling was like from my parents, but I knew what it was from a spouse. Cassie never bought me a gift. Not a Christmas present, a birthday present, nothing.

I thought of Christmases far past where my parents had little to give, but what they had they gave to me, and I always felt love. I hoped Danny would feel love every Christmas. Faith watched the Christmas tree. I hoped Faith spent every Christmas from here on out feeling love and connection.

We sat there in silence and enjoyed the Christmas tree.

"What about your Christmases as a kid?" Faith asked.

I rubbed the sleeve of her shirt. "It was pretty similar to this." I looked down at her. "Although Santa had to make do with the burnt cookies." I remembered Dad choking down burnt meals, each one with a smile and thank you. "With my ex though, it sounds like it was more like your childhood." I sighed. "It took me a long time to realize we wanted different things."

She spun her ring and stared at the tree. "It took me a while to step away too. Mom's still saying I'll come crawling back when I run out of money. But I'm not going back." She glanced up at me. "I'm sorry about your ex."

I looked down at her. "Sorry about your childhood." Her mom trying to get her to come back home had to be difficult. Did that mean she would eventually leave? She mentioned only her mom. "What about your dad?"

She sighed. "Oh, he is there in every family portrait anyway." I felt her shrug. "I hardly saw him, and he took a 'mother knows best' approach with me."

"My dad died when I was in junior high. A heart attack."

She rubbed her hand down my arm. "I'm sorry," she whispered. "I'm sure that was very difficult for you and your mom."

I looked at the Christmas tree. "It was hard, but we found our new normal before too long."

We sat there in silence, but it didn't feel uneasy. It felt safe and warm.

"What do you love about coaching?" Her hand reached up and was splayed out on my chest, and my heart rate skyrocketed with the touch.

I tilted my head in thought. "There is something powerful in helping a group of kids come into their own, and learn to be their best selves." I raised my eyebrow. "That and I don't mind the friendly competition. It helps me stay in shape."

Her lips were curving into a grin. "Well, it has done wonders for you." Her cheeks flushed pink, and the compliment boosted my ego.

I laughed. "Thanks." I rubbed my hand up and down her side, enjoying the feel of her shirt under my hand. "What about teaching? Do you love it?"

"I love it!" Her smile lit up her face. "There is something so loving about children, the way they accept each other and any differences without a second thought." She shrugged. "My mother really struggled with some of my own differences."

I nodded. "Sorry."

"Thanks." Her eyes studied my face, my mouth. "Um." Faith shook her head, trying to come up with another question. "What's one of your pet peeves?" she asked.

My forehead burrowed. "I guess it's when people pretend to be something they're not."

Faith's breath caught in a soft gasp. "What do you mean?" She sat up and her eyebrows dipped in concern.

I missed the way her hand felt over my heart. "Too often, people wear masks; they hide their true natures. Hide who they really are and what they really want. I don't like games."

Faith's brow furrowed and she faced away slightly.

"I feel like my life before the divorce was nothing but hidden agendas and intentions. Like I was a player in a game, but I never got the rules and could never win." I never wanted to pretend to be someone else again, and that so many people did, rubbed me the wrong way.

Faith's vibe had definitely shifted. Her big reaction didn't sit well in my stomach. I waited for her to say why. The silence stretched, no longer with the same comfort as before.

"Well, I better get home, so Santa doesn't catch me." She smiled, but it didn't reach her eyes. Faith stood to go. I knew it was because of what I had said before.

I stopped myself from reaching out to her, even though I was already missing her warmth pressed into my side. I wondered if I should take back what I said, so she might stay.

I didn't.

I warred with my emotions, wanting her to stay. Wanting to kiss her lips. Wanting her to open up about her past. I want to trust her and have her trust me.

I sat still as my brain and heart yo-yoed with what to do.

Faith grabbed her jacket off the back of the couch, and I stood to help her slide her arms in the sleeves. Her golden hair brushed over my hands, and I bit back my plea for her to stay. I would not spend another second of my life convincing someone else to choose me. I opened the door for her and slipped my boots onto my feet as I followed her outside.

She opened her car door, leaned in to start the car, then stood and studied me. I felt like she was going to say something, but then she looked away.

I pulled her into a hug. Her body was soft against mine, and I leaned down to rest my head on her soft hair. "Thanks for saving me again."

She looked up at me; the cold air had turned her nose and cheeks pink. "Thanks for letting me come." She gave me a sad smile. "This is by far the most magical Christmas Eve I've ever had." Her eyes shone and she blinked rapidly. Her breath turned to steam in the cold air and wrapped around me. She pulled me closer and my heart closer to hers.

I pressed my lips to her cold forehead, taking in her floral scent. The gaping hole in my chest shrank a tiny fraction, reaffirming I was ready. Ready to try again. Ready to trust. Ready to love.

But this time around, I needed to make sure I stayed true to myself.

The moon reflected off the snow and reminded me how cold I would be once she left.

I wanted to ask her out.

I wanted her back inside my house, on my couch, and in my arms.

She leaned back from my chest, and her gaze met mine. "Merry Christmas, Adam."

There was a slight sadness behind them. Why?

"Merry Christmas, Faith."

She pulled out of my arms, and I forced myself to let her go, even though every part of me was screaming to hold on tighter.

She got into her car, backed up, and drove away.

Was I reading too much into things?

Chapter Twenty

ADAM

I was not reading into things.

The rest of the Christmas break passed, with Danny making snowmen, us going to bed at ten p.m. on New Year's Eve, and texts from Faith that were vague and distant. I even asked Faith if she wanted to spend New Year's Day with us. She said she had plans, but didn't elaborate.

I needed to constantly remind myself that until Faith was ready to be honest with me, space was best.

Maybe I had, in fact, just been lonely.

Stupid Christmas.

After a week of no practice between Christmas and New Year, bellies full of junk food, and what I could only assume were very late nights, the other team was outrunning us with a full-court press. Having a game two days after break was brutal.

I gestured to the passing referee that I wanted a time-out. He blew his whistle, and they stopped the clock. I had thirty seconds. I gestured for the benched players to stand and let the other players sit for a second.

Danny ran to the boys and handed out water bottles.

"All right, let's go zone, they are beating us man to man." I made eye contact with Jacob. He nodded his head in agreement.

"Connor, I want you under the basket. Remember to set your feet. Maybe we can draw the foul." He took another drink. "There's only three minutes left. Let's give it all." I made eye contact with each of them, and they nodded.

The buzzer sounded, causing Danny to flinch and drop a water bottle. "It's all right, Champ." I tossed him a towel and turned my focus to the team.

Mustang number 12 drove in for the layup, and Connor set his feet and got the foul.

"Yes!" I punched my fist. "Come on, Connor." I whispered under my breath.

Nothing but net.

"Atta boy, one more."

He missed, but Jackson got the rebound and put it in for two.

"Nice!" I gestured for the team. "Get back. Go zone."

We were still down by three, and with two minutes left, the other team might try to stall. They passed the ball back and forth above the three point line. Minute thirty left. Jacob rushed at the pass, misjudging the position. The other team's guard cut to the basket. The ref started counting off the seconds in the key. The Mustangs kicked it out to the side. Twenty-four shot a three. It bounced off the rim.

"Come on," I muttered. "Get the rebound."

We missed it. Mustangs went up for a shot at the top of the key and they made it.

We grabbed the ball and ran out of bounds to throw it in. Under a minute left. The team rushed down the court, calling that they were open and trying to set up the Danny play. The team was working hard to get open, setting up screens and cutting to the basket.

"Okay, now kick it out," I muttered, willing them a perfect play.

Connor ran through the key, Jackson setting up the screen. Jacob kicked it out to him as soon as he hit the three-point line. Under twenty seconds. He took his shot. The crowd held their breath as the ball flew through the air and erupted into cheers when it sank through the net.

We were down by two.

The Mustangs had the ball with ten seconds left. The Eagles started running back.

"Man to man!" Jacob called, and everyone scrambled to find their man. He was right to switch, otherwise, the other team might have stalled. The point guard pressed hard to the basket, then kicked it out.

Five seconds left.

They passed to their post player. He dribbled, leaned hard trying to draw the foul and went up. He made it. Connor did good. Kept his feet, and raised his hands high. The buzzer sounded.

The team worked hard, but in the end we lost by four.

They met in a circle after the buzzer.

"Hey that's all right! You can't win them all." I shrugged. "I'm very proud of all of you. You guys keep up the hard work, and we might see these guys again at State." I smiled.

"Yeah, we will totally get them next time," Jacob confirmed. "All right, Eagles on three. One...two...three."

"Eagles."

We went through the line and congratulated the other players and the coach. Back at the bench, I called out. "All right, boys, practice tomorrow. I know it's been a long night, but it's time to get back to work."

They wiped off the sweat, grabbed their warm-ups, and headed to the locker rooms.

I went over to help Danny with the water bottles. He was setting them in the wire carriers. I knew better than to fill in the spaces; instead, I handed the water bottles to Danny one at a time so he could put them away according to his system.

"Coach." I felt the tap on my shoulder as the female voice reached my ear.

I looked up to see the cheer team coach, Brandy, and her pointy high heels.

"Good game." She placed her hands on her hips. "I really thought the boys might pull it off."

I nodded as I grabbed Danny's shoes. I'm not sure when he had taken them off. "Yeah, it was close." I gestured Danny to sit, and I squatted in front of him.

"I wanted to remind you that this Saturday is the dance." She tilted her head toward me.

Ahh crap! I forgot. "Uh…"

"And don't forget, you need to bring a date." She gave a small wave and rushed away.

I growled. "Great." I tied Danny's shoe tighter than necessary. His eyebrows scrunched together, and he looked at the floor. Great. Danny picked up on my negative energy. He shot a questioning look my way.

"Sorry about my shoes. I am faster without them."

I rolled my eyes and ruffled his hair. "I don't know about that, but I'm not upset about it." I let him see my face and that I meant it. "I'm not frustrated with you, bud, it's other things."

I grabbed his bright orange jacket and slid one arm through the hole. "Are you mad about the game?"

I tilted my head. "Nope, the boys played hard, and that's all I can ask of them."

Danny stared at the retreating cheerleader coach. "Is it about the date thing?"

"Yeah, I guess." That and the fact I couldn't stop thinking about Faith. I put his other arm in its sleeve. "But don't you worry about that."

"You could ask Ms. Faith. She isn't a date, remember." Danny nodded, happy with the solution he had come to.

"Yeah, maybe." I directed him toward the gym doors. It was already past his bedtime. I helped him up into the truck and made sure he was buckled.

"Can I play on your phone on the way home?" Danny asked.

I grabbed it out of my back pocket, checking once again for any missed calls or texts. There were none. Not that I was expecting any.

I handed it over. "Please don't download anything this time. The thing can barely handle what's on it, and I really don't want to have to get a new phone."

Danny took my unlocked phone.

I walked over to my side and started the truck, cranking the heat. Pulling out of the parking lot and onto Main Street, I glanced over at Danny. He definitely wasn't playing a game. He was scrolling through my contacts and he pressed send on Faith's name.

"Danny!" I reached for the phone. "What are you doing?"

He leaned out of my reach. "I'm helping you not be grumpy." He scrunched his eyebrows.

"I'm not grumpy. Now, hand the phone over." I growled and snapped my fingers and pointed at the phone while flicking my eyes to the road.

"You are grouchy. I figured it was because you missed our friend Ms. Faith. If she goes with you to the dance thing, then you won't be grumpy." He held the phone out of my reach.

I sobered at his reasoning. I hadn't realized I had been moping, and that Danny had noticed. "Look, Champ, you can't just call Faith."

"Why not? She was my friend first."

I sighed. I never should have blurred the lines between teacher and more than friends.

"Hello?" I heard Faith's faint voice from the phone in Danny's outstretched hand. "Hello?"

Ugh!

"Hey Faith, my dad is grumpy and needs a date."

I rubbed my hand down my face.

Great.

"I'm sorry, what?"

I cleared my throat and gestured to Danny to give me the phone. He handed it over, happy knowing he had accomplished his goal. "Hey, Faith, sorry about that. Danny called you."

"Oh." Her voice fell. "Sounds good, good night."

"No, wait..." I sighed.

Danny was right. I had been grumpy since Faith had started shutting me out. Was it better to walk away right now? I wasn't sure I could be around her and not want to be in a relationship with her. I wasn't sure she was ready for that.

But who else would I take to the dance?

"Adam?" Faith paused. "Are you there?"

I groaned. "Yep, sorry." I took a deep breath. Danny gave me a thumbs up and a grin.

"I was curious if I could ask you something." One of these times I was going to ask to spend time with Faith, and it wouldn't sound like a charity event.

"Okay, what can I do to help you and Danny?" Her voice brightened a little.

"Um..." I turned off the main road. "Well," I huffed, "it's not Danny that needs help."

I sounded like such a loser.

"Oh." Her voice was smaller.

"I need a date."

The silence was palpable.

"Are you there?"

She cleared her throat. "Um, yep."

"You don't have to, but I need someone to go with me to the dance on Saturday. I have—I kind of volunteered to chaperone."

"And you want to ask me?" Faith asked.

Part of me wanted to demand she be ready to tell me everything, and the other part of me wanted to trust.

Trust. It wasn't my strong suit. But there was no one else. No one else I wanted to spend time with, no one else that made me feel whole.

Somehow, this quiet, resilient woman had softened my heart, and I wasn't ready to give up the chance.

"Yes, I'm sure."

I hadn't wanted to fall for anyone ever again, especially someone who I barely knew. But here I was falling. Like an idiot.

"Only if you want to though. I don't want you to do it out of some weird obligation or favor."

She cleared her throat. "So you are asking me on a date to a high school dance?"

I chuckled. "Yep. I guess so."

The pause stretched and pulled between us.

"I would love to go to the dance with you, Adam."

My heart and smile needed to remember it wasn't a big deal. It was a date.

A date.

A date I wanted to go on, not one I was set up on or tricked into. I hadn't been this excited in a while. I kept trying to remind myself it wasn't a big deal.

"Awesome. Can I pick you up on Saturday at six p.m.?"

"Mmhm," Faith replied.

"All right. Night, Faith."

"Night, Adam."

I moved the phone away from my ear to end the call, and I'm pretty sure I heard happy squealing. My whole chest was lighter, like I could take a full breath of air for the first time in days.

"I told you that you were grumpy because you missed Ms. Faith," Danny murmured as he looked out the window.

Chapter Twenty-One

FAITH

Rose added glitter near my eyes. "Girl, Adam won't know what hit him." She raised her eyebrows suggestively.

My cheeks flushed.

Marissa swiveled on a nearby chair at the kitchen counter. "Ohhh." She saw me and shimmied her shoulders, holding the gingerbread cookie that she had taken a large bite of.

My fingers reached to spin my anxiety ring, but then I remembered I had taken it off for the dance. "Is this even okay? It's kind of public, and what about Danny? What will people think?"

Rose rolled her eyes and picked up her eyeliner, adding a layer with her practiced hand. "People will think what people will think. That has nothing to do with you or what you choose." She tilted my chin up, turning my face toward the light.

Marissa nodded. "That's true." She swallowed another bite. "Other people aren't in your sphere of influence. You can't waste time worrying about something out of your control." She bit another big chunk.

"Sounds like someone has been making good use of therapy," I teased.

"Maybe you should look back into it." She raised her eyebrows. "I know someone if you need." She grinned.

I chuckled. Marissa had been using my friend Sarah as a therapist.

"What really matters is what do you think? What do you feel?" Marissa added.

What did I think about Adam? What did I feel? How would this affect Danny? Then there was the fact that my past clung to me, refusing to let me go.

"I think...maybe it's not that simple." My brow furrowed.

Rose grabbed her lip stain. "It never is, especially once men are involved." She unscrewed the lid. "It's easy to fancy yourself special to someone in the glow of night, but in the morning the truth comes out." She applied the stain a little rougher than necessary to my lips.

I pulled away from Rose and looked at her. "Rose..." My eyebrows lowered. Marissa hopped off her stool and came to her side.

Rose shrugged off our concern. "I don't want to talk about it. I'm fine. I promise." She stiffened her shoulders. "Besides, you should see what I did to his car."

Marissa flinched.

Rose set her lip stain in her makeup carrier. "I stuck maxi pads all over his car. I hope it freezes and rips all the paint off." She raised an eyebrow.

"Wait, I thought you said it was over with Blake already?" I pinched my brow.

"Oh, um, yeah." She looked away from me and shrugged. "We just met up one more time." She focused on her make up bag. "Anyway, enough about that. Follow me."

Marissa and I followed her down the hallway to her bedroom. We stepped into Rose's room with the black and white male model posters all over the walls, and there on the bed was a baby-blue gown. It had a one shoulder design and flared out above the knees.

Rose held up the dress. "Thought the princess might need a dress for the ball."

I gasped, and I went and felt the soft silk. "It's beautiful, but I can't wear your dress."

Rose laughed. "There is no way you would fit into my dress." She pointed to her chest for emphasis. "I borrowed it from Shayla. She already wore it twice and won't wear it again." Shayla was a friend of Rose's that lived in Haven Falls. When she went down for a weekend, that was usually who she stayed with.

Marissa touched the fabric. "That color will look amazing on you! It matches your eyes."

"I think it will look great with your silver heels too." Rose raised her brow. "Will you do something for me tonight?" Rose asked.

"Of course." I reached forward and grabbed her hand.

"When you get back, I need details of how Adam fell at your feet." Rose wiggled her eyebrows. "Because he definitely will."

"For sure." Marissa chuckled.

I took a deep breath. Ever since Christmas Eve, I thought over and over about what Adam said about his pet peeve being people who were pretending.

He deserved the truth, especially if we went on more dates, but Marissa and Rose deserved the truth first.

I clenched my fingers and forced a deep breath into my lungs.

"Okay..." I pursed my lips together. "I need to tell you guys something." I sat down on Rose's bed.

Marissa sat beside me, and Rose waited, her eyebrow raised.

"It's about my past." I took a deep breath and held it for three.

Marissa's eyes widened, and Rose gestured for me to continue.

I closed my eyes, unable to look at their faces, and see the disappointment flash in their eyes. "My real name isn't Faith." I peeked at their reaction. Marissa's eyebrows were furrowed, and Rose was rolling her eyes. "Well, I mean it is, because I legally changed it, but my birth name is Astrid..." I fidgeted with my fingers, missing my ring, and cleared my throat. No going back now. "My birth name is Astrid Luxe." I closed my eyes and bowed my head, waiting for the exclamations and outrage.

"Who?" Marissa sounded confused.

"Astrid Luxe," Rose repeated, with no shock in her voice.

Marissa was shaking her head. "Sorry, but I have no idea who that is?" She looked towards Rose. "Should I?"

Rose huffed. "Yes, and you do."

"No, I really don't think I do." Marissa's eyebrows lowered.

"Yes. You do." Rose threw her hands in the air. "Astrid Luxe, as in the Luxe fashion icon in New York, heir to the Luxe fortune, and 'new face of the brand.' The one who randomly went radio silent a few years ago...about the same time Faith moved here." Rose raised her brow.

Wait.

Marissa shook her head and popped the last bite of gingerbread into her mouth. "Nope, sorry."

"Did you know already?" I asked Rose.

"Of course I knew." She waved her hand. "You showed up in designer shoes, bad hair dye over perfect extensions, and Luxe handbags. Not to mention the number of times you dyed our sheets pink and burnt ramen noodles. It was obvious you had no idea what you were doing." Rose checked her nails.

I sat there with my mouth hanging open. "I...I don't," My eyebrows scrunched. "So you knew the whole time!"

Rose grinned.

"Wait, so you're super rich?" Marissa's eyes were wide.

"Technically, my family is. Not me." I shrugged. "I don't get any of it unless I agree to take over the company, and I don't want it. It was fashion shows, front pages of magazines, and full of fake relationships and anxiety."

Marissa leaned back on her elbows and stared at the ceiling. "Huh...weird."

"So why are you telling us now?" Rose crossed her arms.

I sighed. "I had a lot of friends who were only with me because of my last name. I was worried once you knew who I really was, I would lose you too."

Rose rolled her eyes. "That's stupid."

They handled the first deep dive into my past, but how would they do with the worst part?

"Well, that's why I didn't tell at first. But there's more." The tears gathered at the corners of my eyes, and I cleared my throat. Rose knew my name. But I bet she didn't know what I did. "I'm not who you think I am."

"We've already been over that." Rose waved her hand.

"No, like...besides that. I'm not a nice person," I whispered, afraid that if I said it too loud, my past would rise up and claim me.

"What are you talking about?" Rose scoffed. "You are literally the nicest person I know."

I crumpled in on myself, unable to close the door to my past. "My senior year of high school..." My lips quivered. "I changed." I cleared my throat. "I tried to be who my mom wanted. I was the mean girl, the popular girl, who shattered people's self-esteem and confidence in my wake. I knew what people were insecure about, and I used it." I bit back my sob and cleared my throat. "I hurt them on purpose." I pursed my lips into a tight line. "My rapidly growing friend group loved it. My mother loved that I was finally embracing my popularity and stepping into 'my own.'"

Marissa reached over and picked up my hand, squeezing it tight.

I stared down at it. Instead of seeing our hands together, I remembered walking by the partially opened door to the home office. I heard my name and leaned closer to the door and peeked inside. My mother was in one corner and the family lawyer in the other. "There was a girl in the hospital for self-harm because of me. I can still remember the smell of the flowers on the side table. I caught my reflection in the hallway mirror, and I stared at myself, and I saw myself for the first time for the monster I was, maybe I am?" I shrugged.

"I don't understand." Rose stood stiff.

I took a shuddering breath. "Because of things I said, and things I did, a girl no longer wanted to live." My heart broke again as I remembered. "The crazy thing is"—I shook my head—"I wouldn't have even known." I shook my head. "I overheard the lawyers talking to Mom about how the family would be taking the whole thing to the press if we didn't cover the girl's medical bills." I balked, disgusted in myself. "Mom waved her hand as if it was of no consequence." I scoffed, reliving the moment. "Like a girl hadn't almost died." I wiped the tears now running down my face and glanced up to see Marissa with tears on her cheeks and Rose leaning away.

"What if I never overheard, what if I never knew?" My shoulders sagged. I was somehow both heavier and lighter saying it out loud.

Rose tipped her head to the side. "Wait. You...were a bully?" Her voice held confusion, and knowing about Rose's past, I could understand why. Her middle school was full of people who were vicious to her repeatedly.

A sob voice caught in my throat, I pressed my hand over my mouth, and nodded.

Hurt grew in her eyes. "You sat there and listened to my stories, and you didn't say anything?" Her hurt was replaced with anger.

I closed my eyes and nodded. "Yes."

Marissa sighed as she looked between us.

"I can't fix it. I know I can never undo it, who I was," I said. "The person I was follows me everywhere I go." I clenched my fists.

"I apologized to the girl when I saw her at school a week later." I shrugged. "I changed and refused to hurt others for my personal gain ever again." My shoulders shook, as I gasped for air. "My friends made fun of me and moved on. My mother was never more disappointed in me in my fall from popularity." I placed my hands over my face. "I would never be who she wanted, and I refused to let myself change to appease her." I wiped off my tears with my palms. "I wanted to start over, try to see who I could be without her." I took a shuddering breath. "I knew I wanted a fresh start." Marissa leaned her head on my shoulder. I flexed my fingers and cleared my throat. "I remembered I had this elementary teacher in second grade, Mrs. Carlson." I smiled as I thought of her crazy cardigans and big dangly earrings. "She was sweet, and kind, and made me feel special. Not special because of my last name, Luxe, but special because I loved the color yellow, my favorite animal was the polar bear, and I was great at drawing jellyfish. She saw me, really saw me, and it made all the difference." I chewed on my lip. "I decided I wanted to pay it forward, I wanted to be that for some child somewhere else. I wanted to be an elementary teacher." I pursed my lips. "I started going to an online college, and then found this rural program to finish my degree on the other side of the world. It was perfect."

Rose studied the wall opposite of me, her eyebrows lowered.

I wiped a stray tear with my shoulder. "That was when I came here."

Marissa's eyes held kindness I didn't deserve as she looked back at me. "Faith, or, I guess, Astrid?" She pulled the last word out, unsure.

"I'd rather be Faith," I whispered. I wanted to be known as the person I was trying to become. Plus, the world of Astrid Luxe comes with its own set of rules and drama that I wanted nothing to do with.

She nodded. "Okay, Faith." She looked at me. "I'm really sorry for the way you were raised." She closed the distance between us and pulled me into a hug. "I'm sorry about how you felt unloved and unappreciated. I can't imagine being in the spotlight was easy for you either." She squeezed my hand. "But I also hope you recognize the person you are now, and that the choices you have made say far more about who you are as a person than any when you were in the process when you were finding yourself." Marissa, still holding my hand, reached for Rose. "I'm sorry about your childhood. That humans can be so mean." Rose looked at the ceiling, refusing to meet Marissa's gaze. "I'm sorry you were alone when you had a storm going on at home too. You had nowhere that felt safe." Marissa frowned. "I'm sorry I wasn't here to help beat those jerks up for you."

Rose scoffed and chuckled, her eyes finally meeting Marissa's.

"I'm so sorry for you both, and the way you didn't feel you could be who you were and feel safe." Marissa sagged.

I covered my mouth, trying to hold back the sob, and glanced up into Rose's eyes, which were now glossy. She cleared her throat and blew out a tight breath. Rose was almost in tears. Rose never cried.

Marissa looked between us and she pulled her hands together, causing me to stand in front of Rose. Any control I had up to that point, I lost. I threw my arms around her in a hug and bawled.

I cried for the people I hurt, I cried for the girl in me who wasn't accepted and loved, I cried from the stress of carrying this lie and hurting people I had grown to care about.

Rose awkwardly patted my back and sighed. She slowly leaned away and wiped my tears off my cheeks and shook her head.

"Seriously!" She rolled her eyes. "I'll have to start over with your makeup now. You look absolutely terrible."

I laugh-cried and hugged her tighter. "I'm so, so sorry," I whispered, and Marissa wrapped her arms around us both.

"You're such a drama queen." Rose wiped at her tears.

They didn't leave.

They didn't hate me.

Those few minutes in that hug did more to heal my broken heart than the years of trying to make up for it ever had. Being held by friends who knew the real me and loved me, flaws and all.

"I love you guys."

"I love you," they both repeated.

"All right, that is enough of that!" Rose stepped out of the hug and shook off all the emotion surrounding her. She pointed to the hallway.

"Now go wash your face and put on that dress." She rolled her eyes. "Looks like I should have gone with waterproof mascara after all. Oh!" Rose clapped. "Now you can finally tell me if Jonathan West is really as hot as he looks in the movies and papers. I have been dying to ask for years!"

Chapter Twenty-Two

FAITH

The doorbell rang, and I rushed over and pulled it open. Adam's hair was styled and stiff with gel, and he wore a blue button-up shirt and khakis.

"Wow." His eyes opened wider as they traveled over me and my dress. "You look beautiful," he whispered.

I blushed. "Thanks, you're not so bad yourself."

"Here." He handed me a bouquet of roses and daisies, with a little stuffed snowman. "These are for you." His cheeks flushed, and he put his hand on the back of his neck. "Danny helped pick the flowers, and he insisted the snowman went with them." He fidgeted with his hands.

His nervousness was adorable.

"Well, Danny was obviously right." I smiled. "The snowman is the perfect addition." I searched his eyes. "Thank you, both of you."

He visibly relaxed as I accepted his gift. Did he think I wouldn't like it? I nodded behind me. "Want to come in? I'll go put these in water." I turned and headed toward the kitchen. Adam followed me through the house.

"Faith?" The question was clear in his voice. I turned to see him pointing to my Christmas tree in the living room. My very dead and crispy Christmas tree.

"That tree needs to be thrown out. It's a fire hazard."

"I know, but I can't just throw it away…" I furrowed my brow.

I sighed and grabbed a stool, pulling it over to vases on top of the fridge. I went to stand on it, and Adam rushed over.

"Here allow me."

I put my foot back down as he easily reached the vases on the fridge and handed me on a clear cylinder one.

"Thanks." I took the base and began filling it will water.

"What are you planning on doing with the crispy tree?" Adam tilted his head.

I chuckled. "Okay, I know. It needs to be thrown away. It just felt wrong. It was such a kind gift." It was turning brown, and the pine needles were falling everywhere.

Adam rolled his eyes. "It's just a tree." He squatted down and started loosening the bolts at the base.

I placed the flowers on the counter and walked over to him. "It's a near-perfect tree, actually."

"Well, I'm taking it outside. I can't be the reason your house burns down." He hefted the tree out of the base; needles fell everywhere. He held it out at a weird angle trying not to make a mess.

"Thank you. For the gift, and the disposal." I rushed past him down the hall and opened the front door. He walked past. "The dumpster is over there on the left." I pointed.

I sighed. I was really sad to see it go. It brought such happy memories.

After he dropped the tree near the dumpster, he came back toward me. I giggled. "You look like you have tree sprinkles all over you."

He brushed off his sleeves, and pine needles fell around him like confetti.

"Here, let me help." I went on my tiptoes to reach up to get the ones in his hair. I wasn't tall enough. Our eyes met and I froze. "I can't reach your hair, you need to bend down."

I kept all my wild fantasies to myself as he lowered his head. His hair was stiff in my fingers as I picked out the needles. He was close enough I could smell his citrus scent and feel his warm breath on my skin. My arms got goosebumps from the cold, but a jacket would ruin the look of this dress, so I chose the cold. "You ready?"

"Yep." He walked me over to his truck and held open the door for me.

I might have flashed more leg than intended, but it was a big step into his truck. I could be wrong, but I think he noticed. Adam hopped into the truck and glanced quickly at my legs again.

He had! I held back a giggle.

This sexy man was checking me out.

"So, is Danny with your mom?" I shifted slightly and crossed one leg over the other. His eyes flicked back to my bare legs, and then traveled up the length of them. I was definitely going to be thanking Rose for the dress later.

Adam cleared his throat and focused back on the road as he navigated the familiar streets. "Sorry. What were you saying?"

I bit back my grin. "I was asking about Danny."

Adam kept his eyes firmly on the road. "Oh, he is good, other than he felt that since it was his idea, he should also come to the dance."

"He has some great dance moves."

Adam chuckled. "Better than mine, that's for sure."

We talked for the rest of the drive. I usually hate small talk, but there was something about Adam that calmed my nerves. He pulled into the parking lot, opened my door, and helped me out of his truck. We walked into the school, my hand pressed into his elbow. Streamers flowed over the entrance as Adam led us into the dance.

The lunchroom had been converted to a dance floor, complete with Christmas lights and fake Christmas trees. There were teenagers holding hands and whispering, a group surrounded the food table, and a horrified girl gawked at the dance floor at what I assumed were her parents dancing and kissing.

"Adam." A lady with an enormous smile and high ponytail patted his arm. "I'm so glad you could make it. Even if you were a few minutes late." She checked her watch.

"Sorry, Danny didn't see why he couldn't come."

She rolled her eyes, and then her gaze landed on me. "I'm Brandy." She held out her hand to shake.

I shook her hand. "Hey. I'm Faith."

"Have fun." She winked at me and then raised her brow at Adam.

What did she mean by that? I panicked and reached for my ring. But it was gone. I started rubbing my finger where the ring usually sat.

Adam reached over and grabbed my hand in his, nodded, and led me through the outskirts of the dance floor to the far side. We walked by a dark corner where a set of teenagers were making out, and Adam kicked the shoe of the boy softly. The boy looked up, glaring daggers, but when he saw it was Adam, he immediately muttered "Sorry" and held his date's hand, looking anywhere but at his date or Adam.

When we reached the corner, he leaned against the wall, and I waited for him to drop my hand. But he didn't.

The song changed from a slow one to a fast one that a bunch of girls must have known a line dance to as they rushed the dance floor. Groups of teenagers danced and jumped around, screaming song lyrics.

A boy came over with a cute blonde by his side. "Hey, Coach."

"Jacob."

"I was wondering if we should try switching to conditioning after practice, when our muscles are already tired. I also saw this thing where you scrimmage but you can't shoot till you have passed the ball at least four times."

Adam listened thoroughly, weighing and respecting the boy's opinions. I made eye contact with the girl, she was not impressed that her date was talking about sports while they were at a dance. We both waited a few minutes, but the conversation didn't seem like a quick one.

I bumped Adam with my shoulder, and he immediately gazed down at me. I gestured to the boy's date. "Maybe this can be handled later?"

I held my breath, waiting for him to dismiss me or be frustrated that I had made him look a certain way. Adam looked at Jacob's date and smiled.

"Yes, of course. Thanks for the idea. I will think about it, and we can talk about it"–he winked down at me—"later."

The girl grinned at me and then dragged her date away.

Speaking up had left me a little shaky. "Sorry, Adam. I shouldn't have spoken up like that when I had no idea what I was talking about." Now that the moment was over, anxiety flooded my system.

"What are you talking about?" Adam's eyebrows pulled down.

"With your captain and the date and sports and I just..."

"Hey." He looked down at me. "You have every right to speak up when you think or feel something. You know that, right?"

I studied my feet as a new slow song came on. "I wish I could do it without this." I held up my other hand to show him it was shaking and rolled my eyes.

"Faith, will you dance with me?" He held out his hand.

I stepped closer. "Yes." I bit my lip and placed my hand in his. He slowly pulled me closer and led me out onto the dance floor as the slow song played through the budget school stereo system. He put one hand on the small of my back, his large palms warming my skin through the soft fabric. I placed my hands on his shoulders and felt his muscles shift underneath them as we moved to the music.

He held me, creating peace and safety from the storm in my mind.

Adam's mouth lowered to my ear. "Have I told you you look beautiful tonight?"

I grinned and glanced up into his eyes. "You have, but I don't mind the repetition."

"In that case, you look beautiful." His brown eyes stared into mine, and he leaned closer, his lips resting on my forehead.

My breath caught. "Thanks." Even in heels, I barely made it mid biceps. Time slowed, and I felt safe in his arms, safe and like I never wanted to leave. Like the whole world melted away, and it was just the two of us.

Adam's hand increased pressure on my back until there was no space between us. I studied his eyes, I wanted to remember everything about tonight. The curve of his lips, the warmth of his eyes. Time stood still and I found myself pulled into a world I never wanted to leave. A pull to be closer physically and mentally. I wanted to know Adam. I wanted to know his favorite dessert and favorite color. I wanted to know his favorite song, and whether he snored when he slept.

I think I was falling in love with Adam.

And for tonight, I could pretend he was mine. The song ended, and he grabbed my hand and kissed it. I felt like I was glowing. "I'm going to go grab some water. Do you want some?"

"Sure." I pursed my lips together to keep my happy squeals inside.

Adam stepped away to get us some drinks, and a hand clamped tightly around my arm and pulled me spinning around.

"Wha... What?" I was suddenly face-to-face with a furious Jessica.

"You might have Adam fooled for now, but it won't last. He'll get bored and move on. Just like he did with me." Her face was red as she leaned close to my face.

My brain whirled, trying to come up with something to say, but nothing would come. I stood there, rooted.

"You're a joke, with your fake sweet persona, but who are you really?" Jessica raised her brows. "I bet Adam would be interested in who you were before you showed up here."

I searched her eyes in a panic, feeling like I was falling through the air. Did she know about my past? "Wait. What?"

"Ha!" Jessica smirked. "I knew it! Sweet little Faith has a past. Well." Jessica raised her right eyebrow. "I'm going to find it, and I'm going to make you wish you never came here."

My breath caught in my throat.

Adam put his hand on top of Jessica's, pulling it off my arm. "Jessica, that's enough." He growled as he stepped between Jessica and me.

She ripped her arm out of his grasp. "Did you see that?" She smirked. "I told you, she's hiding something."

The room began staring at us and whispering. What were they saying? I wasn't sure how to hold my arms, and I cleared my throat. I wished I could shrink and disappear. The air was heavy, too heavy to breathe in. My throat tightened.

"Jessica, go home." Adam's voice left no room for discussion.

"I'm volunteering." Jessica folded her arms across her chest and raised her brow. "I can't leave."

I just stood there like an idiot. Wanting to say something, wanting to run, wanting to scream. I did absolutely nothing.

"Well, then we are leaving." Adam turned away from Jessica and reached for my hand. I placed my palm in his, and he gently guided me toward the edge of the room, pulling up the roots my feet had grown, and led me to the side.

"I don't know what her problem is. I gave her the benefit of the doubt, but last time I was very explicit that I wasn't interested." Adam shook his head, and I noticed several people lean in closer to hear the one-sided conversation.

Anxiety prickled and climbed its way up my spine. It grew large enough to swallow me whole.

No, not right now! Get your crap together, girl! I rocked slightly, feeling my breath coming faster, but not deep enough to slow my racing heart.

Adam stood in front of me, blocking Jessica from view. He handed me the cup of water, I took it with shaking hands.

I could feel eyes all over the room on me, and the air felt sticky on my skin. I rubbed my throat, trying to clear my airway. I reached for my ring, frustrated to remember it was still gone. Sounds were muffled around me, and I gasped for air, but there was none.

Where was the air? I couldn't breathe. The walls pressed tighter at every angle.

"Hey, are you okay?" Adam's voice found its way through the panic in my mind. He took the shaking cup from my hands and lowered so he was at eye level with me.

"Um, yes...kinda..." My breath caught. I needed to get out of here. "I'm just going to get some fresh air." I stepped out of his arms, head down, and started rushing for the exit. I couldn't leave fast enough, but I needed to concentrate or I would collapse into panic right here. *Just make it outside.*

"I'm coming with you." I felt Adam's presence at my side. He wrapped his arm around my shoulders and led me to the exit. The pressure he applied at my side held me together.

Chapter Twenty-Three

ADAM

We stepped out of the school dance and into the cold.

"I'm sorry." Faith gasped for air. Her breathing was fast and shallow. "So many people were staring." She tipped her head back as if she were trying to clear her throat. "And I don't do well with confrontation."

"Hey, you're okay." I led her to my truck. At least, I hoped she was okay. Should I take her to the hospital? I could feel her body shaking against my side.

I reached for the door handle but stopped. Would she want to sit in the truck, or was it better to stay outside?

"Sit in the truck or stay outside for now?"

She was still trying to catch her breath. Her jaw flexed, and she cleared her throat. "You should be inside," she gasped. "I'm fine." Her hands reached up and pushed weakly against my chest. "Please, just go. Please leave."

She rocked back and forth as she pulled her arms tight around her torso.

"No." My voice was strong and final. I reached up and brushed a tear from her cheek, and I searched her eyes. "I'm not leaving." This was more than some nerves or being upset with Jessica. I didn't know what was going on, and hated watching her go through this.

Her shoulders collapsed in and she covered her face with her hands. "What will everyone think? This is so embarrassing." The muscles on her neck tensed, and she shook her head.

I reached over and pulled her against my chest. She seemed to like the pressure before. "Would you stop worrying about other people? Focus on you. I couldn't care less about anyone else right now." I placed my chin on top of her head. "What do you need, Faith?" I rubbed my hands down her arms, trying to release the tight muscles.

She rubbed her hands down her throat. "Just stop. Please stop..." she begged.

I stepped back and held my hands in front of me. "Sorry, I'm not sure how to help."

"No." Her neck flexed, and she took short gasps. "Not you."

It seemed difficult for her to answer besides clipped answers.

I nodded. Her jaw tensed over and over.

"Faith."

She looked at the ground, gasping. I grabbed her hands in mine and leaned down so I could see her eyes. She seemed miles away. "Faith, please look at me," I whispered, not wanting my voice to add to her stress. I reached into my truck and grabbed my coach jacket and put it over her shoulders. Her gaze met mine before they flicked away. She tilted her chin up, her breathing still too fast and too shallow.

My blood ran colder than the freezing temperature outside. Was she okay? What should I do? "Faith, I don't know how to help?" The weakness in my voice was something I would break apart later. "Do I take you to the hospital?"

She shook her head no. "Hold me." She muttered between gasps. "Tight."

I closed the distance between us, pulling her body against mine, grateful for her direction of how to help. Her tiny frame was completely swallowed by my own. I reached down and grabbed her hand in mine, and then I placed her palm on my chest, so she could feel it rise and fall.

I took slow, deliberate breaths, hoping she would follow subconsciously.

It seemed to help.

Breathe in...hold for three...breathe out.

Repeat.

We stood there, her reeling, and me desperately trying to protect her from some unseen danger.

I hadn't seen her jaw flex for a bit.

I kept up my slow, exaggerated breathing.

She released a tight, shaky breath of air.

"Good." I whispered.

Slowly, she seemed to reset with her breathing and her whole body was shaking.

She groaned. "Why am I like this?" She buried her face into my chest, and I squeezed her hand under mine. "I'm so embarrassed."

I could tell her body was resetting, and by her response, this had happened before. "Hey, you're okay. Nothing to be embarrassed about."

"Yeah, right." She shook her head against my chest and avoided my eyes. "I just want to be normal." She whimpered.

I looked at the snow that was falling in tiny flurries around us. "We all came unique. Kinda like snowflakes." I shrugged. "Think of how boring everything would be if we were all the same."

"Well, I think my snowflake is bad." Some of the color was returning to her face, and the muscles in her arms were now relaxed.

I laughed, my fear settling. "I remember someone telling me once there wasn't good or bad, just different." I winked at her.

"You can't use my own logic against me." Her cheek rested on my chest. I hoped she didn't feel my own erratic heartbeat.

"You know, if you wanted to get me alone outside, you could have just asked."

She scoffed, leaned back. "Whatever!"

I chuckled. She pulled herself tight into my arms once more. Her body relaxed as she melted against my chest.

"So, what was that?" I whispered.

She sighed. "That was a panic attack, courtesy of my extreme social anxiety." She huffed. "I don't do the best in crowds or with attention, especially if it's confrontational. I can usually handle it, but sometimes it's just too much. I'm so, so sorry. I had already had an emotionally charged day, and I just couldn't—"

"Hey." I placed my hands on her shoulders, looking in her eyes. "You never have to apologize for how you feel." I shook my head. "Not with me, or anyone else, and hopefully not to yourself." I ran my thumb along her jaw.

She leaned into the touch, and her forehead shone with sweat. If she wasn't already freezing, she would be soon.

"Let's get you out of the cold." I opened the truck door and helped her inside.

I rushed to my side, started the truck, and blasted the air, willing it to heat up fast. I pulled her near my side, not wanting her to get cold, but also wanting to feel her and know she was doing better.

She leaned in to me. I rubbed her arms to keep her warm and started humming a song into the silence. It usually seemed to help when Danny was overwhelmed.

"Is that Frosty the Snowman?" She asked through a smiling yawn.

I hadn't even noticed. I chuckled. "Yep. In my defense, it's all I've listened to for a month straight." Now that her muscles were relaxed, she was tired. I smiled and rubbed my hand down her side. "You must be exhausted. Let's get you home."

Faith gazed up at me. "You are a wonderful father. I hope you know that."

I raised a shoulder. "I know I get a lot of things wrong, but I keep trying."

She pressed tighter against my side. "I'm a little tired, but honestly I'm feeling much better. Sometimes I try so hard to outrun the panic, but sometimes all you can do is let it pass through you." She sighed and pressed her face into my shoulder. "Thanks for your help tonight. Even if it was mortifyingly embarrassing."

"I'm not sure I helped at all, but I was glad to be there with you." I rested my lips against her forehead. Her hair smelled like roses. I put the truck in reverse and backed out of the parking spot.

"You helped. Trust me." Her eyes flicked up to mine. "It's not my favorite thing, and I hate it when people see that side of me. But you knew what to do." She shrugged. "Maybe that's why you are so aware of Danny's needs."

I rubbed her arm, unsure of what to say. The truth was, I had no idea what I was doing most of the time. Not with Danny and definitely not with her.

She sighed. "Jessica was right though. I do have past mistakes. When I was in high school, I made some choices I'm really not proud of."

I shook my head. "I think you'd be hard pressed to find anyone who didn't."

She draped her arm around my waist. "You're amazing, just so you know."

I chuckled. "I don't think you're so bad yourself."

"Do you think we will hurt Danny if we date?"

I sighed. I didn't want to hurt Danny, and I didn't want to get hurt either. But it was a risk I didn't want to run from anymore. Faith's kind eyes shone up at me. If it worked out in the end, it would all be worth it.

"I know you are worried about how anything between us could affect Danny. And I like you all the more for it." I rested my head on top of hers. "We will try to keep Danny unaware. Nothing in life is ever guaranteed, but that doesn't mean it's not worth trying."

"I feel like I am pretending, that I will wake up from this dream, and realize none of it is real."

I turned on my blinker and drove onto the main highway. "I'm not pretending, and I don't think you are either." I glanced down at her.

"I'm not, but what if"—she sighed—"what if it doesn't work? Everyone will talk."

I pursed my lips and raised my right shoulder. "Let them."

"I wish I could be more like you," she whispered.

"What do you mean?" I'm pretty sure by all standard testing available I was well below average. To top it off, I was a single dad, divorced, working in a job I loved but that barely covered the bills.

"I love that you don't care what people think."

Ah, that.

"I used to care what people thought, mostly my ex-wife. I wanted to make her happy." I hoped that bringing up my ex-wife at this moment wasn't a faux pas, but she was part of my past and therefore part of me. "I wanted to give her the life she wanted. I wanted to be who she wanted me to be." I thought back to the depressed shell of a human that was left of me once she left. "I gave all of myself." I sighed and leaned my head on top of Faith's. "But in the end, it still wasn't enough. We were both very unhappy." I turned down Park Street. "That's when I had to learn that all that matters is what I think about my life, about myself." I shrugged. "Those are the only things I am in control of."

"How mature of you." She shook her head.

"Okay, therapy and time also helped." I squeezed her side.

I pulled up to her duplex and put the truck in park. She sat up, and I missed her warmth at my side.

"I admit though, I'm spending a lot of time wondering what one other person is thinking and feeling." I searched her blue eyes. "It scares me a bit."

She gave a shy smile. "Who?"

I rolled my eyes. "You, Faith."

She chuckled and leaned in closer. "I might spend all my time thinking about you too."

I swallowed as I stared down at her pink lips. They had been teasing me all night. Between that and the soft blue of her dress, which looked amazing against her skin, and her lean legs, which my hand begged to touch, she was driving me crazy.

"Thanks for tonight," she whispered. "For all of it." Her gaze dropped to my mouth, and my throat went dry.

"I'm happy to take things at whatever pace you want. If you aren't ready for this kind of relationship, I get it. I come with baggage." I smirked. "Cute baggage, but still, baggage. But, Faith, I desperately want to try." I ran my hand down her arm. "I haven't felt like this in years, and I would hate myself if I let my fear ruin this."

Her mouth curved into a grin "Trust me, your baggage is way cuter than mine." She leaned into my touch. "I'm still trying to find out who I am. I have past issues I'm working through, and I don't know how to let them go." She gave me a sad smile. "But I know I have never been this happy."

She pulled me toward her, and whispered in my ear. "I want to try." Goosebumps ran down my back. It took every ounce of strength I possessed not to pull her mouth to mine in that second.

But I didn't want to rush, I wanted to take my time. I put my hand on her cheek, and she leaned into my palm, her bottom lip brushing my thumb. I wrapped my other hand around her hip, the soft fabric of her dress against my palm. Faith tilted her chin toward me. I closed the distance between us, hungry to have her hands on me and her mouth on mine. My stomach tightened as I held her tighter to my chest. Her lips were soft as they melted with mine.

It wasn't enough. I couldn't get close enough to her.

I thought a kiss would satiate my hunger, but all it had done was leave me ravenous.

Her tongue traced the bottom of my lip, and she pivoted to face me better, and a groan escaped my lips.

Heaven help me, but I was lost. I wanted this woman in my life.

"You are so beautiful," I whispered, unable to keep it to myself any longer. "I don't know what spell you've cast on me," I muttered between kisses as my mouth traced her jawline.

She leaned away. "Me? You're the dangerous one." She placed her hands on my neck and pulled me back to her mouth, and I happily obliged.

Chapter Twenty-Four
FAITH

Despite the negative temperatures, I had never felt warmer as I replayed that kiss with Adam over and over in my head. The way Adam's eyes devoured me as he said that I held him captive.

Me.

Shy and slightly boring me. I bit my lip. I absentmindedly walked around Mason's desk and bumped into it with my thigh.

"Ope, sorry, Mason."

My entire world finally felt right. Rose and Marissa knew about my past and still stood by my side. And Adam... Well, Adam had been amazing. He swept me off my feet with those big biceps of his and I still haven't landed.

"Why are you smiling weird?" Danny's voice pulled me out of my daydream.

I refocused on the task at hand, which was math facts and not Adam's biceps or his lips. "Oh, I'm just happy."

"Why?" Danny's eyebrows scrunched.

This was not a discussion I was going to have with a group of second graders. I cleared my throat. "There are lots of things that make me happy. One of them is helping you guys learn." I pointed to the papers on their desks, hoping to refocus the attention there, and not on my weird facial expressions.

"My dad tries to help me with spelling, but Mom says he's lexic and not to listen." Lydia always loved a chance to be heard.

"What's lexic?" Sophia's eyebrows lowered.

I grinned. "She was probably referring to him having dyslexia. Just like everyone looks different on the outside, everyone's insides can be a little different too."

"Like how my mom can't eat cheese or she has to go to the bathroom?" Mason asked.

I cleared my throat. Parents would be appalled at the things I've been told about them. "Yes, like that. Some people are allergic to things, but that doesn't mean everyone can't eat cheese, right?" I asked the class.

"I love cheese," Mason added.

"Me too," Sophia said.

"My mom says we can't eat sugar because it's bad for us, but she still eats it; she just hides it." Harper shrugged. "I know where though."

I had better get this back on track before I hear more secrets. "Okay, so back to dyslexia. Just like some people's tummies handle things differently, some people's brains work a little differently too. With dyslexia, they have a hard time keeping letters facing the right way and lined up. Which can make things like reading or spelling extra challenging."

Sophia's eyebrows lowered.

"For example, I have ADHD and social anxiety." I was proud of my class and how accepting they were of differences.

"Dad bought a new HD TV that I can't touch. Is it like that?" Caleb asked.

"Kinda." I held back a smile. "Everyone needs different things to be successful." It was obvious this was much too deep for my second graders. I thought back to how Adam had talked about it. "You remember when we talked about snowflakes and how they are all unique?" The class nodded. "Well, a friend told me that's how people are. We all have different traits, strengths, and weaknesses. Not better or worse, just different."

"I think my strength is speed." Harper's eyes widened.

"I think mine is eating cheese." Mason nodded with a serious expression.

Soon the class was calling out all sorts of strengths, and I barely held back my laugh. "All right, let's focus back on your math facts. You have four minutes until recess, and if you can focus the whole time, I will let us have a wiggle song before lunch."

They all started shouting song requests for "Go Noodle."

The freezing temperatures had kept them in for recess, so the extra distractibility was expected.

"I will set a timer on my phone, okay? Three minutes' focus time, then a wiggle song." I grabbed my phone out of my back pocket.

They focused on their papers. I was so lucky. I truly loved my life. I loved being a teacher, loved these kids, I loved this little town...and I'm pretty sure I loved Adam. I admit I would love for my parents to still be a part of it, but not at the risk of my own happiness.

My phone vibrated. I had a text from Adam. I tucked my hair behind my ear and bit back a grin. The timer had two minutes left. Surely it would give me enough time to respond. I opened the text thread.

Adam: When can I see you?

Faith: I mean, I should see you when you get Danny at pickup, so like 3:50? Right?

I tried to keep my squeals to myself as the three dots danced as I waited for a reply.

Adam: I mean, when can I see you when Danny isn't nearby? (wink emoji).

I bit my bottom lip.

Faith: Hm, I guess we will have to get creative.

Adam: Can we meet in my office at lunch?

There was a palpable energy between us, and I felt like I would never need to sleep again.

Faith: Lunch date it is.

The alarm went off in my hand and I jumped slightly. Danny frowned as he watched me.

I cleared my throat. "Okay, class." I double-checked the weather again. "Looks like it's after-lunch recess in the gym again."

The class groaned.

"There aren't swings!" Sophia whined.

"They said we couldn't play tag!" Harper added.

I listened and nodded. "Sorry, but it's school policy that if the weather isn't above twenty, it isn't safe to send kids out for recess." I didn't want kids getting cold and sick, and even though I sent reminders for boots and gloves, some continued to arrive in shorts.

"Okay, let's do the 'banana song,' and then we will line up for lunch." Some kids protested, but they all stood by their desks and prepared to give the best performance of their lives.

The music started, and little arms and legs flailed about to the song. This would hopefully get us down the hall and to the lunchroom with fewer incidents. The song ended with freestyle dance moves, and they did not disappoint.

"All right, let's line up." I glanced at the board. "Caleb is the line leader. Then home lunch and then school lunch." Kids rushed about the room as I waited. Once in a line, I put up my hands in my quiet coyote shape. "Eyes up here, please. Okay, this time let's play silent soldiers in the hall." Some eyes lit up and others fell. "Shoulders up, arms tight to sides." I opened the door behind me. "Okay, I want to see the best and quietest soldiers you can be."

We made it to the lunchroom with only a few squabbles, but nothing that needed intervening. I passed the responsibility off to the lunchroom staff. Then I grabbed a Dr Pepper and my chicken salad croissant and headed to Adam's office.

I tried to keep my pace to walking; I didn't want to get yelled at for running in the halls. I knocked on Adam's door and heard him rushing to open it.

His smile was wide as he looked me up and down.

"You know you are really nailing the whole sexy school teacher thing." He raised his eyebrows and reached for my arm and pulled me inside his office as I giggled, and he closed the door behind me.

"Is this all about some secret fetish?" I rolled my eyes.

He pulled me tight against his chest and leaned down to my ear. "Oh, it's no secret." Goosebumps erupted along my arm, and I gave an involuntary shiver.

Adam laughed.

"That's not fair." I slapped his firm chest. "You can't throw your sexy self at me like that and not expect a reaction."

He raised an eyebrow. "You're the one dressed up as a sexy school teacher." I chuckled as he led me to the couch that held Danny's tablet. A basketball game tape was playing on the TV in the corner, and he pulled me onto his lap with my legs on his left side. My lunch was forgotten on the seat beside me.

With my arms draped around his neck, I brought my face to his. I had thought of nothing but recreating our first kiss experience all morning. Could the spark of pure adrenaline and attraction be a fluke?

My lips parted, and his tongue teased me.

Phew, holy Hannah! Not a fluke. I could spend my whole day kissing this man, and never regret a moment. My lips tingled from the contact with his and a shiver ran up my spine.

"Wow." I sighed.

"I agree." He sounded as breathless as I felt.

Part of me wanted to be embarrassed at my obvious attraction. But what did it matter if I was open about his kissing? He knew I was head over heels for him. Besides, I had lived my life with secrets for too long.

"I missed you." Adam kissed down the length of my neck.

"We talked last night." The trail of kisses was both hot and cold.

His mouth curved against my skin. "Talk, yes, but I wanted to hold you." His hand pressed against my back. "I wanted to taste you." He kissed my collarbone. "It was torture."

My stomach did flip-flops at his declarations. "I might have been thinking about kissing you too." I smiled. "Danny mentioned to the class I was making funny faces." I shook my head. "That kid misses nothing." I sighed.

"Maybe it's a neurodivergent thing?" He raised the back of my hand to his lips.

Did this mean he was more accepting of Danny's possible diagnosis? "I actually love to watch how their brains work. It's kind of amazing. They notice different things."

He slowly kissed each finger, and I shivered. "Okay, I better let you eat, or you will waste away."

I rolled my eyes but hopped off his lap and grabbed my lunch and opened up my Dr Pepper.

Adam grabbed his lunchbox with Minecraft characters on it and sat next to me, our legs touching.

"Nice lunch box." I grinned.

Adam shrugged. "Danny wanted to pick out my lunch box this morning. I figured it didn't bother me, and it made him happy, so why not?"

How was this man even real?

He bit into his PB&J. "So, why Hillsdale?" He covered his mouth with his hand as he asked the question.

My mind blanked. How much do I tell him? I didn't want secrets anymore, but I also didn't want to trauma dump on him either. This was all still new. "That's complicated."

He pivoted, so that he was facing me more fully, actively giving me all his attention.

"Um." Even after telling Rose and Marissa, acknowledging my past was still difficult. I blew out a tight breath. "Well, I spent most of my childhood trying to change who I was and to be who my mother wanted." I tilted my head. "I realized later, I wasn't who I wanted to be." I spun my ring and flexed my hands. "I grew tired of everyone being disappointed in me, especially my mom, so I left. I found something that was as far away and as different from my old life as possible."

His eyes were full of questions.

I shrugged. "I know life is full of unmet expectations with relationships." I took a bite of my sandwich. "Maybe none more so than a parent-child one." I lifted my drink, hoping the Dr Pepper would spark a change in conversation. My hand started shaking.

Adam scooted closer and held out his hand for mine. I set down my Dr Pepper and placed my hands in his as he squeezed them. "What do you mean?"

The weight of his hands over mine grounded me, and my panic eased slightly. I sighed. "Most parents envision their children destined for an exceptionally perfect life, and children are bound to disappoint by being their own unexceptional human beings with their own wants." A tear betrayed my pain, and I wiped it with my left shoulder.

Adam's brow furrowed in my peripheral.

I took a deep breath and let it out slowly. "Whew! That was maybe a little dramatic." I rolled my eyes. "It's not a big deal." I looked down at the fabric of my dress pants. "I'm still not used to talking much about my past though." I pushed out a tight breath. "That might take a bit of practice before it doesn't sting."

His eyebrows scrunched down. "You're wrong."

Wait. "I'm wrong about what?"

"You are extraordinary." He reached up and ran his thumb down my jaw, wiping a stray tear I hadn't known was there.

I gave a self-deprecating chuckle. "Well, I sure wasn't what my mother wanted."

Adam tightened his grip on my hands. "You might not be who your mother wanted, but that doesn't mean you aren't exceptional." He dipped his head so that his brown eyes pierced mine. "And you get to decide who you are supposed to be, no one else."

"I spent most of my life hating myself and the way my brain works." The tears burning behind my eyes, I cleared my throat.

He rubbed his hand down my arm. "You get why that doesn't work, right?" His left eyebrow raised.

I tipped my head. "What do you mean?"

"I don't think having differences can be something that is 'unique and amazing' in other people, but bad in you." He gave me a small smile.

My forehead creased.

"I think the way your brain works, and the experiences you've had, have made you the exceptional person you are." He pulled me tight into a hug, and I was grateful for the space to hide my ugly tears.

My breath caught, realizing he might be right.

"You're the person who notices when someone is feeling isolated, like Dotty at the Christmas party. The person who notices my son is not eating lunch and helps him in a way that makes him feel comfortable. The person who will stand up to an adult about what a child might need, even though confrontation literally makes you sick. You are hyperaware of others."

He was making me sound far too glorious. I scoffed. "Okay, but it's also the reason I had a panic attack at the dance. I can't walk into a room of people without getting in my head about what is the right thing to do, and why my mom and I can't find any common ground."

He pressed his lips against my forehead. "I still think you made it out ahead." He shrugged. "Who cares if you don't like crowds or get nervous? You are kind, which is way more important than either."

I leaned away from him to look into his eyes, needing to see him, needing him to hear me. "I haven't always been kind. When I was a senior in high school, I was actually a bully for a bit, and I hate myself for it." I looked down.

Adam pursed his lips. "I think that's partly the cost of growing up." He rubbed his hand down my arm. "Not that it's okay, or that it doesn't matter." He tilted his head. "Just that we might need more grace as we grow."

I nodded as I thought that over.

I whispered. "I also pretend like I don't care, but I actually hate it that my parents are disappointed in me."

He rested his palm against my cheek. "I know a little about being a disappointment." Adam shrugged. "I was depressed for a long time, even before Cassie and I separated."

Adam sat there helping ease my pain, when he knew what it felt like for the people who are meant to love and cherish you to belittle and shred you apart instead.

"My divorce and then learning to be myself was the hardest thing I have ever experienced." Adam kissed the back of my hand. "I was broken and sure I could never be whole." His eyes closed. "That I would have to make the best dad I could out of the pieces I had left." His thumb traced the back of my hand. "Then there was learning to forgive myself for the choices I made while trying to survive." He sighed. "I hurt people. I cut off communication with my mom and everyone from my past. I was self-destructive at times, and I lost my patience with Danny often." He bit the inside of his cheek. "I had to change parts of myself to be someone else, and there was a cost that I paid for it." He looked at me and raised his right shoulder. "Trust me, I get it."

I looked at him and saw the weight that pressed down on his shoulders, the pain of his mistakes. It's obvious it wasn't an easy process, but he wasn't left with a half-self. He was whole in a way that was beautiful. A way I wanted to be.

Adam shifted. "I eventually grew tired of hating myself for everything I wasn't and tried to love what I was instead." He studied me. "Life is too short to spend any of it hating yourself."

"Huh." My forehead creased. I hadn't thought of it like that.

"I saw this quote once. I think it was by Dolly Parton, maybe." He tipped his chin in thought. "It said, 'Find out who you are, and do it on purpose.' That became my resolution. Being true to me, on purpose." He leaned his head on mine.

"Go, Dolly." I chuckled and then reached up and rubbed my thumb along his jaw and his eyes met mine. "And go you." He leaned into my touch. I knew I wanted something different from the relationship I had with myself. I wanted to be me on purpose. I wanted to focus on the good pieces of me and not stare only at my weaknesses.

"The people who are meant to be in my life will accept me for who I am. The ones who won't..." He shrugged. "I'm better off knowing sooner rather than later."

He took my hand and pressed his lips onto my palm. "I was sure every other relationship would leave me with even less of myself. That no one could be trusted not to want to change and mold me into someone else." He shook his head. "I couldn't go back to who I was, so I avoided any relationships at all."

I nodded. "I mean, that makes sense."

He moved closer to me, I laid my head on his shoulder, and he rested his hand on my leg. "Thank you." His voice was soft. "Even if it doesn't work out between us, I can now see that it is possible. That maybe one day, I can trust and be in a healthy relationship with all of me."

I looked up at him and placed my hand over his. I don't think anyone has said anything more beautiful to me. "I'm not perfect. Not by a long shot." I leaned back. "I'm sure I will do and say things that might unintentionally hurt you." My shoulders dropped. "But I can promise I have no intention of changing you."

His eyes were now shining with unshed tears, and he tipped his chin toward my mouth and paused, asking and searching in the most vulnerable way if he could kiss me.

This lunch meeting had not gone as expected. I planned on way more kissing, but somehow this was even better.

But that was enough healing for now.

"Are we done with all this healing garbage so we can just make out now?" I smirked.

"Definitely." Adam smiled. His lips pressed against mine. They were soft at first, like we were holding all the broken pieces of each other and trying not to hurt the other person further.

I didn't want to be careful. I wanted passion and fire. I wanted something so real and deep, there was no denying it. I pulled myself closer to him and kissed him harder. I wanted him to know all the pieces of me; I wanted him to know he mattered.

He matched my intensity, and the heat that passed between us welded our hearts into something a little more whole. Like the Japanese art kintsugi, where broken pieces of pottery and dishes are fused back together with lines of gold, we created something stronger, and more beautiful than it was before.

My alarm went off in my back pocket, and I sighed against his lips. "Time's up."

He grumbled as I pulled away from him and traced my hand along his jawline. His mouth went to my palm and kissed it again.

"Can I walk you back?" He smirked and laced his fingers through mine and kissed the back of my hand as we stood.

I felt my heart speed up, but not in an anxious way. "Sure." I grabbed my lunch, and we walked hand in hand to his office door.

"So." Adam sighed. "How would testing and labeling help if Danny is neurodivergent?"

I gathered my thoughts. "Have you noticed things you do that help with Danny? Like before you leave in the morning or at basketball games? Or how you can tell when he is feeling overwhelmed, and how to help him?"

He tilted his head. "Yeah." We walked through the gym and into the elementary building.

I shrugged. "So the hope is that testing and setting up a plan will help the teachers and other people who work with Danny know what he needs to be successful." We walked through the hall. "There can also be extra support, resources, or accommodations too."

"Hm." He put his hand that wasn't holding mine on the back of his neck.

"It can be challenging. Just like anything else." I raised my right shoulder. "There can be pros and cons. And labels can be scary." I squeezed his hand in mine. "But regardless if you label him or not, it doesn't change who Danny is. He will always be Danny."

Chapter Twenty-Five

ADAM

The first Saturday of February came, and with it the elementary business fair. I had helped by calling and reminding parents, helped some kids come up with a supply list, and helped others finalize their choices.

And, I got extra time with Faith, which I would never complain about.

After trying to change his mind twice, Danny had decided that for his business he was going to answer questions about space and snow.

I was glad that I had talked him into returning the erasers that he had found in a supply closet at the school. He decided he wanted to sell the pink erasers back to the teachers at two dollars apiece. I had to give it to him; the kid was resourceful. After returning the erasers, I decided that selling Danny's wisdom was looking like a great idea.

We arrived at the school at eight a.m. with a group of volunteers. I grabbed the "Space and Snow Questions" sign and two camping chairs and handed Danny the bucket full of suckers. At least I convinced him to hand out suckers with his advice, so hopefully other kids didn't feel cheated.

We went into the cafeteria and to the second graders' section. The room was set up with tables and poster board signs. There were many things to choose from: fresh bread, cookies, plants, coloring bookmarks, painted rocks, and hot cocoa.

This money could really help with PE equipment, but it also helped the kids practice selling and doing math with giving change. The kids who earned the most money won a teddy bear and a gift card. Danny loved winning anything, especially if it resembled money.

I wondered if part of that was my fault. Maybe I talked too much about budgeting. I made sure he got what he needs, but not all he wants.

Money was only part of the problem; the things he could ask for were the other part. After all, the kid asked Santa for the ability to stop time for Christmas. Luckily, he seemed happy with the stopwatch.

Danny rushed over to his shared table with Lucy, who was raising funds for unicorn research. Her mom looked up at me and smiled. She had brown hair and a pink sweater.

"It seems like our kiddos are going to make a good team." She nodded toward Danny's sign, and I chuckled.

"Good call with the suckers." She pointed to the bucket. "I had to convince Lucy she needed to give away coloring pictures of unicorns after a donation." Lucy was sitting at the table, ruffling through coloring pages and putting them into piles.

I noticed Faith as she came in through the double doors. She was carrying a small ladder. I looked at Lucy's mom. "Excuse me."

I rushed toward Faith. "You didn't tell me to bring a ladder."

Her blue eyes met mine. She blew stray hair out of her face and shrugged. "I didn't know I needed one."

My brows lowered. "Did you just have a ladder?"

She quirked an eyebrow. "I'm five-one. I always know where the ladder is."

I leaned down and took the ladder from her hands, feeling her soft skin under mine. My throat tightened, and I tried to focus my thoughts. "Where to?" I nodded toward the ladder.

She pressed into my side and rested her head against my shoulder, and my heart picked up speed.

"Against the wall over there." She pointed to the section behind the second-grade tables.

I did my best to keep the thoughts of my racing heart and the way my body reacted to Faith to myself. We had been dating for three weeks, and the excitement of it just kept growing. I made eye contact with Dotty across the room, she smiled and raised her eyebrows.

I shrugged, blushed a little, and followed Faith.

After an hour of hanging signs for everyone who was "vertically challenged"—Faith's words, not mine—the business fair started, and Danny straightened his shirt and sat in his chair.

I hoped people would be kind.

The first to come for Danny's knowledge was Mom. She put one dollar in his jar and sat down in the chair opposite him. I could never repay her for all the help she had given me these last years. I wished I could do more for her. Mom leaned forward and placed her hands on her knees.

"What do you want advice about?" Danny asked.

Mom smiled. "I was curious what advice you might have about space travel?"

Her eyes flicked to mine, and I mouthed *Thank you*.

"What about space travel?" Danny asked.

"Well, if I wanted to go to space, what should I do?" Mom asked.

Danny raised an eyebrow. "Grandma, I'm sorry, but I think you need a new goal."

I nearly choked on my cup of hot cocoa that I bought from one of the third graders.

Mom's eyes went wide. "Why?"

Danny's forehead creased. "It depends, but most people have

to train three to five years, and then they are usually in their thirties or early forties max. I think you might be too old."

I closed my eyes. I didn't know whether to laugh, correct, or console at his blunt advice.

"Well, thanks for the advice." Mom nodded and rose from her seat. I had a feeling this was going to be a long day.

Next in the hot seat was Faith's roommate, Rose. With her were Marissa and Scott, who own the B&B, and if looks were correct, maybe Scott's brother or twin, and another guy.

"Hey, long time no see," Rose said as she sat in the camping chair.

Danny merely nodded toward the cup holding the dollar. She chuckled and pulled a dollar out of her pocket and placed it in the jar.

"What's your question?" Danny sat tall.

Rose tipped her head up to the ceiling, thinking of a question.

"How about why I am so violent and scary?" Scott's assumed brother muttered. "Or, I know. Am I in the habit of sticking things to cars?" He raised his eyebrows. Rose's head whipped in his direction, her dark hair flying with the movement. He stepped back slightly, raising his hands in front of him. There must be a story there.

"Those aren't about space or snow?" Danny added.

"Right, Michael! Wait your turn." Rose growled and then faced Danny again. "What is your favorite planet?"

Danny pursed his lips. "Well, we don't know if all the planets have been discovered." He raised his hands.

Rose held back a smile. "True. What's your favorite of the known planets?"

Danny answered immediately, "Jupiter. Did you know that a day on Jupiter is only ten hours? That means school would only last like two hours tops."

Rose smirked. "I like your reasoning." She stood up, and then

Marissa sat in the chair and added a dollar. She extended her hand toward Danny.

"Hi, I'm Marissa, a friend of your teacher."

"Nice." Danny nodded.

"What's your favorite thing to do in the snow?"

"I like making snowmen, and getting Christmas trees."

Marissa grinned. "Oh yeah, I heard about that. Faith had so much fun." Her green eyes met mine, and she smiled. She stood up from the chair and extended her hand to me. "Hi, I'm Marissa."

I shook her extended hand. Scott took the vacated chair and added a dollar to the cup.

"You guys took the B&B over for Carol, right?" I asked Marissa. I appreciated the safe space she'd always created for kids in this town.

"Yeah, Scott and I did." She gestured to her husband sitting in Danny's chair. "Never planned on it." She shrugged. "But life can be simply amazing when it doesn't go according to plan."

I looked at Danny. "I hear you there."

"Well, it was great to meet you." She smiled as her husband stood from the chair and his brother took his spot.

Danny looked between them. "Are you brothers or something?"

"Twins," Scott added.

"I'm Michael. I'm the older and better-looking one." He sat in the chair and added a dollar to the cup. "Who would look better in space, Scott or me?" He grinned.

Danny's forehead creased, unsure of how to respond, "I don't think they care about looks. Did one of you get better grades in school, or have pilot or scuba diving experience?" Danny asked.

Michael's shoulders dropped a fraction. "With brains, Scotty definitely wins." He pointed up at his brother.

Rose laughed. "For sure."

"Do you want to go to space?" Danny asked.

Michael shook his head. "Nah. I actually hate even flying on planes."

Danny scrunched his nose. "I don't like the swings. I don't like how it makes my tummy feel."

Michael smiled. "I guess I will need to find a dream that includes my feet being on the ground."

"That's a good idea," Danny agreed.

Michael stood. "Thanks."

The last person in the group took the chair and held out his hand. "Hey, I'm James." He had dark hair and glasses.

Danny gave him a firm handshake. "I'm Danny."

James pursed his lips. "Why did you choose this as your business?" He gestured to the ask Danny sign.

Danny shrugged. "Dad wouldn't let me sell the erasers back to the teachers that I found in the school, so this was the only other thing I could think of that didn't take a lot of work."

James chuckled. "I like it. Well, what do you think is better on a date, a chicken costume or a dog one?"

Danny's eyebrows lowered. "You already asked one question." He gestured to the jar.

James threw his head back and laughed and then put a twenty in the jar.

Danny's eyes grew wide. "Wow! Thanks!" He touched his chin in thought. "A dog costume. Girls like dogs."

"Solid advice." James stood, offering Danny a fist bump, and the group wandered on.

Chapter Twenty-Six

FAITH

I sat on the basketball bleachers, sandwiched between Dotty and Rose on one side and Marissa and Scott and James on the other.

Scott leaned forward, his hand in Marissa's. "So how long have you liked basketball, Faith?" His eyebrows were raised and he had a mischievous smile on his face.

Marissa elbowed him in the side. "Scott!" She tried to scold him, but she couldn't stay mad at him, so she rolled her eyes.

He laughed.

I still didn't know more than the basics of the sport, but I knew how important this game was to Adam. He had been distracted for the last several days as he went over game videos, and I could tell his mind was preoccupied. Not too preoccupied for our lunch kisses and stolen conversations though. He promised he would never be too busy for those.

"What happens if they lose?" I refocused on the group of boys running back and forth on the court and forced myself to pry my gaze away from the coach's backside.

Rose raised an eyebrow at me, and I blushed and shrugged.

Scott looked at the court. "If they lose, I think they might be out. This one is for the district championships."

We were eight behind. The buzzer sounded at the end of the third quarter. Danny flinched at the sound of the buzzer.

He stood and grabbed the water bottles and rushed toward the players. The team circled around him, half on the bench and half standing. Adam squatted in the middle, holding a little whiteboard and marker. He made different marks on the board and nodded to different boys. The boys gave him all their attention. He smiled and pointed his head toward number 44, and the group laughed.

"The coach is such a frickin' joke." A male voice hollered behind me. My back stiffened. And I kept my eyes focused on Danny as one boy helped him put the water bottles away. My heart was so full watching this group of young men. I was in awe of them. The team that Adam had created and the way they all respected one another.

My phone beeped an alarm, along with several people's phones around me. I grabbed my phone. It held a yellow warning symbol. There was a severe winter weather warning for our area for the next three days.

I cleared the message and refocused on the game. We'd had the warnings before this winter, but usually the storm would blow over pretty quickly.

The team put their hands in the middle and cheered, "Eagles!" A group of boys headed out onto the court, and I caught Adam searching the crowd. As his eyes found mine, he winked at me as I gave him a little wave.

Seven tapped his shoulder, bringing his attention back to the court. Danny had spilled a water bottle, so Adam nodded and handed a towel to him. The boys cleaned up the water.

"That kid spills water every game. I don't know why they let him even help." The same grumpy voice from before sounded behind me.

Heat flooded my veins. I was going to rip that man a new one!

I turned and made eye contact with a man with gross, stringy hair and unfocused eyes.

"Excuse me?" My hands shook. I usually shrank away from confrontation, but I didn't feel fear. At least if I did, it was drowned by my need to protect Adam and Danny.

"What's the matter? Don't like me bad-mouthing your lover boy?" The man smirked, showing missing teeth and cold eyes.

I glared at him and wanted to come to Adam's defense. I cleared my throat and stiffened my spine.

Marissa grabbed my hand, and she leaned toward me. "He's not worth it," she whispered. "Tony has filed more complaints at the law office than the whole town put together." She scoffed. "The man is a terrible excuse for a human and father, and the whole town knows it." She leaned near me. "Don't waste your time or energy on him."

I huffed and tried to calm the fire in my stomach. I faced the game again and took a deep breath and spun my ring.

Danny waved up at me. "Hey, Ms. Faith, did you see me?" He started up the bleachers in my direction.

I nodded. "I did. You did a great job."

The man behind me scoffed, and it took all my willpower to focus on Danny.

"Thanks." He stopped in front of me. "Can I sit with you?"

Marissa and Scott scooted farther down the bench and patted a spot for Danny, and he plopped himself down next to me.

"Did you hear we are getting snow tonight?" Danny's legs swung back and forth as he smiled.

I shook my head. How was he still excited about the snow? It was February, and I was ready to see spring colors and the sun. "Yep. My phone gave an alert. Sounds like it might be a big storm."

Danny nodded. "We already went to Grandma's and put extra salt on her driveway. Dad let me help."

I saw Adam's spine go rigid as he looked at the end of the

bench. He turned around in a panic and began searching the bleachers. I assumed it was for Danny.

I whistled.

It instantly caught his attention, and his eyes shot to mine and then to Danny at my side, and his shoulders relaxed. He smiled at us and then turned around to refocus on the game. There were three minutes left, and we were still down by four. Our team had the ball, and my breath got stuck in my throat.

"Come on," I whispered.

Danny started spouting off some space facts that I couldn't focus on.

"Right, Ms. Faith?"

I shook my head and looked at Danny. "Um, sorry, what?"

We scored, and now were down by two, but the other team had the ball.

Scott leaned forward. "Hey, I heard the moon is actually made of cheese?"

Danny giggled. "No way!" He turned his energy and space facts toward Scott.

I made quick eye contact and mouthed *Thank you.*

He nodded.

We had the ball, and Adam seemed unaffected under all this stress. It had to be crushing. He chatted with the same energy as before. I blinked rapidly.

We were still down by two. Twelve had the ball and passed to seven. They passed it around looking for a shot, but there was under a minute now. I blew out a tight breath.

They passed under the basket to forty-four, and he went up for the shot as the buzzer rang. The person in front of him shoved him hard to the ground, but the ball still went in. Tie game.

"Come on!" I waved my hand in the air. "Surely they can't just push like that, right?" I looked at Scott because I didn't actually know.

"Sorry, I wasn't watching." Scott looked up to the game.

The referee blew the whistle and made hand gestures I didn't understand.

"Wait, what does that mean? Are we not still tied?"

Dotty leaned forward so she could see me better. "No, they still counted the points. He gets an extra shot because of the foul."

I nodded as if I understood, even though I had no idea.

Adam stood, his shoulders relaxed, hands on his hips. The energy coursed through me, and I needed to fidget.

Forty-four bounced the ball a few times and lined up for the shot. I spun my ring and tried to take a normal breath.

He shot; the ball hit the backboard, traced around the rim, and then fell in.

Without realizing it, I was on my feet, jumping, clapping, and cheering.

Adam smiled and clapped. He patted the boys on the back as they came over to him from off the court. They had won the game.

I honestly believed that if they had lost he wouldn't have treated them any differently. I shook my head. This man was amazing. How was that much amazing even possible?

He went down the line to each one and said something to them and patted them on the shoulder.

I put my hand on my chest, trying to settle my heart. "We won! I can't believe people do this sports stuff all the time. I think I aged five years." I chuckled.

The team circled and cheered and went to shake hands with the other team.

Rose leaned toward me. "See you at home." She winked.

"Have fun." Dotty grinned and raised her brows as she passed with Rose. James stood and joined them as they walked down the bleacher steps.

Danny stood abruptly. "The water bottles!" He rushed toward the stairs but caught on Scott's foot.

"Careful." Scott's hands reached out and steadied him.

"Thanks." He nodded but didn't slow.

Scott chuckled. "That boy is focused." I walked with Scott and Marissa down the steps.

"Yeah, he is." I smiled as he scooped up the water bottles. When we got down to the court, Adam was kneeling near Danny, helping him finish up with the water bottles.

"Thanks for coming with me," I whispered to Marissa.

"Anytime." She bumped my shoulder. "All right, we better go make sure the B&B's roof is cleared before the storm hits. Besides, I think you need to tell someone good game."

My eyes and heart sought Adam.

"I think it's customary to slap their backside when you say it," she whispered and raised her eyebrows.

I chuckled and said goodbye and then went to Adam and Danny. I warred with myself, and I wasn't sure how to act. All I wanted to do was run and jump into Adam's arms and tell him I was so proud of him. But I also didn't want to make things hard for Danny.

"Good game, Coach." I placed my hand on his shoulder. Adam's eyes shot up to me, and he winked. Heat spread through my chest.

"I was hoping we'd get to"—he looked at Danny—"talk, before you left." He stared at me.

I bit my bottom lip as I imagined kissing him.

An older woman with a floral button-up and kindness radiating off her stepped behind Adam and Danny. She stared at me, but patted Adam on the back.

"Great game, son." She smiled.

Right, that's where I had seen her. She was Adam's mom and had been the one to get Danny at pickup sometimes. I thought about the polarizing differences in the vibes our mothers gave off.

Adam turned to give his mother a half hug. "Thanks. I wasn't sure we were gonna be able to catch up after that first half." He shook his head. "I can't believe we got down by twelve and still pulled it off." He looked toward the locker room. "They're good kids."

His mom reached up and patted his shoulder. "I think the coach isn't so bad either." She raised her eyebrows. "Wouldn't you agree?" she asked me.

Heat burned in my face. I had seen his mom before, but we had never chatted. She was usually just picking up Danny.

"Mom." The warning in Adam's voice was obvious.

But his mom didn't back off; she kept staring at me with her eyebrows raised.

"Um, yeah." I blushed. "I'm actually quite a fan."

She nodded in affirmation. "Good to hear. All right, better get on the roads before they ice over." She winked at me and then gave each of the boys a side hug. "Drive safe. Love you both."

As she left, I thought over my answer. Was that too forward? Not forward enough?

Danny looked up at me. "Since it's Friday, Dad said I can stay up late."

"Lucky." I smiled at him, but my eyes kept glancing at Adam.

"Since it's not a school night, can you stay up too?" Adam smiled a mischievous grin.

Danny's eyes widened. "Yeah! You can stay up late with us!"

"Uh." I cleared my throat. I mean, I didn't have other plans.

Adam ruffled Danny's hair. "That's what I was thinking too, Champ." He looked at me and raised his brows. "Want to stay up late with us?" He winked.

"Oh, um...sure." I bit my bottom lip to keep from smiling too wide. "I can come over for a bit."

Adam grinned. "Yes!" He fist-pumped and then gave Danny a high-five.

I chuckled and shook my head. These boys were too stinkin' cute.

I waited with Danny as Adam closed things up and made sure

the boys had their stuff. Then the three of us walked to the parking lot.

"Can I ride with Ms. Faith?" Danny asked.

Adam raised his shoulders and looked toward me.

Being his teacher, I'm guessing I better not. I squatted down near Danny. "I actually don't know. I'd need to see if there is a policy about it. Is that okay?"

His eyebrows scrunched. "I don't understand."

"Okay." I looked up as I tried to think of how to explain it. "There are rules at schools, like in our classroom."

Danny nodded aggressively. "Like no boogers on the desk."

Adam snorted.

"Especially that one." I pointed in the air. "There are rules about teachers and students too." I raised my right shoulder. "I don't know them all. So, I will need to check if it's a rule or not for teachers to drive students anywhere."

He tipped his chin in thought. "Okay." He hopped into Adam's truck and I started my car. I began scraping the ice that had formed in the few hours since I'd driven the car here.

Adam scraped the ice off of his windshield in long strokes. He was much faster than I was and came over and finished clearing mine. He leaned against my side, touching me whenever he was close enough to do so.

"This is my new favorite way to celebrate games we win. If I knew that you coming over for an after party was on the table, I might have been way more nervous with the results."

I rolled my eyes. "You didn't even seem nervous at all!"

He shrugged. "Of course I was. I like to win, but more than that, I just want the boys to do their best."

I sighed. "I knew it." He raised an eyebrow at me. "You are too good to be true."

He rolled his eyes and glanced back at his truck. Seeing that Danny wasn't watching, he snuck a quick kiss. His lips were cold, and his breath was warm. I desperately wanted more. I kissed him again. Danny knocked on his window, so I took a step away. Based on the look in Adam's eyes, he was sorry to step away as well.

"Want me to follow you?" Adam asked.

"How about I follow you?" I stared at his eyes, not wanting to break the contact. He took a step toward me and I knew in his gaze he wanted me too. He reached out and I fell into his arms. His truck horn blared, ripping the silence and startling us both.

He groaned, "Ugh. Fine." He turned back around and walked toward his truck. "Drive safe."

My chest warmed and I felt like I was glowing. We loaded into our vehicles, and I followed Adam's truck out of the parking lot.

Snow was falling, making it look like we were going faster than twenty-five as the flakes shone in the headlights.

The steering wheel was like ice. I reached and put on the gloves in the passenger seat and grabbed a blanket from the back and put it over my legs. My heater always took a while to heat up.

It took much longer to get to Adam's. What usually took twenty minutes was closer to thirty-five. Twice my tires slid to the left. I couldn't tell if my shaking was from the cold or the adrenaline from almost driving straight into a snowbank.

I was happy once we parked at Adam's, and I didn't feel like I had to focus so intently on the road.

Adam opened his front door and then stood in the doorway, holding the door open, waiting for me. Once inside, Danny rushed to take off his shoes and escaped down a hall. Adam's hand trailed against mine. His eyes went wide, and then his hands were instantly cupping mine.

"You are freezing." His eyebrows scrunched in thought, then his eyes widened. "Is your heater working?"

I shrugged. "Yeah?"

Adam growled. "Faith."

I rolled my eyes. "I have gloves and a blanket in there. It was just extra cold tonight. It works, it just takes a bit."

"Why haven't you got it fixed?" He was obviously frustrated.

"Because it still works? I think." I pursed my lips.

His eyes met mine, his brows lowered.

"This isn't your job to fix." I smiled at him, although I had no complaints as he pulled me against his chest and started warming me up by rubbing my back and arms.

Adam grumbled. "There is no way your heater is working right if you are this cold."

"I thought about taking it in a few weeks ago," I admitted as I warmed my nose on his chest. "But then I got nervous." I was glad he couldn't see my face.

"What do you mean?" He stepped back and studied me.

My brow furrowed. "I'm not sure. The thought of taking it in and talking to people, and they might ask questions, and I won't have the answers." I sighed. "I'm worried I might say the wrong thing. And it is working...kinda." I shrugged. "I know it's silly." My shoulders fell. "But it's something that's hard for me."

He pulled me back into a tight hug, shaking his head. "How about we take it in together tomorrow then?"

I loved the idea of him coming with me, but I needed to do these things by myself.

What if he came with me but didn't say anything? Was that cheating? I figured it was better than nothing, and I really needed to fix it.

"Okay, but I want to talk to the mechanic myself. Don't let me chicken out." I looked up at him. "I need to practice being brave."

Adam grinned. "Danny calls it sucking in your screams." He raised his right shoulder. "When you're scared to do something, but do it anyway."

I laughed. "That's a perfect description!"

Adam led me to the couch and we sat. "Thanks for coming to the game. It was fun seeing you there."

"I almost yelled at a grumpy man for you tonight." I raised my brows.

He put his arm over my shoulder and chuckled as I leaned into his chest. "Maybe you're better at confrontation than you think." He pressed his lips on my forehead.

Hm, maybe I was? I could stand up for people when I needed to.

Danny came running down the hall into the living room. I panicked and added space between myself and Adam and I missed his warmth instantly.

Danny sat on Adam's other side and leaned against him, yawning. Adam placed his arm around him. His tablet was open to a video about space. Once he was focused on his video, Adam winked and gestured me over to him.

I quietly leaned onto Adam's other side, and he placed his arm around my shoulder.

My world and heart felt full, and I didn't want to jinx this happily ever after that might be just within reach.

Chapter Twenty-Seven

ADAM

Danny and Faith had fallen asleep on either side of me, and I was torn between losing my arms to numbness and moving them when they seemed so peaceful. I shifted Danny closer so I could reach and pause his tablet.

This was not the night I'd envisioned with Faith, but it wasn't bad either. Somehow, even just sitting on the couch with Faith in my arms was enough. That Danny was pressed in on my other side was even better.

I wasn't sure how I had fallen so fast for Faith, but falling was definitely what I had done. I would be devastated if things didn't work out between us. I looked down at her soft blond hair that draped over her cheek and her pink lips.

I wrestled with my fear of whether she would choose to stay in Hillsdale and with me.

There were no guarantees.

The way she talked about her past and her mother pressuring her to return to New York didn't help.

Danny mumbled in his sleep about stars. I sighed, knowing he would sleep better in his bed.

I pressed a kiss to Faith's forehead and whispered. "I'll be right back, just going to put Danny in bed."

She sat up and rubbed her eyes. "Sorry I fell asleep." She covered a yawn with her hand.

"You're fine." I smiled as I scooped Danny into my arms and walked down the hallway to his room. I laid him on his bed and pulled the blankets up how he liked, and tightened them around him. He flopped over, and I ruffled his hair. "Love you, buddy. Good night," I whispered as I turned off his light and made sure his night light was on.

As I walked back toward the living room, the power flickered twice, causing the lights to turn off and on. I waited. If the lights flickered again, it usually meant the power would be out for a while.

It did.

The house went completely dark.

"Adam?" There was worry in Faith's voice.

I turned on the flashlight on my phone. "It's okay, just the power. Might be from snow on the power lines." I walked into the living room.

Faith's wide eyes looked toward the window in its complete darkness. "What time is it?"

I checked my phone. "Midnight."

Her eyes widened. "Midnight? Yikes, I better get home." She stood and rushed toward my front door.

Dread pooled in my stomach as I thought of the conditions of the road and her heater not working.

I furrowed my brow. "I think you should probably stay the night. I know I would feel better."

"Wait. What?" Faith's eyes shot back to me. "Like with you?"

"Not like that." I tilted my head. "Actually." I smiled. "I would be okay if you stayed like that too."

Her cheeks turned bright red.

I grinned. "But mostly I don't think it's safe." I stepped toward her and held out my hand. "Between your heater and the storm, I think it would be safer to stay in my spare room. Then I can follow you back into town tomorrow, and we can get that heater fixed."

She smiled at the ground and moved a piece of hair behind her ear. "Oh right, 'cause the snow."

"Yep." The snow was at least a convenient excuse.

"Yeah. I guess that makes sense. As long as it's okay." She shrugged.

It was more than okay. The way she fit into my life and my arms felt too good. Maybe Mom's millions of prayers sent Faith to me, but whatever the reason, I didn't care. I just didn't want her to leave.

"I need to grab some flashlights and more blankets." I tried to keep my mind focused on the present. Not where I hoped this was all leading. "Would you like to wait here on the couch or come with me?"

"I'm not sitting in the dark by myself." She rushed to my side and took my hand. She leaned her chin to my ear, so I dipped my head. "I hate the dark and clowns." She whispered as if someone might overhear.

I chuckled. "We should be clown free, and I have some lanterns that will help with the dark." I searched her eyes and found genuine fear. "Hey." I squeezed her hand. "You're safe."

She took a steadying breath. "I know, I feel safe with you," she whispered.

I had a strange surge of male pride at her comment.

We went to the garage, to the bins of camp gear and grabbed some battery-operated lanterns. I turned them on and brought them back into the house. I put one in the main area in case Danny woke up and needed the bathroom. Then I led Faith to the spare room.

I opened the door to the room that's primary use was for storage. But there was a bed made with clean sheets at least. I went into the closet and grabbed some extra blankets.

"Will Danny need another blanket?" She looked toward Danny's room. "The heat won't be working, right?"

"Yeah, I will put an extra blanket on him and then some at the end of his bed, and he can grab them if he wants."

She nodded and looked toward the bed. The silence stretched and pulled. Would she rather not sleep here? I stopped the offer to sleep with me before I blurted it out again.

"Um, do you have an extra phone charger?" Faith stared at her phone with what appeared to be the battery dying quickly.

I smiled. "I do, but I don't think it will help much."

"Why? Oh, right, the power." She shook her head but didn't drop my hand. "My phone is about to die, and I don't have service anymore. I texted Rose before, so she should know I'm here. I'm a little worried about waking up and being disoriented by myself with no light."

I held up the lantern. "I can leave this with you?" I shrugged. Should I offer to let her sleep in my bed? The thought of her next to me was dangerously tempting. Could I keep my hands to myself all night?

"Could I maybe sleep on the couch?" she added before I worked up the courage.

"I don't think you could fit comfortably."

She chuckled. "No, *you* can't lie down on it. I will be fine."

I wished I hadn't hesitated. If I offered now, it would seem weird. I added a few blankets in Danny's room and walked with her back to the living room, with a stack of pillows and blankets for the couch.

Would I even be able to sleep knowing she was this close? The last several weeks were full of stolen moments between work and Danny. I glanced at the couch and then back toward my room.

Screw it. Luckily, I had put the pile of laundry away yesterday.

I cleared my throat and took a steadying breath, and her eyes met mine.

"You know..." I cleared my throat again. "If you are worried about being out here alone." I paused, and she stared at my lips.

Her gaze searched mine.

"Um, I will keep my hands and ideas to myself if you want to share my bed." I raised my right shoulder. "Just in case you wake up disoriented or something?"

She bit her bottom lip and raised a brow. "We'd better not. I'm not sure I could promise the same."

Heat boiled in my stomach as I looked at this beautiful woman. The thought of being loved and held by Faith did something that rattled every coherent thought in my brain.

She yawned and leaned into me.

"Right, so couch?" I nodded. It was probably for the best, I reminded myself before I tried to change her mind.

"Or I can just be good..." Faith gazed up at me.

Forget what's for the best. I wanted her in my bed. I wanted to hold her as she fell asleep, watch her as she woke. I grabbed her hand and started pulling her toward my room.

As we passed Danny's room, he mumbled something about stars, and Faith pulled me to a stop. I looked back at her and she smiled.

I knew what she was going to say. Danny would be confused if he found her in my bed, he might be confused to see her on the couch too, but it was safer for her to stay. My shoulders dropped, and I sighed as I turned. "So, couch?"

She chuckled softly. "Yeah," she said. "Probably better."

I sighed and led her back toward the couch, and I might have been a little pouty about it.

She followed me, and then laid her head down on the pillow on the couch as she yawned. "Good night, Adam."

I kneeled beside her and brushed her hair away from her face. "Good night, Faith." I leaned in and kissed her. I took a fortifying breath, and it took every ounce of willpower I had, but I forced myself to stand and go to my room alone.

"DAD DAD DAD!!"

I woke up with a start as Danny pulled on my arm. I felt like I had just gone to sleep. It took longer than I wanted to admit to fall asleep knowing how close Faith was. I rubbed the sleep from my eyes and lay back down.

"DAAAAD!"

I sat up, and instantly the cold pressed against my skin. "I'm up, I'm up." I yawned. "What's up, bud?"

"Come see! There is enough snow now for a thousand snow-men!" He grabbed my arm and tugged. "Hurry!" I wiped the sleep from my eyes as he pulled me through the hallway and into the living room where Faith was standing at the window, wrapped tight in a blanket. My heart leapt at the sight of her. I wanted to rush to her and pull her into my arms.

Her hair was pulled back in a ponytail, and she moved her feet back and forth on the cold ground. I stood beside her and placed my arm around her shoulder. If Danny asks, I will tell him it's because she was cold. She leaned against my chest, but her gaze stayed focused on the window.

I should have brushed my teeth. What if I had terrible morning breath?

"See!" Danny gestured at the window, drawing my attention to it.

"Holy..." There was a lot of snow.

Where there was a foot of snow the night before, the world was now covered in what looked like a three- to four-foot blanket of white. The road, the trees, everything. I couldn't even make out our vehicles in the driveway. They were white blobs. The wind caused the whole world to see white. The wind would make it even more dangerous.

So much snow.

I blew out a whistle, going over all the worst-case scenarios in my head. It was obvious from the cold that the power was still out.

What if the power didn't come back on?

What if Mom or one of the older neighbors didn't have enough heat?

Could everyone's barns and outbuildings hold up under that much weight of snow?

How long would it take them to plow the roads all the way out here?

"Okay..." I pinched my lips in thought, trying to hide my initial panic. "Looks like we might stay home today."

Faith's wide eyes met mine.

"Wahoo! Snowman day!" Danny ran toward his boots.

Faith leaned close. "The plows will start with town, and it will be a while before they can get this far out. Right?" Her brow furrowed. She glanced at Danny to see that he was occupied. "Is everyone going to be okay? What if someone's car is stuck out there?"

I pulled her toward me in a hug, and her presence instantly calmed my racing heart. I placed my chin on top of her head. "I certainly hope that's not the case. Storms like this can cause all sorts of problems. Roofs could collapse, people and animals could freeze, pipes could break."

"I could have been stuck out in this storm." She whispered, barely audible, and I think it was more for her than me.

But the result of her statement was like ice being poured down my veins. I imagined Faith stuck out there in this blizzard and pulled her tighter to me. I had to know she was still here, to feel her heartbeat against mine.

"Well, I'm very glad you weren't." The words didn't come close to expressing my relief.

Her eyes met mine, and she gave me a small smile. "Me too." She looked back at the window. "But what about everyone else?" She chewed on her bottom lip, and I instantly wanted her mouth on mine. I shook my head, trying to remind myself we were in a bit of a crisis and to focus. "Do you need to call anyone?"

She shrugged. "My phone's dead, but I assume everyone went home and is fine."

A thump sounded beside me as Danny stumbled in his boots and coat as he rushed to the front door.

"Where do you think you're going?" I called after him.

"I'm going to make a snowman!" He pulled open the front door.

"Whoa! Wait a minute there, Champ."

Danny stood frozen in the doorway, revealing snow piled higher than his waist. "Woah!"

A gust of wind sent the snow spiraling into the living room. Danny yelped, and I helped him close the door. His wide eyes met mine. "I think it might take a long time to shovel Grandma's sidewalk this week."

I chuckled. "That's an understatement." I ruffled his hair. "I'm going to call her and make sure she has heat. The wood stove works, so she should be good." I pointed at the pile of snow in the entryway. "How about you play in that snow for now?"

He nodded and grabbed a pile and pressed it together. It packed tight. "It's the snowman kind!"

That meant the snow held more moisture and would be heavier. I met Faith's eyes over Danny.

"I better make sure Mom is okay, then maybe call around and see who needs help." I walked back to my room to grab my phone, praying it still had battery and service.

Chapter Twenty-Eight

FAITH

The power was finally working consistently, but it took most of the day. It was now getting dark again. My phone was plugged in with Adam's charger and finally had enough charge to turn on. The cell phone service was spotty at best. I wrote out a text to Marissa and Rose.

Faith: I'm safe. I'm stuck at Adam's. The roads are impassable, especially with my tires. He said he could try to bring me into town in his truck if needed. Are you both safe?

I hit send and watched as the sending message appeared under the text. I chewed my bottom lip.

Message unsent.

I sighed and held my phone in the air as high as I could as the bars went from none to one. I hit send again. Holding my phone awkwardly over my head as I stared at the screen.

Message unsent.

Adam chuckled. "Here, let me help." He walked to my side and held out his hand for my phone. "If you want." He smirked.

His reach was substantially more than mine, so I shrugged and handed it to him. He held it in the air and hit send.

Nothing.

"Sometimes you can get better service on the road." He went to the front door, grabbed his coat, and started putting on his boots.

"Oh no, it's okay." I didn't want to be an inconvenience.

He quirked his eyebrow. "Really, it's no problem. I'm sure your friends are worried, and I know I would want to know you are safe." He winked, pulled the door open, and went outside. As he waded through the snow toward the road, it ranged from almost mid-calf to above his knees in some spots.

I'd lived here three years and never seen a storm like this. Being farther outside of town added complications as well. The plows would start in town and would work hard and fast.

Adam walked up the driveway, where the snow wasn't as high, and out onto the road. He held his hand in the air, and it looked like he pressed send. His breath floated up in the air toward my phone. He brought the phone down and studied the screen and flashed me a thumbs up.

His shoulders stiffened as he looked down the road. He stepped back into the driveway as lights came into view on some sort of tractor. It pulled up next to Adam, and he started talking to a man in a cowboy hat, coat, and gloves.

Adam leaned in to hear him above the motor.

My stomach tightened. Did this man have news, and if so, was it good or bad?

The man pointed back the way he had come. Adam nodded and turned and ran to his front door.

Well, that can't be great news. What could it be? Was it the road? Was someone hurt? Ugh, it could be so many things. We had sent a few texts, but had gotten nothing back from anyone.

Adam flung the door open and came into the house, along with a pile of snow. He closed the door behind him, stomped the snow off his feet, and handed my phone back.

"Sounds like Frank took a fall off his roof when he was clearing the snow. They need help getting him into town, and they are setting up groups to check on some of the older folks. Said they had already checked on Mom on his way out, and she was doing okay." His eyes shot to Danny playing with the now-more snow pile, and he frowned as he looked at us both. "They really need my help," he muttered and trailed his thumb down his jaw.

They needed him, and he needed Danny to be safe. "Go." I nodded toward the door. "I got Danny. Grab some extra warm clothes though." I thought about Adam out there in the snow. "And you have to promise you will be careful." I searched his face.

He closed the distance between us and put his hand on my cheek. "I will. If the power goes out, just grab one of the lanterns, okay?" he whispered, "And stay inside." I saw how torn he was.

"I will." I gazed up into his warm brown eyes as he placed his forehead on mine. "Be safe," I whispered.

Danny came over to give Adam a hug. He must have been nervous. I should have stepped backed and not let Danny see Adam holding me. But all that mattered in that moment was that Adam be careful and return safely back to us.

He squatted down in front of Danny. "Hey, Champ. Frank is stuck in the snow." He reached up and ruffled Danny's hair. "Do you think you can stay here and keep Faith safe while I try to help?"

Danny's eyebrows dipped as he looked toward me. I smiled at him.

"Thanks, Champ." Adam gave him a quick hug and then stood and squeezed my hand. He ran down to his room, and before I was ready, he was running out the door to go help.

Danny and I walked toward the front window and stared out as Adam hopped into his truck. The tractor had cleared the driveway while he waited.

Adam held up his hand, and Danny and I both waved back. Then he turned and backed out of the driveway.

We both stood there watching the truck for as long as possible.

Then I took a deep breath and turned my mind to helping Danny feel comfortable.

"Okay, Danny, do you have a favorite book or board game?"

He shrugged. "I like my tablet."

"Well, you can show it to me, but some things won't work without the internet."

His eyebrows lowered. "Will Dad be okay?" He avoided my eyes. "Can he get hurt too?"

I took a fortifying breath and decided not to give voice to my irrational fears. "I'm sure he will be very careful." I squeezed Danny's shoulder. "Now, do you have any two-player games on your tablet?"

We played games on his tablet, watched Frosty the Snowman, drew pictures, and then I taught Danny how to make pancakes.

Time passed achingly slow. My phone vibrated in my pocket, going off over and over.

I must finally have gotten service.

I pulled my phone out and looked through the notifications. It was nine p.m. I checked to see if Adam had sent anything in the hours he had been gone.

Nope. I chewed my lip and went to my other messages.

Marissa: We are safe here! We lost a section of the roof of the gazebo, and there was some damage to the house, but not bad compared to some. I'm glad you are safe. I was so worried you'd driven back and got stuck.

Rose: Stupid storm. Snow's the worst. Thanks for texting. I was going crazy. The hair salon looked okay from what I could tell.

I hit reply.

Faith: I'm still here with Danny. Adam went with some other guys to help Frank, and then they were checking on people.

Marissa: There is an emergency town meeting tomorrow to assess damages and see who needs what. We offered the community center-11AM.

My stomach dropped as I wondered what destruction the storm had caused. I hoped everyone was okay.

Faith: Thanks for the heads-up. I'll make sure I'm back for that if not sooner.

Danny was tired, so I helped him get ready for bed. He brushed his teeth, and I helped him find some clean pj's. After I tucked him in "snug as a bug in a rug," which was apparently tight all along his body and the way Adam does it, I went to shut off the light.

"Will you stay and do minutes?"

I turned back to his space bed. "What's minutes?"

"I ask Dad to stay a few minutes, then he tries to sneak out, and then I ask him to stay for some more."

I sat against the wall and smiled. "Sure, Danny. I will stay for as many minutes as you want."

"Even a hundred?"

I chuckled. "If that's what you want."

He rolled over in his bed. I sat against the wall, glancing at my phone more often than I should. Wondering and hoping when I would hear Adam's truck or get a text. Once I made sure Danny was asleep, which took twenty minutes instead of one hundred, I left his room, leaving the door open, and went to clean up the kitchen.

Still no Adam. I couldn't help myself. I went and sat in Adam's room.

It was a bit of a breach of privacy, but he had offered me to stay in here last night, so hopefully that meant it was okay. He had a king-sized bed with blue blankets, a cheap nightstand, and in the corner there was a stack of weights. I smiled and shook my head. I picked up one of his sweaters from the left side of the bed and smelled it. It smelled like him. Like oranges and spices and happiness.

"Come on, Adam." I muttered and looked up to the ceiling. "Shouldn't he be home by now?" I rubbed my tired eyes. I couldn't sit, I needed to be moving. I put on his sweater so I could keep his smell and warmth with me and I went out to the living room and re-organized Danny's toys.

Then I re-cleaned the kitchen and dining room.

Lights flashed in the window, and I rushed over.

A snowplow went down the street, throwing piles of snow to the side.

Not Adam.

At least they were plowing the roads this far out now.

Another snowplow went by, clearing the other side. It gave two fast honks as it passed, and then Adam's truck pulled into the driveway.

He did the same honk back.

I released a shuddering breath.

He was home.

The amount my heart jumped and the tears pricking my eyes were a little embarrassing.

But he was home.

Adam got out of his truck and rubbed his shoulder and stretched out his neck. He looked exhausted. I wondered how I could help. The freezing air rushed in as Adam opened the door. He stomped the snow off his boots and pulled off his gloves as he blew into his hands.

"Hey." The greeting sounded lame in my ears for the amount of fretting I'd done.

His eyes met mine. "Hey." He pulled his arms out of his wet coat.

"Can I get you anything? Tea or coffee or something?"

He pried the other arm out and began taking off his boots. "Nah, thanks though. Honestly, I'm just tired."

I nodded and clasped my hands in front of me.

Do I hug him? Does he want space? He was probably tired enough without my clinging to him.

He stepped into the living room and then opened his arms.

Yes! I rushed into his embrace. He yawned and swayed a little. I grabbed his hand and headed to the couch. "Let's sit. You're exhausted."

He sat beside me, resting his head back on the cushion behind him.

"Do you want to talk about it?" I asked.

He rubbed a hand down his face. "I don't even know where to start."

That didn't sound good. I leaned against his side, and his arm draped across my shoulder.

"Most of the time I was shoveling. We started at Frank's. He should be to the hospital. Doug thinks he probably broke his hip. Jacob's herd is sick after the power shut off all the electric feeders, but he is hoping they will recover." He sighed and shook his head.

I squeezed Adam's hand.

"That's not the worst of it though." His lips frowned. He paused and took a deep breath. It was as if he were worried about my reaction.

I waited.

"Sounds like the school didn't fare well." Adam looked at the ground.

The school? "What do you mean?"

"The newer section of the high school is okay, and the gym, but the portables, most of the elementary, the office, and cafeteria..." He closed his eyes. "Faith, it's unusable. Part of the roof caved in, and there is water damage everywhere from broken pipes."

I leaned back. Wait. "What?" I shook my head. "What do you mean?"

He turned toward me, his brown eyes sad. "There is a meeting tomorrow, but there is talk of closing the school."

I gasped and leaned back. "What does that even mean? What happens to the kids and teachers if they do?" A cold shiver crept up my spine and didn't leave.

Adam rubbed his forehead. "It's all speculation at this point." He looked at the ground. "But there isn't enough room for everyone in the parts that are left... And there isn't the money to rebuild."

"Could we raise it and they rebuild in the spring?" Even as I asked, I knew the unlikeliness of it.

Adam frowned. "Maybe...but the district doesn't have that kind of resources. To pass a grant and get federal resources can take years."

"What about fundraising or something?"

"We could do some for sure. But most people here live paycheck to paycheck. No one has that kind of money." Adam gestured me back into his side. I scooted closer and lay on his chest. "Several of the nearby towns are likely facing similar problems."

"So what, the kids just won't get an education?" My forehead wrinkled as I blinked back tears. That was cruel and would have devastating long-term effects.

"Nah. Sounds like the district is thinking of bussing kids to other towns. Sharing the space that's available. There isn't enough room to send them all to one, so they will most likely split the kids up."

I shook my head. "The nearest town is thirty minutes away. Those kids will be on the bus all day long."

"Yep." He sighed and nodded. "The other option is to go to an online school individually."

Online. No connection with their peers. Those poor kids.

The school also employed much of the town.

What about their jobs?

What about mine? What about Adam's? I spun my anxiety ring. There was too much pain everywhere I thought.

"What about the school's extracurricular activities?"

Adam sighed. "There are so many other people who are facing much worse consequences, I know that." He shook his head. "But I just can't stop thinking about how hard those boys have been working. They really had a chance to take state this year." He sighed and his shoulders fell forward. "I mean, will Jacob still get his scholarship?"

My heart was breaking in more ways than I knew were possible. It broke for the families that would lose income; it broke for the kids whose lives were going to be turned upside down and separated. What would Adam do for work? His life was here. My heart broke for Adam and the team that worked so hard to suddenly have everything taken away.

Adam's head drooped. "I really wanted to hang out tonight, but I'm so exhausted. I think I might take a shower and go to bed."

I sat up. "Are you hungry at all?" The terrible day Adam had was wearing him down physically and mentally, and all I could do was sit and watch.

He rubbed his calloused thumb down my jaw and winked. "Nah. I'm good. Thanks though." He gave me a sad smile. "Sorry I didn't bring better news."

"The storm is certainly not your fault," I challenged.

"True." He nodded. "Thanks again for watching Danny today. It was great to help without worrying." He groaned as he placed his palms on his knees and stood, and I stood beside him.

He seemed as if he might collapse.

"It's terrible, but I just can't see any options." He rubbed his palm down his face and shook his head. "Unless someone randomly inherits millions and fast...we're out of luck." He sighed and chuckled, trying to lighten the mood. "Too bad we aren't in one of those Hallmark movies, eh?" He winked at me and held his arms open for a hug.

I stepped into his embrace numbly.

My mouth dropped open.

Wait.

"Is it okay if I take you home in the morning?" Adam asked.

"Of course." I heard him, but my mind was far away.

"Do you need anything?" He asked.

I looked over to the couch and the pillow and blanket that were there from the night before. "Nope, I'm good, thanks."

"Good night, Faith." He kissed the top of my head softly. "Hopefully, we will get more answers tomorrow and fewer rumors."

"Good night, Adam," I whispered, my mind already racing.

He walked down the hallway to his room slowly as he put a hand on the back of his neck.

No one in this town could save the school—no one but maybe me.

Chapter Twenty-Nine

ADAM

I woke up feeling every bit of my age and then some. I guess nothing prepares the body for five hours of shoveling intensely heavy snow. I sat up and pressed my hand over my shoulder, stretching it. Then I yawned and stood stiffly as I made my way to my bedroom door in basketball shorts and no shirt.

I could hear voices farther inside the house. And from the smell of it, maybe breakfast.

"Can I flip it now?" Danny asked.

"Let's wait until the bubbles pop," Faith added.

I smiled as I thought about how different our life had been in the few months since Faith. I forced my body to walk down the hall and decided I would sneak into the bathroom and brush my teeth.

Looking in the mirror, my hair was as messed up as my muscles. I put water on my hands and did my best to smooth down the unruly mess. The cup that held toothbrushes on the counter now held three, and I smiled at what the future could bring. Faith asked if I had an extra toothbrush yesterday. I quickly brushed my teeth and then I splashed water on my face. I wiped the water off on a nearby towel and headed toward the galley kitchen.

"Do you think you can flip this one by yourself?" Faith asked.

"Sure can. Guess that means I'm a chef," Danny answered.

Her soft laugh filled my heart. "You sure are." I leaned against the wall unnoticed and watched the scene play out before me as Danny slid his spatula under the pancake and dramatically slammed it over. Faith flinched. "Easy there, Champ."

She used my nickname for him. Any lasting barrier around my heart melted.

What would she do if she lost her job? Would she go back to New York and her family?

My stomach grumbled.

One crisis at a time.

"Is someone making pancakes?" I walked toward the pair. Danny threw his hands up in excitement.

"Oh, be careful." Faith held her hands between Danny and the pan. "That pan is hot."

Danny jumped down off the step stool and ran into my arms. "Missed you, Dad."

"Missed you too, Champ." His little body wrapped against mine, filling any existing holes with his love.

"I tried to stay awake last night, but my eyelids were too heavy." Danny sighed.

I chuckled. "That's okay, Champ. I had a hard time opening my eyes too." I winked in Faith's direction, who was staring at my chest, her mouth ajar. She wore my dark blue sweater. It looked good on her, even if the sleeves were too long. Her cheeks turned pink, and she shook her head. I figured she'd seen me without a shirt before with the stitches, so it didn't matter. Although, I liked the effect I had on her.

Danny wiggled in my arms, wanting me to release him from the hug. I eased my grip on him. And he reached for my hand and tugged me toward the table. "I made you breakfast! I made a few black ones like Grandma, but I did better with a timer." I sat in the chair he indicated.

Faith walked toward the table, holding a plate of towering pancakes and wearing a soft smile. This time, she focused on my face. I never wanted this to end. If only we could pretend that life hadn't been drastically altered outside in the snow.

"Good Morning, Adam." Faith raised a brow.

"Morning, Faith." I reached for her hand, and she placed it in mine. I gave it a quick squeeze before she pulled it out of my grasp.

"I'll have you know, it took constant distraction to keep this boy from waking you up for the last few hours. He is quite a determined thing." She chuckled.

Hours? I looked for my watch, which was still by my bed. "What time is it?"

"Ten."

My eyes went wide. I hadn't slept in that long probably since Danny was born.

"Wow."

"The meeting is in an hour, so you have half an hour." She nodded toward the stack. "You'd better get eating." She grinned. "Danny was sure you would eat at least ten."

"Ten?" I grimaced. I didn't want to disappoint Danny, but I wasn't sure that was doable. "I mean, I'm hungry, but, uh..."

Faith went back into the kitchen and returned with two plates. "Maybe Danny and I can help." She winked.

The three of us sat down to breakfast, and Danny told me all about the adventures of the day before. Danny smiled at Faith often, and she smiled back.

I sighed. Better get this meeting over with. If Faith couldn't stick around, Danny and I needed to know sooner rather than later. "All right, let's eat up. We have a meeting to get to."

Danny's bright eyes searched mine. "I get to come too, right?"

I nodded. "Yeah, I think most of the town will be there."

Danny shoved a huge bite into his mouth. "I'll hurry."

I grimaced as pancake bits fell onto the table. "Maybe just focus on chewing real good."

Faith took a small bite, and her eyes traced the walls of the house. It was like she was trying to remember everything, to burn it into her memory.

That didn't bode well.

What would our future hold? Her gaze flicked to mine, and she gave a sad smile and then focused on her plate.

I WAS WORRIED ABOUT FAITH'S CAR, BETWEEN HER TIRE tread and her heater. But, she didn't feel comfortable driving the truck, so I followed behind her as we drove into town. I hated every second of that thirty-minute drive.

Wondering if she was too cold every second we were apart.

Was she worried about no longer having a job?

And if so, what would she do? What would I do?

She had no other ties here, as far as I was aware.

We parked at the B&B and made our way down the shoveled path to the community center.

Once inside, we saw rows of folding chairs facing a makeshift stage. The chairs went from the front all the way to the back, and they were almost all full. I saw my mom several rows up and to the left. She waved us over. I took Danny's hand and headed toward her. She only had two seats saved beside her and instantly looked panicked as she counted the chairs.

I would stand. It wasn't a big deal. "Hey, Mom." She stood, and I gave her a quick hug.

"I didn't think about it. I should have saved three seats." She muttered as she shook her head.

"It's fine. I'm happy to stand." I turned over my shoulder to tell Faith to sit by Danny and I could stand near the sidewall, but where I imagined her being, she wasn't there.

She was stuck in the middle of the aisle, several rows back, with Rose and Marissa on both sides, talking with their arms, and pulling her into a hug. I made eye contact with Faith, and I nodded to the seats near me with raised brows.

Trying to ask if she wanted me to save her a seat.

She grinned and mouthed, *Rose saved me a seat. Thank you.*

I sat by Danny and forced my attention to the front. It was harder than it should be, considering this meeting held most of our futures.

The mayor, George Baker; the town lawyer, Scott; Luke Dennis, the fire department chief; and Dotty sat on the stage in a row of folding chairs. George stood and cleared his voice. The roar of the crowd died as people focused on the front, trying to hold their questions back. There was a sense of uneasiness, like everyone was holding their breath, wanting to know what was coming but also fearing the words.

"Good morning, everyone." He nodded to the crowd. "I wish we were meeting under different circumstances, but here we are."

I appreciated his candid nature, maybe more now than ever before. No need to drag things on. My eyes shifted to Faith, several rows back and to the right. She was sitting by Rose as she chewed on her bottom lip. I forced my gaze to the front again.

"There is much to discuss and much more still to discover." Was it the lighting, or did George look like he'd aged years in a matter of days? "There are many needs within the community, some we are aware of and many we don't know." He sighed. "But I feel we'd best get the biggest rock out of the way first. The few people who knew the extent of the damage were asked to keep it under wraps, so naturally, my phone has been ringing off the hook for the last thirty-six hours." Rumors and secrets spread faster in Hillsdale than wildfire on a dry summer day. He turned to Dotty, gesturing for her to join him. "Let's discuss the future of the school."

George stepped to the side, and Dotty stood. Whatever she had to say, it would not be easy.

Dotty cleared her throat and blinked rapidly. "First off, I'm supposed to express the regrets of the superintendent. He was stuck in the storm and cannot make it today. We have been communicating often through email and phone." She took a steadying breath as she looked at the ceiling. "We have been doing extensive research into our resources and what it would take to get the school up to a functioning capacity."

My stomach tightened. They were going to close it.

Dotty stared at the back of the room while her eyes glistened. "Unfortunately, there are not enough resources to continue the school year. But since education is of such fundamental importance, we are working with different school buildings as well as—"

I leaned in closer as the crowd erupted. I tried to make out what Dotty was saying. People were standing and hollering questions. I caught a scattering of words like jobs, kid's friends, and how this town would dissolve into nothing.

That was a concern. No new families would move here if there wasn't a school.

The businesses that hadn't been hit by the storm would be hit by the rest of us not having income. Not to mention that none of us could survive without income for years. Would the town even survive?

Dotty held her hands up, trying to get the crowd to calm down, but people had gathered energy and weren't stopping.

A sharp whistle pierced the sky. I flinched and turned to see Rose standing. "All right, you barbarians, sit!" she yelled.

The shock must have helped several come to their senses because people started looking embarrassed and sitting back down.

"Screaming at each other won't help." Rose rolled her eyes and focused back on Dotty. "Honestly."

Dotty gave Rose a smile. "Thanks."

Rose nodded.

"We are currently hoping to have the school rebuilt, but with grants and funds, it looks like it will be about two or three years at the earliest." Dotty cleared her throat. "I know this is not ideal. But it is better than not reopening at all."

"Can the kids continue going to school here in non-school buildings until then?" Angie Merritt asked.

"Potentially. They would have to be approved by the district and state education departments and comply with all safety codes." She sighed and raised a shoulder. "But three years is a long time for students to feel displaced like that. I'm not sure if it would be most beneficial."

More questions erupted all over the room.

"What about the boys' basketball team? Can they still go to state?" Tony hollered.

"What are we supposed to do for work in the meantime?" Jessica asked.

"What if we hold fundraisers?" Betty Ann called over the crowd.

"What if we could raise the money by spring?" I'd recognize that voice anywhere. That was Faith.

I turned to see Faith standing in the middle of the room. She stood stiffly and was fiddling with her hands. But she wasn't backing down either. She stood and stared at the front.

"What was that, Faith?" Dotty asked.

She took a steadying breath, her cheeks turning pink. "Hypothetically, of course, what if we could come up with the money by spring?" She swallowed and spun her ring, uncomfortable with the attention. "Could we keep the classes as is for now, and could the kids still take part in extracurricular activities like sports?"

Dotty raised an eyebrow. "Hypothetically, it would be a miracle." She shook her head. "But yes, we would find accommodations and try our best to keep every class together if it was that short term. The boys would continue to be a team if we didn't need to split the classes and bus elsewhere. But honestly," she raised her hands, "I've looked over the damages, and I assure you the repairs will cost hundreds of thousands of dollars."

"Okay, thanks." Faith quickly sat, her face was flushed red. Rose grabbed Faith's arm and pulled her toward her. Rose looked angry.

Dotty shrugged. "I think it may be in the students' best interest, if change is going to happen, that we do so sooner rather than later."

A rumble of disagreement started like a tumble wave through the audience.

What did Faith mean about coming up with that type of money? I turned around. Rose and Faith obviously did not agree about something.

The mayor cleared his throat. "Okay, let's put a pin in that one for now. Scott, would you give us a report?"

Dotty turned and went back to her seat. She sat with a forceful drop.

Scott stood and went to the mic, and I desperately tried to pay attention, but all of me was begging to look at Faith.

Chapter Thirty

FAITH

I refused to sit by and watch so many people that I love lose so much when there was something I could do about it. Rose grabbed my sleeve with her manicured nails and pulled me toward her.

"I know what you're thinking." She scowled at me. "Don't you do it."

"I'm not seeing a lot of options here." I muttered under my breath.

"Um, how about not the one that makes you absolutely miserable?" She scoffed. "I'm pretty sure there is a reason you left."

"Circumstances have changed." I folded my hands in my lap to keep from fidgeting.

"You know your mom isn't going to just give you the money without forcing you to come back, right?"

I rolled my eyes. "Yeah, I know."

Rose raised a brow. "I think it's fair to say everything is still a bit of an unknown right now. At least give it time. Think it through."

I brushed my hair behind my ear. I was worried about saying anything. I couldn't fight the war in my head and Rose at the same time. I didn't want to reason my way out of what was right, and with time, I think I might.

Scott mentioned that Merritt's had lost the whole dining room and she wasn't planning to rebuild. Several in the crowd gasped and Rose's attention snapped back around and refocused on Scott and the meeting.

I opened my phone and clicked on Dotty's name. I needed to do this before I changed my mind.

Faith: I might have a plan, but I need to figure some stuff out. Can you give me a week to look into some things before you decide anything about the school?

I couldn't sit still any longer. I spun my ring and released a tight breath.

This was me sucking in my screams.

Nothing was scarier than my mom. My stomach tied itself in knots at the thought of returning home to her.

I couldn't focus on other town problems. If I were lucky, I might help with one, and that would need to be enough. I leaned over to Rose.

"Hey, my anxiety is doing weird things." I wasn't wrong, but I hated to use it as an excuse to trick Rose, but I needed to be alone. "I'm going to step outside for a minute."

Rose's forehead creased. "Okay..." Her lips pursed. She wasn't happy about it, but she wouldn't stop me either. "No life-altering plans until at least after lunch." Her eyebrows raised as she stared at me. "Deal?"

I nodded but didn't voice a reply as I quickly ducked out of the meeting. My shoes squeaked, and the noise echoed in the room as I rushed toward the exit.

I grabbed the handle and stepped through the door into the cold air outside. I couldn't think about what I was giving up. I had to stay focused on what I was going to be giving to others instead.

I made it to my car and hopped into the driver's side seat.

I took a steadying breath, and I counted to three. I scrolled through my contacts and found Mom/Meredith and hit the dial. I hoped one of the numbers I saved as hers would actually work.

Also for good measure, I started driving home and put the call on through Bluetooth. I needed to be doing something with my hands, and it made it so I wouldn't get caught by Rose or Marissa.

"Astrid?" Her voice held confusion.

"Hey, Mom."

She scoffed, clearly upset, but I refused to call her Meredith. She was my mother, and that was what I needed her to be right now.

"You never call, and the one time you do, it's before noon? You know I have social engagements till late on the weekends."

There was an annoyance in her voice, and next will be smug. I waited.

"Have you given up on this ridiculous notion?" I heard my mother smirk. "Let me guess, you finally ran out of money."

I steadied every part of my shaking soul. Suck in your screams.

"Something like that."

"So what?" Rose came in and threw her jacket on the coffee table. "You're just going to disappear into a life you hate?"

I spooned the flour into the measuring cup and leveled it off with a knife before I dumped it into the mixing bowl. Mom was sending a plane to the nearest airport tomorrow morning to pick me up. I counted the cups of flour in my head. I needed something I could focus on, something I could control. I needed baking.

"What about Adam? What about Danny?" Rose walked over to the kitchen counter and placed her hands on her hips. "What about me and Marissa?"

I glanced at the ceiling, trying to keep my tears in place.

"Why do you think I'm doing this?" I wiped my hands off on my apron before I waved my hands in front of my eyes. "It's for you guys!"

"Such a martyr." Rose scoffed and folded her arms. "And do we even get a say on whether we want you to?"

I rubbed my forehead, feeling the flour dust my skin. "I'm not planning on staying. I hope I can reason with my parents." I steeled my shoulders and looked at Rose. "But if it comes down to it, yes." I cleared my throat. "I will go back to a life I hated, so that the people in this town, including you and Adam, can recover. So you can keep your business, so my beautiful students don't have to have their lives turned upside down, so Adam keeps his team and job, and so this town that I love doesn't dissolve into nothing." My shoulders collapsed. "So many families in this town rely on that school."

Rose's anger broke. She grabbed my arm and pulled me in for a tight hug. "You're stupid even to consider it." Her voice shook as she spoke.

I took a shuddering breath; I had already cried tonight about leaving, and I was determined not to break into tears now.

"What are you going to tell Adam?" Rose whispered as she stepped back.

The broken pieces of my heart shattered even smaller. I rubbed my eyes. "I don't know."

Rose shrugged. "He might move to New York?"

I shook my head, stopping the thoughts before they could form. "He loves his life here. He has fought hard for that peace. I refuse to be like his ex, requiring more and more sacrifices from him for my pretend happiness. I won't even ask. There is no point in us both being miserable." I looked at the pattern on the linoleum floor. "I haven't even told him about my name change. We talked about the life I lived, but not the specifics." I shrugged. "Things felt too new, and now it almost feels too late." I chuckled as I wiped a stray tear off my cheek with my shoulder. "I think I might wonder for the rest of my life if, given more time, we could have worked."

"You sound a lot like you don't think you are coming back." Rose grumbled.

I really wanted to. I hoped I could make my parents see me. The real me. And that they would help, but I wouldn't hold my breath.

Rose sighed. "When do you leave?"

"Tomorrow morning," I whispered.

She raised her brows. "Look, I don't care who your parents are, if they trap you in a life you aren't happy in, just know I will be on the next flight to give them a piece of my mind."

I laughed and cried, because I knew she meant it. "I don't deserve you."

Rose scoffed. "You're wrong. They're the ones who don't deserve you." Rose placed her hands on my shoulders. "Just because someone is family doesn't mean they're right; if they can't see the amazing person you are, they don't deserve to be in your life."

There was no stopping their tears now. They flowed freely from a space that bounced somewhere between happiness and sorrow.

"Sometimes the family we choose, the ones who will stand by us and fight our battles, that's your true family." Rose dipped her head to make sure I was listening.

The tears streamed down my cheeks. I took a deep breath.

Rose nodded back to the kitchen. "All right, what are we making?"

I shook my head. "You hate cooking."

She shrugged. "What has that got to do with anything? If you're cooking on your last night here for who knows how long, then I'm cooking right beside you." She picked up my phone from the counter and handed it to me. "But first, you are going to call Marissa and Adam and tell them to come bake too." She searched my eyes. "I won't let you disappear, like you did from your old life. You have people here that love you and need you." Rose gave me a sad smile. "You would never forgive yourself if you disappeared on them."

I sighed, Rose was right. I owed it to them to let them know I was leaving tomorrow. I planned on telling them, but I was also avoiding the pain as well.

Rose unlocked my phone that was set on the counter, and scrolled down to Marissa. "Maybe start here."

My jaw flexed, and I cleared my throat. "Okay." I nodded.

Rose hit the call button and retreated to her room to give me privacy.

Chapter Thirty-One

ADAM

I rubbed my forehead, trying to stop the oncoming headache. Faith had finally called me back. She had ignored several calls after the meeting, and then she called all serious asking if I could come over. Mom agreed to take Danny for me, and I was sure that whatever was coming, it was going to hurt.

I leaned my head against the back of the seat and stared at the ceiling of my truck, taking a cleansing breath.

"Well, no time like the present," I muttered as I opened my truck door and rang the doorbell. I could hear music blaring inside. I tilted my chin to the side. Strange.

No one came.

I knocked.

I waited, but all I could hear was women screaming a song I couldn't make out.

I knocked louder and rang the doorbell and then waited.

I wasn't going to wait outside all night. I tried the handle, and it was unlocked. I opened the door.

"Hello," I called into the concert of voices as I stepped into their duplex. "Faith?"

I walked down the small hallway that led to the main living

space, and Rose, Marissa, and Faith were all in the middle of an impromptu concert. Complete with flour dusting their cheeks and hair, as they sang into various kitchen utensils. I smiled as I leaned against the wall.

Seeing Faith with her friends and having fun like this was good for me. It reminded me that Faith had other people in Hillsdale too.

That, maybe, she might still stay.

I wasn't sure what all Faith wanted to tell me, but it didn't give me happy, carefree vibes like this.

I joined in. As the song went into the chorus, I rushed to the counter and picked up the spatula. The girls screamed at my sudden appearance as I placed the spatula near my mouth and belted a very high and off tune note, and then, my voice cracked.

We all laughed and continued the concert while enjoying time in Faith's glow and sphere of happiness and kindness.

After two more songs and cookies were placed in the oven, I leaned against the counter. "All right, so is now the part when you tell me you're leaving?"

Faith gasped and put her hand to her mouth.

Rose side-eyed Marissa, and they both left the room.

Their reactions were all too telling. A part of me was holding on to hope that she would deny it.

Faith's lips quivered, and I held my arms open. She rushed into my arms, hugging me tightly.

It broke my heart all over again to feel her soft body press against me. I wrapped my arms tight around her and kissed the top of her head. I wanted to beg her to stay. To choose me.

"Won't you try to stay. We can look for different jobs? Or figure something out." I whispered into her hair, the sadness clear in my voice. I cleared my throat and failed to keep my tears locked away.

She searched my face. "You are the best thing that has ever happened to me." She reached up and put her hand against my face. "My favorite Christmas present." She choked back a sob. "You are proof that I can be loved, just how I am." She chewed on her bottom lip and a tear fell down her cheek.

I reached up and rubbed it with my thumb. This was it then, the end. "Can't we try and figure out a way for you to stay?"

She nodded toward the couch. "Let's sit." Her hand trailed down my side and grabbed my hand as she led me to the couch. Now that I had felt what it was like to be loved and wanted by Faith, I didn't know if I could go back to my lonely existence from before. She added so much light and life to my world. We sat, and she sat cross-legged on the cushion and faced me. Her jaw flexed, and she rubbed her ring. She was anxious. I died a little inside as I reached my hand over to hers so I could give her the pressure that helped her feel safe.

She studied our joined hands and tried to contain her tears. I would sit here with her at that moment as long as she would let me.

I wanted Faith in my life, as long as she could be.

I rubbed the back of her hand with my thumb and studied all of her.

Wanting to remember each breath, each smell, each look.

She cleared her throat. "I have to tell you something about my past."

I tilted my head in confusion.

She sighed. "So..."

She looked at the ceiling. "I..."

She slapped her hand against her thigh. "Ugh! I don't even know where to start."

All I knew about her past was that she was from money and had no desire to return. "Please tell me you're not married."

A laugh escaped her perfect pink mouth. "No, I'm not married." She held her hands out in front of her.

"Thank heavens." I smirked, glad to see some of the tension gone from her shoulders.

"But Adam, I used to live a different life and also had a different name."

"What?"

She took a fortifying breath. "My parents own Luxe Fashion in New York." She peeked up at me. "I am their daughter, Astrid Luxe—well, I was until I changed my name."

I shook my head, trying to make sense of everything she was saying. I remembered the name Luxe only because Cassie dreamed of belonging to their empire.

"Wait..." I held my hands in front of me. "Like the huge fashion brand Luxe...that one?" My eyebrows dipped in confusion.

"Yeah." Her shoulders slumped.

I scoffed. "Cassie's dream job, Luxe?" I raised my eyebrows.

She studied her socks with a frown. "Well, it wasn't mine," she whispered.

I looked around the room. "Is this some weird, sick joke you played on me?" I scoffed.

"Watch it in there, Coach!" Rose yelled from down the hall, and then her voice was muffled.

Faith flinched, spun her ring, and her jaw flexed tight. "No, this wasn't about you at all," she whispered. "This was about me."

I rubbed my forehead. "I don't understand." I shut my eyes. "You lied to me; you lied to Danny." My mind reeled, trying to grasp who this woman was in front of me.

She glanced up at me. Tears streamed down her cheeks as she took a sharp breath.

"I actually didn't." She shrugged. "I legally changed my name to Faith Lyons, although I hated the Lyons part before I even met you." She wiped a tear.

I resisted the urge to comfort her.

Her voice was soft as she looked at the floor. "I grew up in a home I hated. With parents who were indifferent or completely disappointed in me. I grew up hating myself." Her eyes flicked to mine. "I grew up in a world that was loud and fake." She swallowed. "Without my parents' knowledge, I became a teacher, changed my name, and took a job as far away as I could." She spun her ring and flexed her jaw.

Was it becoming too much, was she going to have another panic attack? I hated how bad it made me feel to know I caused some of her distress.

"I hoped to leave the Luxe legacy far behind and find out what life could look like if I was just being me. Not Astrid Luxe." Her brows drew together. "I just wanted to be me." She choked back a sob.

I raised an eyebrow and grimaced. "Astrid..." I think she had said the name before, but I must have been too distracted by the family's last name.

"Yep."

I shook my head and tried to process it all.

Why was she telling me this now?

I stood and began pacing back and forth.

"I meant everything I have said to you. I have loved every moment of this life." I turned to her, and she gave a sad smile. "In some ways, I never lived at all before Hillsdale. Not really."

Broken-down, not-going-to-survive Hillsdale.

I pursed my lips. "So...what are you saying? Are you going back to that life, since your job at the school might not be around?" I tipped my chin as I tried to reconcile the two people that represented Faith now in my mind. The one sitting next to me, who loved baking and teaching second graders, and the one that was filthy rich, self-absorbed, and famous. I couldn't get the two images to match. I rubbed my forehead. "I don't understand."

"I'm going to suck in my screams." Danny's saying brought my eyes to hers.

I blinked rapidly, trying to connect dots I couldn't see. "What do you mean?"

She took a tight breath and held it before letting it out slowly.

"My mom, or Meredith, as she prefers, cut me off financially as soon as I left, hoping I wouldn't be able to survive without the family funds, and would have to come back and 'claim my Luxe legacy.'" She did air quotes around the saying.

She fidgeted with her ring, and I came and sat down beside her again.

"Adam, my parents are rich. Like stupid rich." She shook her head. "Don't you see? They could fix the school! It's the perfect solution." She chewed her bottom lip. "Danny could stay with his class, people wouldn't have to go without their incomes, businesses wouldn't fail from Hillsdale dissolving." She smiled for real now, even though tears shone in her eyes.

It was my Faith smile, the one that brightened whatever space she was in.

"Hillsdale could rebuild, like the Hallmark movie ending you were hoping for. I can fix this; I can save all of you." A tear ran down her cheek.

My stomach sank. I gave her this idea? "So...you're saying you will return to a life you hate, so this town in the middle of nowhere...that never even makes it on a map...can be okay?" My eyebrows dipped.

She nodded. "I'm still hoping to convince my parents without having to stay," she lifted one shoulder, "but I don't know if it will work. Mom has been begging me to come home for a while."

Her cheerful expression faltered momentarily.

I picked up her hands in mine and stared down at them. Faith would throw away the life she loved and return to one she hated so that this town could rebuild. I sighed. There weren't two Faiths. There was only one.

There was only my Faith.

I knew this woman. Just like the basketball team that changed its play name, it was still the same play. She was everything I had grown to love and want. And now she wanted to risk her happiness for everyone else.

I pulled her back into my arms, and her shoulders relaxed into me as she wiped a tear from her cheek. I stroked her back. "I'm not calling you Astrid. That name sounds like asteroids, and that's weird."

She laughed against my chest.

I leaned back and studied her blue eyes. "Faith." I shook my head. "You can't do this."

She leaned back and looked at me. "What do you mean?" She flipped her hand over. "It's the perfect solution."

I placed my hands on either side of her face. "Faith, you can't sacrifice yourself like this. Not for me or Rose and Marissa or Danny or anyone." I wiped a stray tear from her cheek.

She looked down at her clasped hands in her lap.

"You can't," I whispered as I rested my forehead against hers. "I know what it is to give everything of yourself, hoping others will be happy." I rubbed my fingers through her hair and brushed it back. "It doesn't work that way." He shrugged. "You don't get to choose their emotions. You will end up so, so empty." Her eyes met mine. "I would rather lose a million towns than see you lose that light in your eyes." I rubbed my fingers across a tear. "Faith, it would kill me. Please don't do this."

A scoff from somewhere down the hall. "Oh sure, he says it and you listen," Rose grumbled.

"Shh!" Marissa chided. "If you make it so I can't hear this, I will never forgive you."

Faith rolled her eyes. "Maybe for once my parents will listen to me and want to help?" she whispered, but I could tell she didn't believe it.

"That's not good enough." I brought my lips a fraction away from hers, wanting to kiss her, but wanting her to know I meant it. "I need you to promise me you won't go back to a life where you were so unhappy." I kissed one cheek and then the other before I met her eyes again. "Not for anyone."

Her shoulders sagged, and her head dipped. "How else am I

supposed to help?" The pain was clear in her voice. "What good is having secret access to a bunch of money if I can't save the people I love?" Her eyes met mine. "All the people I love."

Love. My heart soared.

I loved her more than I even thought was possible.

She healed my broken pieces in ways I could never repay. I leaned in, resting my forehead on hers. "I love you, Faith."

"I love you too," she whispered back.

I kissed her, and I hoped she could tell how much she meant to me with every second of that kiss.

I squeezed her hand in mine. "You can suck in your screams." I sighed. "You can face your parents and ask to see if they can help save our town." I dipped my chin so I could see her blue eyes. "But you cannot offer yourself as a sacrificial lamb to do so. And I will hope and pray that regardless of what your parents agree to, you will come back to Hillsdale." I died a little as I thought of what life would be like without her. "Faith, I don't know that I could go back to living without you. Not now that I know how beautiful and whole life can be."

She raised her shoulder. "Hillsdale is my home." She gazed at me. "You're my home."

Somehow, in the course of a few minutes, my heart had broken and healed. The person who held it together was Faith.

Then she spoke to the hallway, which I noticed held Marissa and Rose. "And all of you are my family." She took a steadying breath. "Although I would be lying if I didn't say I also want my parents to accept me and want to be a part of my life too." She gave a sad shrug.

I lowered my head, bringing my face closer to hers. "Want me to come with you to New York?" I would do it. I would drop everything to go help her face this battle.

She smiled. "I appreciate it, but I think this is one I need to face alone." She put her hand on my cheek. "Besides, Danny and your basketball team will need you here."

Every part of me wanted to take this fight away from her. To march in and demand her parents be kind to her and recognize the amazing person she was.

But this wasn't a wound I could solve.

I sighed. I knew Faith needed this; she needed to face her past.

And I needed to trust that she would come back to me after she did.

Chapter Thirty-Two

FAITH

I didn't know if I was being brave or going to jinx myself, but I packed only a backpack of clothes for my trip home. Maybe I was trying to assure myself that I would come back. Although, let's be honest, my parents could replace everything I owned without a second thought.

I shook out my hands and took a deep breath as I climbed up the steps into one of Luxe's private jets.

I'd never been able to truly defy my mother before, but I guess there was a first time for everything. Or maybe Dad wouldn't be as indifferent as before?

Stepping into the jet, I was met by my mother's assistant, Janice. She gave me the same curt smile as years ago. "Astrid." She nodded for me to follow her in her black tailored dress suit and with her hair slicked back into a high ponytail. It looked so tight, I imagined she had to have a headache. "Meredith instructed me to assemble a full team and ensure you look presentable once we land." She gestured around the cabin, which held at least fifteen other people I didn't recognize. That part didn't surprise me; my mother changed wardrobe and hair assistants faster than the trends could keep up with. That she believed it took an army and an entire flight to make me look "presentable" was slightly offensive.

I glanced down at my yoga pants and soft blue sweater. My hair was up in a loose, messy bun. This was the real me, and I didn't want to change back to who I had been. Was this the first step of many I would concede on? Or do I start by standing my ground from the start? I rubbed my forehead; I thought I would at least get the flight to New York until I had to be brave. But I should have known better. I bit my bottom lip.

Janice leaned in. "Meredith also informed me that if you didn't comply, to let you know she would refuse your new business idea you plan on proposing." Janice cleared her throat and looked to the side. "If you are choosing to return to Luxe, I'm afraid you must look the part." Her eyes went over my hair and clothes, and she shrugged.

"And if I am just trying to see my parents and nothing else?" I wasn't sure there was a difference between the two, but I was hoping there was. This was more than I had resisted anyone associated with my parents before, and although I was proud of my newfound strength, I could feel my hands shaking and my stomach filling with nausea.

Janice leaned in close and whispered, "Then I might add that whatever you are hoping to accomplish, it will be much easier if you choose your battles wisely."

"Spoken like a woman who knows my mother well."

Janice hid a smile and cleared her throat.

"Well, let's get this over with." I sighed. Choosing my battles was wise. This wasn't one that was worth the stress.

Janice stepped behind me and gestured me forward, and the assembled makeover team headed behind the curtains beyond my view. I followed them and grimaced at the piles of tools, machines, and product. I could remember the hours with similar torture devices before, but I had gotten so used to my easy routine of a little light makeup and simple hairstyles.

"Choose your battles." I murmured under my breath. "For Hillsdale." I closed my eyes and was led to the first station.

Over the next several hours, I felt like Sandra Bullock in Miss Congeniality. I was waxed, tweezed, dyed, and dressed up to be someone I no longer recognized in the mirror. Something that seemed more product than person.

Although I would never admit it to my mother, I loved the new hairstyle, not that I got to choose it. It was full of subtle highlights and now rested below my collarbone. Also, these leopard print heels weren't bad either. I'm keeping these for enduring her makeover torture.

As the plane landed, I thanked and gave a quick hug to everyone who was assigned to help with my current status. Each stiffened and glanced around in fear before they gave a small smile and a nod in return. I knew my mother would hate to see me "talking with the help," but I refused to be that person. Each of these people gave of their time and expertise, and I was grateful for it.

The door opened, and before I went onto the first step, the clicking of cameras reached my ears and the reporters started yelling over one another to be answered.

"Astrid, where have you been?"

"Astrid, have you been sick?"

My hands shook, and nausea climbed up my throat. My mind recalled years of flashing lights, cameras, and questions yelled in my direction.

I took a deep breath, held it for three, and slowly blew out. I spun my anxiety ring and took another deep breath. "Okay, suck in your screams."

"Astrid, we heard you had been in France?"

"Astrid, are you home to stay?"

I put a practiced polite smile on my face. Slowly building a barrier between the real me and the version people got to question and exploit. I sighed. Janice tapped my shoulder.

"Here." She handed me a pair of sunglasses. "I feel like these help."

I looked over at her. "Thank you, Janice."

She grinned and then stepped behind me, returning to an almost invisible presence.

"Astrid, is it true you were pregnant?

Wait what?

I held my head high as I walked down the stairs. I kept my smile tight as I went toward the limo that was parked on the tarmac. Wesley, our driver for as long as I could remember, opened the door, and my mother stepped out with full lips, blond hair, and a body that statistically was probably younger than mine.

I stutter stepped.

I hadn't expected to face her until we were at our New York house—the one designed by Andrew Stern. I'd always called it Stern House, though Mother never approved. With it being March, I knew they would stay there from now until summer.

She held her arms out in a forced gesture.

Did she want me to hug her?

"Astrid, my darling. We are so glad you have finally returned home." She added loudly enough for the reporters to hear. Dad stepped out next in his stiff suit and blue tie.

I stopped in my tracks. Wait. Dad?

I rarely even saw him at the house growing up. He was like a glimmer that flickered in and out of view, but never stayed long. Always rushing to the next appointment or next golf something.

But he came here now? To the airport? Was it to see me? My brain couldn't keep up with all the new input it was receiving.

He walked around the car and stood near Mom's side. He seemed older than before, and his shoulders drooped in a way they hadn't before. Had he lost weight? His gray hair was parted and gelled to the left.

"Look at us," my mother added for the benefit of the reporters.

"The Luxe family is back together at last." She smiled larger for the cameras than she ever had for me.

"How about a family picture?" Someone called from behind me.

"What a wonderful idea!" Mom held her hand to her heart, as if surprised. Like this publicity stunt hadn't always been the plan.

I stood in front of my mother, who pulled me in for a stiff, awkward side hug, keeping her "good side" to the cameras. Physical connection was never a strong suit for her.

I glanced at Dad. He opened his arms wide and pulled me into a hug, and he held me tighter than he ever had before. Strange.

"Hey, Dad."

"Hey, Astrid." He rested his chin on top of my head, and I leaned back and looked at him, my eyebrows furrowed. His blue eyes drank me in, and his grin seemed just for me, like the cameras weren't even there. "I've missed you, kiddo."

I smiled back. He hadn't called me that since I was little. He pulled me in for another hug.

"Alexander, you're going to ruin her makeup with your theatrics." My mother grumbled as she turned me around for the cameras.

I thought her word choice was rather ironic.

"Family picture." My mother called out in a cheerful voice for other people's benefit. "Lose the glasses." She growled at me.

"Of course, Mom." I said. Her hand tightened on my shoulder. "Or do you still prefer Meredith?" I raised a brow as I met her eyes and squeezed my hand into a fist to keep it from trembling. "Or is this another one of those not in front of the cameras type topics?" Everything was always not in front of the cameras, and then ignored and deflected once home.

She didn't give a verbal response, but her eyes held daggers as she gestured to the cameras.

I turned, posed, and smiled like I had been taught to do since the time I learned to walk. My dad squeezed my shoulder, but somehow it felt different from Mom's.

Mom earned one point for my appearance and cameras, but I'm saying I get a point for talking back to her, when I was terrified.

"I can't believe my baby is back to stay!" Mom glowed for the cameras.

Chapter Thirty-Three

FAITH

After the cameras, we sat in the limo and headed to Stern House.

"It's so good to see you, Astrid." Dad smiled at me.

"One heart attack and you think you're dying." Mom rolled her eyes.

"Wait, what?" I studied Dad.

Dad's eyebrows furrowed. "Didn't you know?" He looked at Mom. "You said you told her."

I blinked, trying to absorb the information.

"I told you I called her, and I did, and she said not to call back."

"Wait." My forehead creased. "When did it happen?"

"Just before Thanksgiving," Dad replied.

My mind searched back to before Thanksgiving, the first time I heard my mother's voice, and I wondered if it had been sad.

"Wait...that's why you called?" I glared at Mom.

Mom glared. "Yes and then you asked me not to call you."

"You called and told me to stop being ridiculous and to come home to the family business. You said I was dramatic and you were embarrassed of me." I held out my hand palm up. "You didn't say anything about Dad having a heart attack."

"It's okay, Astrid, you're here now." Dad shrugged. "Was just a little scare."

"Little?" Mom rolled her eyes. "Please, you were in the emergency room and ICU for days. We barely kept it out of the papers."

My eyes shot to him. Maybe that was why he looked so much older. "I can't believe you didn't tell me." I looked between them on the opposite side of the limo.

Mom scoffed. "You made it obvious you wanted nothing to do with us." Mom's shoulders were stiff and straight.

"That isn't completely true." It wasn't false either though. I had avoided any interaction. I rubbed my forehead.

The car pulled into the large bricked circular driveway in front of an ostentatious house, with large white columns, grand entry steps, and gold door frames. We walked through the entryway and into the living room.

"You're right, I should have communicated more with you both." I studied the floral pattern on the Victorian chair as I sat. "I think I was worried the only thing you would want to talk about was Luxe and make me feel guilty." I raised my right shoulder.

"Never mind, and now that you're here, there are a lot of business affairs to catch up on." Mom crossed her bronzed legs.

I spun my ring and took a deep breath as I looked at the coffee table.

Suck in your screams.

"I never meant to separate myself from you both." My eyes flicked between them. "I, however, intended to separate myself from the business." I flexed my jaw and cleared my throat. "It's not who I am. I tried to force myself to be that person, and I was miserable." I closed my eyes. "I'm introverted. I enjoy bubble baths, reading, and cooking. I love quiet nights at home and hate crowds and publicity. I don't want it."

Mom huffed. "We are the business." She folded her manicured hands over her blazer jacket.

I nodded. "Yes, but I'm hoping there might be another option." The anxiety in my stomach started to swirl and rise up my throat. "That you might just be my parents."

"What do you mean? You're staying here and working for LUXE. Right?"

I shook my head no.

Mom slapped her hands on her toned legs. "Great!" Her hands flew up in the air. "I already told them to print in the paper that you were."

I flinched. "That is unfortunate." I reminded myself that this wasn't my fault. I never told her I was coming to stay.

"So why are you here then?" Dad leaned forward and studied me.

I took a shuddering breath. "I meant when I said I wanted to retry our relationship, but honestly, there is more as well."

Mom huffed, and Dad gestured for me to continue. I had thought of this conversation a hundred times and never found the right way to share my whole life in Hillsdale. My parents sat on chairs on the other side of the coffee table. I stood and walked over to them. "I want to show you something first." I squatted between them and opened my photos and scrolled back.

"These are my best friends." I showed them a picture of Marissa and Rose. "This is Marissa." I pointed at her. "She is married now and running a B&B slash community center slash law office." I chuckled as Dad's eyebrows shot up. "It's a super tiny town, so often people do multiple things to pick up the slack." I shrugged. "There isn't a large box grocery store, movie theater, mall, or even hospital nearby for over an hour."

His forehead creased as I'm sure he tried to picture a world so foreign, and I looked at Mom. Her arms stayed folded and her leg was crossed, pointing her body to the opposite corner of the room.

She ignored me and my phone, but I caught her quick glances, so I decided to just continue.

"This is Rose. She is my roommate and, honestly, she's the best, and a little feisty." I smiled.

I scrolled through my pictures from Hillsdale Trunk or Treats, pumpkin weigh-ins, Easter egg hunts, Fourth of July parades, and so many other community events. I briefly explained the events and different people in the pictures.

Then I showed them my second-grade classes over the past three years, each child's face bringing with it distinct memories of happiness and learning. Was I willing to never teach again? I cleared my throat and my tears. "I teach second grade." I sighed and raised my right shoulder. "I honestly love it so much." I grinned. "I love the kids and helping them learn and grow. I love the things they say and the moment their eyes light up when they learn something new." The tears pricked my eyes as I thought of all of my past and current students and the hardships they were currently facing.

I scrolled through the pictures until I got to one of Adam, Danny, and me getting Christmas trees.

"Who's that?" Mom's voice was icy and her lips pinched in a frown.

I wasn't sure how much to share, but if we were starting over, the truth would probably be best. "That is Adam and his son is Danny."

Dad's eyes shot to me, looking puzzled.

"In these we were getting Christmas trees. It was pure magic up in those mountains." I felt a warmth and peace spread through my chest.

There were pictures of my class as reindeers, desserts I'd made, my decorated Christmas tree from Adam and Danny, pictures of the dance I went to with Adam, and the last one was of the basketball game.

"Is that the same guy?" Dad squinted at the picture.

"Yeah." I grinned. "He is the coach of the basketball team. He loves those kids, and honestly, they love and respect him too. And they are kind to Danny."

Dad gave a sad smile. "He is crazy about you." It wasn't a question. "You can see it in his eyes."

I smiled. "I'm a little crazy about him too."

He nodded again.

"Oh, please." Mom waved her hand. "You mean you would rather live on a teacher's salary in some tiny town, with a bunch of nobodies, than be here, with us, and the successful life we have built for you?"

I gazed into her eyes and hoped for kindness.

There was none.

"Yes." I sighed. "But I'd love for you guys to come visit and see it. And I'd like to visit here more too. But the town is truly amazing!" My smile faltered. "Well, it was amazing."

Dad tilted his head. "What happened?"

I shrugged. "Mother Nature, I guess." My shoulders sagged, and I found pictures of the storm and damage to the town. I handed the phone over to Dad.

"I hoped that maybe you guys would give a large charity donation and help the town rebuild. We can do whatever publicity you like for it? We will hold other fundraisers and try to make it part way, but there isn't enough money to do it on our own."

"So, this is why you're home." Mom sneered. "We have already agreed which charities we are supporting this year." She rolled her eyes.

"Yes, but you run a business. This could be good for Luxe. Think of how it would look for the papers. You guys would save a whole town. But regardless of Luxe..." I took a steadying breath and blew out the tightness in my lungs and glanced at my parents. "I was hoping you would do this for me, as my parents." Tears gathered in my eyes. "I love this town, and I love these people." I wiped a stray tear with my shoulder. "They don't have the resources to fix the school. Most of the town lives paycheck to paycheck or from harvest to harvest. Without the school, they will have to bus kids to other towns, split up friendships, and require long bus rides. I rolled my ring. "That's just the start. Over 60 percent of the population of Hillsdale earn their wages from the school, and they will all be jobless, including me." I sighed and looked at the floor. "I know I don't deserve to ask for this, when I ran off like I did."

Mom scoffed. "That's for sure."

Dad's forehead wrinkled.

"If we did this, would you come back and work for Luxe?" Mom folded her arms and raised her brow. "Seems like a small price to pay if you love them as much as you say you do."

This was it.

The moment that mattered most.

Would I be willing to sacrifice what I wanted and worked toward in life so others could live the life they loved?

I breathed in and held it. I couldn't tell what was right.

My friends would despise me for it, but they would despise me in a functional town.

"Would that be required?" I whispered.

Chapter Thirty-Four

ADAM

It had been several days since I had seen Faith. Several days of quick phone calls, both of us overwhelmed in our own spaces. I wanted to go with her to New York; I wanted to make her come back, but neither of those things were up to me.

The team had several days before the state basketball game. Considering there was so much uneasiness in their lives, they were doing well. They pushed themselves as they ran ladders on our half of the gym.

It would be ideal to use the entire floor, but sacrifices needed to be made by everyone. Part of the elementary school was currently using the bleachers and the other half of the gym for their lessons. There were also classes in churches, the firehouse, and the B&B community center.

Again, not ideal, but necessary. Our next practice would be full court.

The bonus was I got to watch Danny interact with his classmates a little during practice. It was a lot for him with the recent changes, and the way noise echoed in the gym. Faith mentioned headphones might be helpful while in the gym.

We had started the paperwork for testing Danny a bit ago, and we were still waiting to meet with the pediatrician.

I hoped I was doing the right thing by Danny.

The team ran across the black line; several placed hands on their knees as they tried to catch their breath.

"Nice job!" I walked toward the group. "Let's run through some plays."

Jacob nodded and took the ball up to the three-point line as the other boys got into position. He held up the number three, and I watched the players shift around accordingly.

Somehow, even though I'd lived here most of my life, everything had a newness that now included memories with Faith.

We were slotted to go in third at state with a single elimination bracket. I was happy they kept the state championship going. The kids could use some normalcy in their lives. They moved the venue a little farther away to accommodate the storm, but other than that, things were going forward as planned.

Fifteen minutes later, I blew my whistle. "Four foul shots each, a ladder for the team for each shot missed." The boys started lining up around the key. "State is coming up at the end of the week. I know life is a little hectic right now, but let's try our best to focus on the good."

The phone call with Faith last night had been short. She sounded exhausted, but at least she answered this time. I tried to remind myself that she had a lot to do there, and she felt a lot of pressure to succeed, which might be why she seemed somewhat distant last night.

I searched for plane tickets to New York, and wondered if it would be worth the extra cost to see her, even if only for a few hours. But then real life kicked in, real life as in Danny, who had recently decided four a.m. was a perfectly acceptable time to rise and shine. Or rather, rise and demand.

I needed to focus on the life in front of me and what was in my control. For now, that was Danny and basketball.

Jessica, who was currently helping with half of Danny's class, including Danny, was struggling to get him to calm down.

These class conditions would be hard under the best of circumstances. That he was supposed to practice math facts while watching other kids play jump rope was pure torture for him. Adding in lots of changes and sounds, and he was not adapting well.

Jessica waved her hands in the air as she talked with Danny. They were obviously going the rounds, and Danny was not backing down.

I jogged toward the commotion and Danny screamed. "You're not my teacher!"

Jessica raised her voice to match his volume. "Yes, I am now. Faith isn't coming back, so you better start listening to me." She slammed her hands to her hips.

I stuttered to a stop, my tennis shoes squeaking on the gym floor. Why would she say that? Did she know something I didn't?

"I wish you wouldn't come back!" Danny called back as he crossed his arms and swiveled his body away from her.

Jessica clenched her fists.

Faith later, Danny now.

"Hey there, Champ." I called before Jessica screamed back in retaliation. They both looked in my direction, with flushed cheeks and tight shoulders. "Let's give Ms. Jessica a break. She's doing her best." I went to the bottom of the bleachers and ruffled Danny's hair, blocking Jessica from his view.

"She said Ms. Faith isn't coming back." Danny's eyes filled with unshed tears.

Poor guy, I never should have let him get so involved. He would miss his teacher either way. Faith was special. But I should have tried harder to keep him from getting even more attached.

Hopefully, this didn't end up hurting us both. But especially Danny.

I glanced over my shoulder at Jessica.

"Look, I'm sorry to be the one to tell you, but..." She grabbed her phone from her pocket and turned its screen on and faced it toward me. The screen showed a news article saying "Astrid Luxe back to stay" and had a picture of what I assumed was Faith's family, with a very different-looking Faith.

My mouth was dry, my lungs tightened, and my stomach dropped. I cleared my throat.

"I told you she was hiding something." Jessica raised her brows. "She didn't even tell us her real name." Jessica grumbled under her breath and rolled her eyes.

I glared at Jessica. "Her name is Faith. She legally changed it."

"You knew?" Jessica eyed me suspiciously. "And what, you just didn't care that she was pretending to be someone else the whole time? You still picked her?"

I glared at Jessica until she fidgeted and then I whispered, so the surrounding kids couldn't hear, "You don't know what you're talking about, not that you care, but Faith is currently sacrificing a lot to save your job. Why do you think she went back when she did?" I shook my head in disgust. "And yes, Jessica. I choose her, and I will choose her every day that she lets me. You have no idea who Faith is."

Jessica gasped and stepped back. Maybe I took things too far, but I was sick of her. I turned back to Danny, who was clearly upset and likely wouldn't settle soon. Leaving him with Jessica would only make it worse. "I'll keep Danny with me for the day. Give both of you a bit of a break."

The fight had leaked out of Jessica. She stared at the ground as her shoulders slumped. She stared at her phone, which held Faith's picture.

Danny reached over and put his hand in mine and hopped down the last step of the bleachers.

"All right, Champ, how about you help me coach for a bit?" We walked back toward our half of the gym.

"Is Ms. Faith coming back?" Danny whispered.

I stopped walking and squatted down to face him. "Faith is trying to suck in her screams right now. She is being brave and going through some things." I wouldn't add that she was trying to save the school. That was too much pressure for her if it didn't work. More than anything, I wanted her to come back, regardless of what her parents said. "I still think she will come back." I chewed on my cheek, trying to not show Danny how desperately I wanted her to come home too. "But we don't get to know all the answers." I frowned.

"That's stupid." Danny's eyebrows lowered. "I hate not knowing."

I laughed. "Me too, Champ." I stood, and we walked back to the team. "Do you want to see if anyone needs water?"

Danny nodded, excited to have a task to keep him busy, and ran toward the water bottles. While everyone was preoccupied, I pulled up the article I'd seen on Jessica's phone. My heart squeezed as I read the article posted the day Faith landed in New York.

Surely, if she had decided to stay, she would have told me, right?

I scanned the article but learned nothing other than the source was Faith's mother and she was excited to have the company back together.

"Have the company back together?" I shook my head. What a piece of work.

I scrolled back up and studied the family picture. Wondering if I could still find my Faith in the picture, underneath the layers of makeup, fake lashes, and high-end clothes. Her current style reminded me of Cassie, and I knew the comparison wasn't fair.

I zoomed in on the picture. Faith's smile was different. It wasn't the one that lit up her entire face that I loved. It was restricted and fake, and her eyes looked sad.

I sighed. "Please, Faith." I rubbed a hand through my hair. "Please come back."

Chapter Thirty-Five

FAITH

"What makes you think you deserve to come ask for money when you just plan on leaving?"

The sharp point of my mother's words dug at my skin, and I closed my eyes. I sighed. It had been the same conversation for the last three days, but I wasn't ready to give up. "I honestly probably don't deserve it. But I'm hoping you will consider it, anyway."

After the discussion about not coming back to LUXE, Mom had screamed and stormed out.

I agreed with Dad to meet again to talk at lunch the next day, after Mom had a good night's sleep, and give everyone space to digest the new information. The only problem was Mom left early that morning and didn't come back all day. I talked to my dad, but I really doubted he felt like he could agree to anything without Mom's permission.

I hadn't slept for the last few nights. All I did was replay the conversations over and over in my head. Would my parents still choose me, even if I weren't the child they had hoped and planned for? This was too important; I had to figure out a way to get them to help.

I rubbed my forehead and placed my hand on the dining room

table. I had to shout to even be heard by her from where I was sitting. I stood from my seat, grabbed my plate, and walked over and sat in front of my parents. I'm sure Mom hated it, but I hated sitting so far away.

I decided to try to picture everything through my mother's eyes. "I know you raised me to replace you in a company you cherish and are very proud of." I reached over and placed my hand on top of hers. She scoffed and pulled her hand farther away. I pinched my lips together. "But, it isn't the life I want, and my life is mine to choose." I looked at my parents' eyes, my mother's full of anger and my father's soft.

"Yes, you have made that very clear." Mom rolled her eyes. "The money you ask for, however, is mine to decide." She pointed to herself.

"Ours," my father added.

I glanced at Dad. He rarely spoke, and it was never in opposition to Mom.

"Excuse me?" Mom glared daggers at Dad.

He cleared his throat and sat taller. "The money is not yours to choose, it's ours." He raised his brows at her and refocused back on me.

My eyes shot back and forth between them, unsure what I was supposed to do.

"Oh, silly me." Mom's brows lowered. "I didn't realize that with your heart attack and taking a step back in the business meant you would suddenly decide how to raise our daughter."

Dad frowned. "That's just it; she is our daughter." His shoulders stiffened. "For years I was trying to build the business, to the point I couldn't see anything else." He looked at me. "The next thing I knew, she was six, and you had her in lessons and pageants. It was a world I knew nothing about. You insisted you knew more about raising our daughter. And I let you convince me." His blue eyes drank me in as he shook his head. "I think it may always be one of the greatest regrets of my life." His lips pressed into a thin line, and he cleared his throat. "That I was content with allowing someone else to raise my daughter until one day I realized I had no space in her life." He shrugged. "That I was too late." He stared down at his plate and his salad. "It took almost dying for me to know my greatest regret was you kiddo."

I sat back in my seat unsure where to look or what to do. Wait, what?

"When I asked your mother to call you, and see if you would come visit, she told me you were upset and said never to call again." He shook his head. "I knew I deserved the response. I'd done nothing to earn your respect or love, but I made a promise in that hospital. I would do better. I would choose better." He closed his eyes. Then he looked up at me. "I knew right then, if I was ever given an opportunity to start over with my little girl, I would take it." Tears ran down the worn lines of his face. He glared at Mom. "So yes, it is our money, and Astrid is our daughter." He looked back at me. "But this is my chance to try again, and to be better." He faced Mom. "And I'm going to take it."

My breath caught in the back of my throat, and I leaned back. Could he mean it? Did he really want to try again?

My mom threw her cloth napkin onto the table. "Alexander, we don't run a charity!"

Dad shrugged. "I mean, we donate to several charities for tax purposes." He raised an eyebrow. "So we kind of do."

"Not this much!" Mom snarled. "If you do this, she will never come back!" Mom stood. "It will all have been for nothing, the legacy, the sacrifices." She threw her hands high in the air. "What about the business? What will people say when they realize our own daughter doesn't want it?"

Dad raised a shoulder. "I couldn't care less. At the end of the day, it's just a business." He stared at me. "And Astrid deserves to choose the life she wants. If she doesn't want LUXE, then I don't want her to have it."

Mom's face turned bright red, and she screamed before she

stormed out of the formal dining room, out the double doors, and to the grand staircase.

I blinked rapidly. What should I do? Do I run and give him a hug? Was that weird? "Do you think Mom will ever forgive me for not wanting LUXE?" I whispered.

"There's no knowing what your mother will or won't do."

I peeked up to meet my dad's eyes. "Are you sure?" I whispered. "You're willing to help Hillsdale?"

Dad's eyes squinted, he frowned as he shook his head no.

I gasped and leaned back in my seat. Had I misunderstood?

"I uhh, I don't understand."

He smiled. "Astrid, I'm willing to help *you* in whatever way you choose."

I pushed back my chair and rushed along the long dining table and fell into my father's open arms. He stroked my back. "Oh kiddo, I'm so, so sorry." He hugged me a little tighter. "I hope one day you can forgive me, but even if you don't, I won't give up this chance to do one thing right by you. I want to get to know the woman my daughter has become."

I leaned back and looked into his eyes. "Thanks," I said, hugging him again. "I'm excited to get to know you better too."

THE NEXT FEW DAYS WERE SPENT TALKING TO DAD about Hillsdale and my life there, and with Mom avoiding us both. I learned my dad actually hated golf, but Mom had pressured him into it because it's what successful men do.

He told me that if he learned anything, it was that life was short and could be gone in an instant. So choose your time wisely.

It was almost time to go, so I made my way up to Mom's bedroom and knocked.

"What." She obviously wasn't in a great mood.

I eased the door open. "Hey, Mom, just wanted to say goodbye and ask again if you want to join Dad and me." Her bedroom was decorated in teal and gold. It had a diamond chandelier hanging over the four-poster bed. "I think if you saw Hillsdale you might like it?"

I was lying. She wouldn't get it. She would see the rundown shops, outdated fashion, and lack of press and feel her skin itch like she caught some invisible plague. I wasn't like my mother, but maybe I was more like my father than I ever knew.

I nodded to Janice and waved hello as I walked past her and went to Mom's bedside.

"I'm surprised you even want me to come." She shifted on her silk sheets to be farther from me.

"Of course we want you to come." Maybe.

"Well, I refuse to make a fool of myself, and your father should reconsider as well. Think of what this could do to our brand." She shook her head and turned away from me.

I was glad Dad wanted to come see his "future investment" and, as a way of trying to appease Mom, I even agreed to come back for holidays and call more often.

She wasn't appeased, and she wanted nothing to do with my life in Hillsdale.

"Bye, Meredith." If that's what she preferred to be called, I would do my best to honor her wishes.

Her eyes met mine; they were watery. "Mom is fine, just not at big public events."

I smiled. "That should be an easy promise to keep."

"Don't remind me." She groaned as she looked up at the ceiling.

I plopped onto her bed and gave her a brief hug. "Thanks, Mom."

She gestured for me to go. She didn't like it, but she wasn't asking me to reconsider anymore, so I figured that's a win.

I rushed down the stairs and met Dad near the front door. He opened his arms wide to show me his new maroon and gold sports jacket with an Eagle mascot on the back.

I chuckled. "That's perfect! I can't believe you found that."

He shrugged. "Money has its perks." He winked and brought his hand out from behind him. "I had one made for you too." He held out the sports jacket, and I squealed in delight as I put it on. He wrapped his arm around my shoulder as we made our way out to Wesley and the waiting car.

I figured the best place to break the news about the school would be at the State Basketball game today.

Dotty, the superintendent, Dad, and I had been on video calls late into the night. We wanted to make sure everything was set before we said anything. I couldn't give this broken town false hope.

Once the jet landed, we ordered an Uber to the high school gym in Clifton. It was Dad's first time in an Uber, and he spent the whole time asking the driver way too personal questions about his life. I think the driver and I were both happy when we parked outside the gym.

We stepped out of the car, and Dad gave the driver a tip he would never forget. I looked at Dad's smile. He seemed brighter than I had ever remembered. I pulled him toward the gym doors in our matching jackets.

"Are you ready to become everyone's favorite person?" I asked him.

He shook his head. "Oh, I'm sure I could never replace you in their eyes."

I rolled my eyes. "I'm not exactly the social butterfly type. I do have some favorites though." My cheetah-print heels clicked on the linoleum floor.

"So I heard." Dad chuckled.

I probably told Dad too much info about Adam, but this parent-child thing was all a bit new for us both.

Marissa said it had been a close game so far. I knew this meant so much to Adam and the team. I spun my ring and hurried for the gym doors.

"Excited to see someone?" Dad raised his eyebrows as he glanced at my hands.

"Maybe?" I pursed my lips.

"It does me good to see you so happy." He squeezed my shoulder.

"Oh, just wait till you watch her kiss the coach. She glows."

I spun around, searching. "Rose?" My best friends were standing outside the doors. Rose with her arms folded, Marissa beside her, and Dotty came too. I screamed and rushed over and hugged my friends. I could feel tears prick my eyes.

The fact that we were going to save the town was sinking in, and I felt such a wave of relief.

"Come meet my dad." My smile was wider than possible as I turned and pulled them in his direction. "He has agreed to help save the school!"

My dad reached his hand out toward them. "Thanks for being so kind to my Astrid."

"Dad, it's Faith now, remember."

He shook his head. "Right. That might take some practice."

Marissa, Dotty, and Rose shook Dad's hand and thanked him for his upcoming help.

"Does Adam know you are here yet?" Marissa asked.

"I texted him, but I don't think he ever got it." I said.

"Well, that's convenient." The cheer coach, Brandy, came down the hallway and stood near us with Jessica pressed against her side.

I was suddenly nervous and unsure of what to do with my hands. Was Jessica going to make a scene? The last time I talked to her was when she was screaming at me at the dance.

I took a step back as Rose went to step in front of me. I placed my hand on her shoulder and took in Jessica. She had tears in her eyes.

She cleared her throat. "I heard what you did for the school, and all our jobs."

I scrunched up my nose. "That was supposed to stay a secret," I muttered.

Jessica took a steady breath, taking a little step closer. "I'm so sorry, Faith." She pursed her lips and studied the ceiling. "I wanted it to be me, and when it wasn't, I couldn't stand it." She shook her head. "I was so desperate to be loved that I became someone I wasn't proud of." She wiped off her tears, cleared her throat, and then pulled a big poster board from behind her back. "I made this for you." She shrugged. "Thought you could surprise him when the team runs out after halftime." She held the poster toward me. "Consider it my first attempt of many to apologize." Jessica looked down.

It had school colors, and written in big letters, it said, DIBS ON THE COACH.

I recognized in her the person I once was. A person who changed to be loved. The girl in me that was lost and scared and desperate. I stepped closer to her. "I know how easy it is to get wrapped up in trying to be enough that you lose your way." I whispered to her. "It's okay."

I held my arms up, and Jessica closed the distance in the hug. I wondered if, at that moment, I was hugging a past version of myself more than Jessica. I knew it was time to forgive myself too, to move past my mistakes, and to keep trying. We are all human and make mistakes, but what matters is how we deal with them when they come.

As I stepped away from Jessica, I noticed Rose staring daggers at her.

"She might have forgiven you, but I haven't." Rose glared.

"Stop." I chuckled. I loved my spicy friend. Marissa gave me a side hug.

"Okay, so here's what we should do." Brandy drew us all into a huddle. Even Dad.

Chapter Thirty-Six

ADAM

I didn't get to talk to Faith last night, but the day before, she said she was going to try to be here for the state championship game. I pried my hand away from my pocket, which held my phone.

I desperately wanted to check and see if she had texted or landed or, well, anything. But the boys deserved my full attention for now. We were currently up by four against the Mustangs, but with this game, that could change in an instant. I rubbed my hands together.

"All right, boys, that was a great half. I saw a lot of good communication." I nodded toward the boys. "I'm proud of this team. I'm proud of you guys out there, win or lose." I smiled at each of them. "But...since we have worked this hard," I grinned, "we may as well try to win. Right?" The boys erupted into cheers. "Any pointers, Captain?"

Jacob leaned forward to see Connor. "Watch it in the key. The ref will keep calling for three seconds." Then he looked to the other side. "Jackson, don't be afraid to go for the layup if they double guard me." He smiled. "Other than that, I'd say let's make sure all those laps weren't for nothing."

The team cheered and huddled around the captain. "Eagles on three. One, two, three, Eagles!"

Danny came running around the corner into the locker room.

"There's a tunnel!" He bounced on his toes, unable to keep the excitement in only his voice.

He reached for my hand and dragged me to the door. I peeked out the door to find the "tunnel" of people.

"Looks like the whole town is in that lineup." I chuckled. "They came to support you today. Let's give it our all."

The boys yelled again and ran past me as I held the door open. Everyone was waving signs and pompoms and supporting our school's colors.

This town was something else.

"You too, Coach," someone hollered in my direction.

"And me!" Danny cheered.

"Oh, why not?" I took Danny's hand and ran through the tunnel.

The smiling faces of a town I loved surrounded me. A town I was proud to be a part of. Even though it had been hit hard this last month, they were still here for each other. People who don't live in small towns don't know what they are missing.

At the end of the tunnel, waving a poster and cheering, was Faith.

My Faith.

I stopped, my heart picking up speed that my body refused to follow.

The sign said, DIBS ON THE COACH.

She came back. Faith came back. I shook my head and couldn't stop my stupid grin.

"Ms. Faith!" Danny ran over to his teacher. "I knew you wouldn't let Ms. Jessica be my teacher!"

She tipped her head back and laughed. "I'm glad you at least had someone trying to help while I was gone. I was worried about you kids."

"So you are staying this time though, right?" I was glad that Danny wasn't afraid to ask the hard questions.

Faith smiled as she hugged Danny, and then her eyes met mine. "Yep, I'm here to stay. Hillsdale is my home."

My breath caught in my throat and I closed the distance between us. I pulled her into my arms. "I have desperately missed you," I whispered to her as I felt the warmth of her against my chest. I leaned back so I could see her eyes.

"I missed you too." She put a hand on my cheek.

I brushed my thumb down her jaw; she leaned into the touch. "Thanks for coming back."

"Thanks for giving me a place to come back to," she whispered, bringing her face closer to mine.

I nodded at the sign that she'd been holding. "I like the sign."

"Me too." She chuckled. "Jessica made it."

My eyes widened. "For you or her?" So help me if I needed to talk to that woman again...

"Me." Faith smiled.

"Huh?" My forehead creased. "I don't think I will ever understand women."

Faith giggled.

"I love you," she whispered.

"I love you." I rested my forehead against hers. I felt like I could take my first breath of air in a week. I could survive without Faith, but I felt like I was on life support, barely existing. I looked at her blue eyes and felt like all my broken pieces fit together into something whole. I kissed her and hoped she felt every ounce of my love for her in that kiss.

Forget the town, forget the game, I had Faith and Danny.

Brandy, the cheer coach, ran over and cleared her throat. "Excuse me, you two."

I sighed and leaned away from Faith, but I refused to drop her hand until I had to. Brandy handed Faith a megaphone. Faith tried to push it back at her, but Brandy shook her head and handed it back.

Faith sighed and grabbed the megaphone. I dropped her hand and quirked an eyebrow.

She focused on the crowd still lined up as the walls of the tunnel. "I have an announcement. Turns out we have received a very generous donation from Alexander Luxe." Faith looked around the crowd. "We're going to save the school!"

The tunnel collapsed, everyone cheering, hugging, and crying. She did it! I shook my head. Of course she had. I closed the distance between Faith and me and I gently took the megaphone from her hand. She handed it over with a puzzled expression.

"Let's be clear," I said into the megaphone. The crowd quieted and looked my way. "There is no *we* about it. Faith and her dad saved our town. Let's hear it for our own Ms. Faith." The crowd cheered, and Faith blushed.

I set down the megaphone, lifted Faith in my arms, and kissed her soundly.

At that, my basketball team whooped and cheered, slapping me on the back.

"Wait," Danny protested. "Where did you get that coat?" He had his arms folded in front of him as he stared down Faith's dad.

Alexander chuckled and smiled. It was a wide-open kind smile, like Faith's. "I had it made." He shrugged. "Thought if I was sponsoring the school, I needed to show up in full support."

Danny frowned. "I think since I help with the water bottles, I should get one too."

"I think you're right. I'll see that it's taken care of."

Danny nodded. I extended my hand toward Alexander. "Hello, Sir, I'm Adam. Thanks so much for being willing to help our town." My eyes went to Faith. "But even more so, thank you for Faith."

The buzzer sounded again.

"Everyone off the court," a ref called and blew his whistle.

"Guess we have some catching up to do later." Faith winked as she stepped past me. "Go get 'em, Coach." She swatted me on my backside.

This woman would keep me guessing and smiling for the rest of my life if I was lucky.

The rest of the game was close, but after double overtime, we won. The boys whooped and cheered. Today was like a dream come true.

At the buzzer, students and parents from the stands started rushing the court, cheering and crying.

"Free pie at Merritt's!" Angie cheered. "Tomorrow morning at ten a.m. Bring camp chairs to sit on."

The restaurant had taken a hit, but it didn't stop people from giving and being generous. Angie wasn't going to rebuild, but between James funding the repairs at no interest and the town begging, she decided she would reopen.

We won. I shook my head in disbelief. Even after the crazy weeks we had. We won. I looked up in the stands to see a blonde in her maroon and gold Eagles jacket jumping up and down screaming. When her eyes met mine, they were filled with happy tears, and the sight of her took my breath away.

Actually, I had already won before the game. Faith saved our town. She had saved me. I charged toward her, taking the steps two or three at a time. I couldn't wait to pull her into my arms.

Chapter Thirty-Seven

FAITH

Today was the last day of school.

Adam and I both agreed until I was no longer Danny's teacher, we would try to keep things in the friend zone, at least in front of him. Even though the entire town, and all my students, already knew we were dating.

Dating.

It seemed like such a simple word for the feelings I felt.

The timer on my phone alarm rang, signaling it was the end of the day. My group of second graders grabbed the cards they signed for one another, their last-day-of-school sugar cookies, and their backpacks from the side of the community center.

It wasn't the classroom setup that I loved, but it was my class, and that was all that really mattered.

I couldn't believe Dad was helping rebuild the school. I owed him so much. Mom was still keeping her distance, but Dad kept saying she would come around.

Hillsdale was amazing. James was putting a new technology center in the school and helping to fund some business rebuilds— I'm pretty sure Angie Merritt is paying him in pie. Michael has been here every weekend, hammer in hand, and Scott and Marissa were letting people stay at the B&B for free. Rose even offered free manicures to anyone whose house was damaged. I wasn't sure if it was all small towns or just mine, but I was proud to be a part of it.

My students lined up for the last time.

"Bye, Ms. Faith."

"Bye, Ms. Luxe."

I'd changed my last name back to Luxe, and told the children they were welcome to call me either. I never liked Lyons anyway, and honestly, I was proud to be a Luxe.

Lucy came toward me, her big doe eyes watering. "I'mma miss you, Ms. Faith."

"Me too," Lydia said.

"Me three," Mason said. "Can you come to my house too, like you do Danny's?"

I smiled and cleared my throat. No matter how hard we tried to keep things quiet, I'm pretty sure there was no such thing as quiet in Hillsdale.

"I will miss you too. Don't forget, next year you are always welcome to come and say hi. Once you are one of my students, you are always my students." I held my arms open for anyone who wanted a hug. It was crazy to spend so much time with these kids, only to pass them off to someone else the following year. I didn't know if I would ever get used to that part.

They wiped their eyes and noses on their sleeves.

"I hope each of you has a happy summer! And I'm excited about next year and the new school!" I clasped my hands in front of me. "Who's excited to see the new school?"

All the hands went up, including mine.

I walked the students out to the parking lot, then returned to clean up the rest of my makeshift classroom.

I picked up the pencils, scissors, and crayons and put them in boxes. I cleared up the smeared sugar cookie frosting, gathered the loose garbage, grabbed Mason's dinosaur jacket to give to his mom when I next saw her, and turned off my computer.

Running footsteps sounded from outside the door, followed by a familiar jovial knock.

I couldn't help my answering giggle as Adam pushed the door wide open and rushed toward me.

"School's out!" Adam fist-pumped as he rushed into the room, showing off my favorite biceps, which still caused me to swoon. He was more excited than any kid I'd ever seen that it was summer. I chuckled as he ran over to me, picked me up in his arms, spun me around, and kissed me thoroughly.

"I've always loved summer," Adam said as he wiggled his brows. "But I think this is going to be the best one yet."

I ran my fingers through his hair at the back of his neck. "I love you."

I looked into his brown eyes and was amazed at how much this man had changed my entire world. He didn't feel the need to fix my broken pieces or to save me from my problems. He saw me for me—and loved me and held me through all of my uncertainty, as I found myself, and that made all the difference.

"I love you, Faith." He rested his forehead against mine as his lips took on a devilish grin. "Did I say I was glad it's summer yet?" His head drifted closer to my mouth. "Because I'm really glad it's summer."

I bit my bottom lip. "Oh, yeah?"

He nodded. "Yep. And I think it's officially starting right now."

He pulled me in and his lips found mine, and in his arms I was home.

THE END

Epilogue

FAITH

I sat on the faded sofa with my hot cocoa, staring at the Christmas tree in the early morning light. The tree was an eclectic sight. I helped Danny make a snowflake garland this year with paper and glitter, and the new kitty, Mittens, was constantly climbing up in its branches and knocking the ornaments off. Danny sat on the floor, ripped wrapping paper pieces cascading around him. He picked up a package with red wrapping and gold ribbon.

"What's it say, bud?" Adam leaned forward, resting his elbows on his knees. Danny squinted at the writing.

"To Adam." His blue eyes pinched with focus. "From Faith."

I bit my bottom lip as Adam's brown eyes shot to mine.

"I thought we said no gifts?"

I shrugged.

Adam's eyebrows dipped as he grabbed the package from Danny. He felt the edges as he looked at the ceiling with a furrowed brow. "I think it's a book?" He tilted his jaw toward me. "If this is one of your romance books, I'm still not reading it."

I chuckled and gestured to the package.

Adam began tearing off the paper. I bit back my laughter as his eyes took in the title and he rolled his eyes. He chuckled and flipped the book around to show Danny. "Baking for Beginners."

I couldn't hold back my laughter.

"That's a good gift cause you need it." Danny nodded.

"I'm joking!" I grabbed a small gift bag from behind the sofa and handed it to him.

"You..." Adam wrapped his arms around me, pulling me onto his lap, and I leaned against his chest. I loved being in his arms and feeling his breath on my neck. He kept his arms around me as he dug through the gift bag.

Adam's scruffy jaw pressed into my cheek as he pulled out the Santa hat and black bow tie.

He threw his head back and laughed then leaned in and kissed my neck.

I raised an eyebrow. "That way you can show me how the push-ups are really done." I nodded to the bag. "There's still one more thing."

Adam reached back into the bag and pulled out a silver ring. He looked at me in confusion.

"You have to read it." I smiled.

Adam sat up and took the ring in his hand, slowly turning it over. He read out loud as he turned the ring. "Loved, just the way you are – Faith." I watched as his eyes widened and he shook his head. "Wow." He cleared his throat. "Thanks."

I hoped he knew I meant it too. I loved him, all the sharp and soft edges, and I never wanted him to feel that he wasn't good enough just how he was. I sighed and lay back on Adam's chest as he pressed his lips against my temple. "This has been the best Christmas." I sighed again and it phased into a yawn, the early morning catching up to me already. "Thank you. Both of you." I hoped every Christmas I ever spent would be here, in their lives and in Adam's arms.

"There's still a present on the tree." Danny tilted his chin.

"Are you sure?" Adam asked.

"Yeah, see." Danny reached into the tree branches and pulled out a little square gold box. "I don't think it's going to be my invisibility cloak."

Adam chuckled beneath me. "What does the tag say?"

Danny picked up the tag. "To Faith." He moved the tag. "It doesn't say who it's from."

I looked up at Adam's warm brown eyes.

"Well, go on, you better open it." His low voice near my ear caused my arm to erupt in goosebumps.

I sat up off his chest and scooted to the front of the couch where Danny handed me the box. Whatever it held, it didn't weigh much. I started unwrapping the paper and pulled out a little black velvet jewelry box.

I glanced toward Adam, and he gestured for me to continue. I tried not to get ahead of myself. It could be a necklace or earrings. I didn't want to make assumptions. I took a deep breath.

I slowly opened the box, my excitement overflowing to my eyes.

The box was empty.

Wait. What?

I looked over at Adam.

He scooted off the couch and knelt in front of me. He reached into his flannel pajama pants, and now in Adam's large hands was a beautiful petite gold ring with a teardrop diamond. It was simple, beautiful, and perfect.

"Faith." Adam's eyes shone as he smiled at me. "You are my sunshine, my light in darkness. When you're not in my arms, I feel lost. Would you do me the honor of becoming my wife?"

The tears couldn't be stopped at this point. I pressed my hand to my mouth. I couldn't picture a better happily ever after than the one I was living.

"Does this mean I will finally get to call her Mom now?" Danny stood up, and walked over and sat on Adam's bent knee.

"I guess it depends on what she says." Adam shrugged and searched my eyes.

I wanted to freeze this moment forever. Capture it and never let it leave my heart. Both my boys sat there looking up at me in the glow of the Christmas tree lights. They both had morning hair sticking up in different directions, and their eyes held such happiness. My boys. My family. My heart was full to the point of bursting.

"Yes!" I grinned so wide my cheeks hurt. "Always and forever, yes!" I nodded my head.

Danny fist-pumped. "Yes!" He jumped up, and ran into my open arms. "This is better than an invisibility cloak."

I pressed my lips to his forehead. "I would love to be your mom, Danny." He leaned back and smiled as I hugged him even tighter.

"It's my turn." Adam grumbled near my right ear.

I stared up at his hungry eyes. "You boys might have to learn to share."

Adam raised one of his eyebrows in challenge. "Danny, I plan on spending the next long while kissing your future mom, and my future wife."

Danny shuddered. "Gross. I'm going to go play with my new space rocket." He wiggled out of my arms and ran to his pile of presents. My dad had sent Danny a whole collection of space toys.

Adam smirked at my now empty arms. "What were you saying?" Adam stepped closer, slowly and deliberately.

I couldn't let him win that easily.

"If you want to kiss me, you're going to have to catch me first," I squealed as I jumped and ran for the kitchen. Adam laughed as he rushed after me. I didn't even make it halfway there, with his stupid long legs. I giggled as he scooped me up in his arms.

"Anything else?" He quirked his eyebrows.

"Well, I guess I wouldn't mind wearing the ring." I bit my bottom lip.

Adam smiled and picked up my hand and kissed the palm before he slowly turned my hand over and slid the ring onto my finger. It was a perfect fit. The style, the size, the life. All of it.

I placed my hands on either side of his face and I studied his eyes. I was going to marry this man. "I love you," I whispered and felt it in every piece of my soul. "I love you more than I knew was even possible." I studied his lips, and the stubble on his jaw. He gave me a soft smile. "I don't think I will ever get over how much I love you." Tears formed in my eyes. "I am so happy, more so than I deserve."

Adam shook his head. "You deserve everything. I love you, Faith. I love you with all I am, and all I will ever be." He kissed my forehead, and he nuzzled my hair with his nose.

All the single women in Hillsdale may have wanted him, but I was the only one who caught him. I closed the small distance between us, and my mouth found his, soft and strong. His arms flexed, bringing me even closer to his body.

I was home. I was home and loved and accepted in a way that I had never thought was possible. I looked down at the ring on my finger and squealed as I kicked my feet in delight. "Guess I won the coach after all." I bit my bottom lip.

"Trust me." Adam smiled as he stared at my eyes. "I'm the one winning."

FREE BONUS WEDDING SCENE — SIGN UP FOR MY newsletter at www.kiripatterson.com

<h1 style="text-align:center">Author's Note</h1>

This book is my attempt to give the past me grace, and to accept all my pieces without feeling like they might secretly be failures. Out of every story I've written so far, Faith is the most like me. Well, other than I don't have access to secret wealth.

I learned later in life that I have ADHD and anxiety. Shocking, I'm sure, to those who see me in public, awkwardly standing still, while freaking out in my brain about what to say or where to sit.

It's easy to pick apart pieces of ourselves and be frustrated that we're broken or different from others or what we expect. Winters can be tricky for me, and I remember I was grocery shopping and was panicking every time I went to the point I would often have panic attacks.(Sorry to the employees of WinCo who found my abandoned cart when I decided I couldn't be around all the people and ran to the car.)

I was talking to my cousin, whom I adore, and who is so helpful for my mental thought check-ins. I told her I was so frustrated with myself. This was a normal human task; people do it all the time, and I was being ridiculous. I probably used a bunch of loaded language about what it meant about me as well. Her response stuck with me, and I try to remind myself of it often.

"Kiri, grocery shopping is a morally neutral task. It's not like the people who grocery shop versus doing pick up are morally better because of it. You are neither better or worse by doing it. If you know it's a struggle for you, work with your body, and establish systems to help yourself. Just do grocery pickup."

I wonder how often we attach a moral or significant weight to things and what they 'mean' about us that really doesn't exist.

I am neither better or worse because I struggle to be in large social settings, especially with small talk/ mingle situations. I am neither better or worse that I have anxiety and occasional panic attacks. I am neither better or worse that I can feel others' emotions and can be overwhelmed by them. These are just pieces, pieces that add to the whole that makes me, me.

I hope each of us gives all our pieces grace and understanding. I hope we learn to love all of us, and to be the truest you on purpose.

Thanks to my Adam, Joseph, who understands my mental storms and how to ground me.

The other reason I wanted to write this book was the idea of expectations or failed expectations. I think I have always been worried about not meeting expectations and letting others down, whether as my own parents, school, religion, as a parent, as a sister, as a wife, anything.

Adam's fear of not being a good enough parent for Danny and Faith's fear of disappointing her parents both came from that space.

Danny is partially based on my Benson.

He is the last of my four kiddos, and my parenting energy and skills did not in fact increase with each child. I was tired, and I felt to blame for anyone's frustrations about friction when they had rough interactions with Benson. My initial thought was, this must be my fault. I let him watch too much TV, I didn't pay attention to him enough, and any other thing that I could think of.

I remember the first few times people asked me, "What's up with Benson?" and "Have you thought about testing Benson?" It felt like a punch in the gut. Benson was just Benson. Just because he didn't sit or like transitions didn't mean anything.

A few years later, his teachers approached the subject of ADHD and his being on the spectrum. Again came the rushing thoughts of how I must be to blame and caused this additional struggle in his life.

I began studying and trying to get him tested. (Did you know the wait list can be 2 years long!) and I felt like I was thrown into the deep end of a swimming pool without floaties. There were acronyms and a language all its own with learning about disabilities.

My Benson is still just my Benson. I do understand him better though now, and know how to better support him. He sees the world through a different lens, and I am amazed by the thoughts, stories, and conclusions he comes up with.

One time on the way to school I saw a little kindergartner with a too-big backpack and I said something like he was so adorable I could eat him.

Quietly from the back seat I hear, "Mom, that's weird, and it has to be illegal."

He makes me smile, and see the world in a different hue, and yes... socks can be a real struggle.

But I adore him, and I love how his brain works.

Acknowledgments

Thanks to Ms Fry and Mrs Petross. Both of you were so important in helping me understand and find support for my son. You approached the subject in a way that helped me see his strengths and how additional support could help him succeed. You changed our world for the better.

Thanks to teachers. They are angels on earth, with the ability to shape and mold more lives than perhaps any other profession. Thank you to all the good ones.

As always, thanks to the tribe of women that keep me writing and support me.

Melody Williams and Tanya Strong, thanks for the initial feedback, and cheerleading Marco Polos where you believed in my ability to hit unrealistic deadlines.

Casi Holman, thanks for our weekly writing sessions, feedback, and plot chats. They keep me consistent when life is chaos.

Ali Fields... Girl, you read this book twice in tight timelines. You are amazing! I appreciate the help and comments that you give that push the story to improve. Tell your family thanks for sharing you with me.

To my family.

To my husband, who believes in my ability unabashedly. He believes I can create and hit deadlines when all I feel is fear and doubt. He believes in what I do, and that I am wildly capable.

To my kiddos- Thanks for your support. Thanks for being patient when I'm on a deadline. I know everything else falls apart in the chaos, so thanks for helping me put it all back together in the aftermath. Although Danny in this story is similar to Benson, I hope you know you all inspired it. Your individuality and personalities are some of the brightest spots of my day.

I am beyond excited to see what you each achieve in life. Thanks for letting me be a part of your story. I hope you always have the courage to be true to you.

About the Author

Kiri Patterson grew up in small town Idaho and communicates through movie quotes and song lyrics.

She taught herself to read before Kindergarten and has loved reading ever since. Especially books with sweet love stories, strong characters, and lots of witty banter—ingredients she wants in all her stories.

She tries to survive on chai tea, Dr. Pepper, and dark chocolate ...but throws in the occasional vegetable for good measure. Other guilty pleasures include marathons of the Great British Baking Show, BBC period dramas, Harry Potter anything, and French Fries.

Kiri currently resides in Star, Idaho, with her hot husband, four rapidly growing children, a strong belief in happily ever afters, and her pink laptop—a nod to her belief that everything is just a little better in pink.

Also by Kiri Patterson

Seasons of Hillsdale

No Plans to Fall

Novellas

Cupid and Cupcakes